The Cowboy's Second Chance

THE COWBOY'S SECOND CHANCE

THE COWBOYS OF SWEETHEART CREEK, TEXAS
BOOK 3

JEAN ORAM

The Cowboy's Second Chance
The Cowboys of Sweetheart Creek, Texas Book 3

By Jean Oram

© 2020 Jean Oram
First edition
All rights reserved

This is a work of fiction and all characters, organizations, places, events, and incidents appearing in this novel are products of the author's active imagination or are used in a fictitious manner unless otherwise stated. Any resemblance to actual people, alive or dead, as well as any resemblance to events or locales is coincidental and, truly, a little bit cool. Unless your names rhyme with Travis or Shauna, in which case it's still not a coincidence. At least, not really.

Printed in the United States of America unless otherwise stated on the last page of this book. Published by Oram Productions Alberta, Canada.

COMPLETE LIBRARY OF CONGRESS CATALOGING-IN-PUBLICATION DATA AVAILABLE ONLINE

Oram, Jean.

The Cowboy's Second Chance / Jean Oram.—1st. ed.

ISBN: 978-1-989359-33-4, 978-1-989359-34-1

Ebook ISBN: 978-1-989359-32-7

First Oram Productions Edition: January 2021

Cover design by Jean Oram

ACKNOWLEDGMENTS

Sometimes the most memorable event at a conference is one of the sessions. The one that makes you look at everything differently, sending you charging back home to make big changes.

And sometimes the most memorable event is a simple supper in a pub with author Patricia McLinn. She'd collected a few of us conference orphans at the end of RAM 2019, selecting a table with a good view of the football game, asking the waitstaff not to interrupt during a play. (To which they obliged with humor and grace.)

Patricia patiently taught me almost everything I know about football during that supper. Explaining patiently and expertly everything from what the numbers on jerseys meant, to what high school football might look like in Texas—the cheerleaders take a different bus to events, for example. She used terms like "the green team" to help me keep track of what was going on as she explained.

It was the best in a conference full of greats. It's always a pleasure to sit with Patricia and I owe her a debt of gratitude for her help making Ryan's story that much more rich in detail.

Obviously, any oversights or errors are my own.

As for some of the 'game talk' and strategy—that comes from years of listening to my husband talk about volleyball. Always the volleyball. In several short years he went from having never watched a game to coaching at a competitive level.

Carly's tips on mixing up the plays, throwing the other team off guard and being unpredictable are something he might try. (See? I do listen, even when there are tears of boredom streaming down my face or I'm trying to do my morning meditation.) And the feeling of not earning the win due to what happens to the other team in one of the scenes—that's him, too. Him and his big heart full of empathy. It's what makes him, him.

As well, besides thanking Patricia and my husband for the sports element, I'd also like to thank my 'make it better' team. A heartfelt thanks goes to Margaret Carney and Tessa Shapcott for patiently accepting my numerous series scheduling changes as I dealt with life during the pandemic as well as a big thanks for your suggestions, edits, and overall help to make this story all that it is. I'd also like to thank my beta team: Margaret C., Donna W., Erika H., and Lucy J. I'd also like to thank Stefanie Brame for her sensitivity read and suggestions. And finally, to my error finding team. You're the polish, girls! Thanks for your help.

A NOTE FROM THE AUTHOR

When you sit down to write a book sometimes you think you know how things are going to go. You know who your characters are and what they are striving toward. And then things happen. Things change. The characters begin to insist on some things, or some things appear on the page and feel so right.

As I write this note (June 2020) our world is in the midst of dealing with the COVID-19 pandemic and my neighboring country is dealing with riots and protests of various kinds. Many are related to discrimination based on color.

It is a confusing time filled with pain. As a woman raised to believe that every single life, story, and perspective matters and that kindness and caring matters more than a person's color, it is especially confusing for me. Discrimination and racism is not right, and it does hurt.

Maybe that's why I love writing so much. It's an escape for me as much as for my readers.

Enter my dear heroine Carly Clarke who is a woman of color. Carly walked onto the page from the start as a strong woman with beautiful dark skin and a hurt soul. She is like me and you with her hopes and dreams for a future where things will finally go right, and where she entrusts her heart to the right person.

My books are always about hope, love and following one's dreams. And this is the heart of Carly's story, too. Just like it's mine. Just like it's probably yours.

If I have misstepped, please forgive me. And if our society's perspectives change over the years, as they always do, and the things I have written today are no longer relevant or appropriate, please forgive me. My only intention is to assist in making the real world line up with what is in my heart: compassion, kindness and caring, where every life matters greatly and where a person's character matters more than their color.

I hope that I have done justice in telling Carly's story. I hope that I have helped give more women a voice. I hope that, thanks to Carly, more women will see themselves on the pages of my books. And I hope that those who assume they will see themselves reflected back on the pages of these stories will also see themselves in Carly. We are more alike than we are different.

Every person deserves love, kindness and compassion.

Let the healing start here.

With love,
Jean Oram
Alberta, Canada 2020

For McPat

You are probably beyond needing or wanting to have a book dedicated to you, having written so many of your own and having shaped so many moments and careers in your life already.

Just the same...

Cheers, girl! This one's for you.

---

*R*yan Wylder searched through the ranch house fridge, on the lookout for his mother's semi-famous lasagna. He was certain there'd still been some left when he'd gone over to the neighbor's at one in the morning and just about gotten himself shot.

"Already ate it," his brother Myles said, entering the room.

"All of it?" He checked his watch: 7:40 a.m. Myles must have had an extra early start to his Saturday to have consumed that much lasagna already. "Hey, how high does our forklift go?" Ryan asked, closing the fridge.

Myles studied him for a moment. "Why? Looking to go next door and get yourself shot at again?"

"She didn't shoot at *me*." Carly Clarke, their gorgeous new neighbor, had shot out the yard light above him when he'd returned her loose goats in the middle of the night. He may have also been enjoying the view through her slightly translucent nightgown. That woman had more curves than any road he'd ever driven down in Texas Hill Country.

She hadn't been a fan of his gawking.

"Doesn't she wear a wedding band?" Myles asked, no doubt reading Ryan's expression and coming to conclusions.

"What kind of husband sends his wife out alone in the dead of the night to take care of an intruder?"

"Maybe he wasn't home."

"Has anyone ever seen him?"

"I'm not sure," Myles said thoughtfully.

Ryan headed to the pantry to rummage. He didn't live on the family ranch any longer, but regularly helped with chores and felt entitled to raid the kitchen when hunger struck.

He let out a sound of triumph as he held up a tray of their mother's extra gooey cinnamon buns.

"Mom's saving those for later," Myles stated.

Ryan groaned and returned the cinnamon buns to the shelf.

The purposeful clack of cowboy boots landing on floor tiles signaled the arrival of their eldest brother, Levi, now thirty-five.

"Any lasagna left?" he asked, heading to the fridge. He adjusted his cowboy hat, appearing very much like the ranch owner he was, as he leaned down to look inside the old appliance. Technically, the five Wylder brothers shared ownership in the Sweet Meadows Ranch, but Levi was in charge and frequently reminded Ryan of his recent status change. Levi was no longer simply the I-Know-Best bossy big brother, but also the one taking the lead in the family business that fed every one of the Wylder clan, whether they had retired, like their grandfather and parents, or had jobs off the ranch, like Ryan and Brant.

"Myles ate it," Ryan said.

Levi eyed the second youngest Wylder, who was built like the linebacker he'd once been. "Where do you put it all?"

Myles shrugged. "Since I know you won't let us take a break until we're done moving Brant back to the ranch, I thought I'd better pack on some reserves." He patted his flat stomach with a grin.

Ryan had almost forgotten about Brant moving out of the

apartment above his veterinarian clinic today. The plan was to let Ryan's best quarterback's pregnant girlfriend live there. After last night's important playoff game—one that had brought the high school football team one step closer to the elusive state championship trophy—Robyn's parents had kicked their daughter out of the house.

Not great timing for Ryan's starting quarterback to have a personal crisis. Area football playoffs were in six days, and the state championships four weeks after that. These next few games were what their entire season had been leading up to. And if Blake Hernandez was fretting over Robyn, then he wasn't focusing on the game. And if he wasn't focusing on football, then goodbye championships, and goodbye scholarships for him and several other players on the team.

The crazy thing was that Ryan hadn't even thought about that mess once this morning. Apparently getting shot at by a feisty neighbor on her hobby farm was an excellent way to take one's mind off of a potential crisis.

"Karen said Robyn'll be ready to move her few bags of stuff into Brant's around noon," Myles stated, his voice warming as he said his girlfriend's name.

"So if we can get all of Brant's personal effects moved to the ranch before then," Levi said, selecting an apple from the fruit bowl, "we should be set."

"I'll be late," Ryan told them.

Levi blinked at him, asking around a mouthful of apple he'd bitten off, "How can you be late? You're already here."

"There's something I need to do."

Myles smirked, carrying a bowl of cereal to the table near the windows, where he had a coaching textbook open.

Levi let out a frustrated sigh. "Well, when you're not too busy with your projects, our brother needs your help."

"I said I'd help and I'm here, aren't I?"

"The ranch could use more of your time, too, you know."

"I hired Hernandez to do my morning chores." That way Ryan could focus on being a high school teacher and football coach, as well as keep a finger in the other pies he had on the side. His star quarterback could also use the money, with the baby coming next summer. "And didn't you hire another farm hand?"

"I need your analytical brain to look over a breeding schedule I want to test next spring."

"I can't focus on anything but football right now," Ryan replied. Mentally, he was trying to remember where he'd find the keys for the ranch's ancient forklift.

"This schedule could save the ranch a fair amount in feed costs. We may also lose fewer calves due to dehydration during heat waves."

Ryan wasn't falling for his bait. Levi was trying to lure him into asking questions about his "plan." He'd hook Ryan's curiosity with some details he'd want to research, and then before long it would be Ryan's project.

"Brant's already doing some casual research on that stuff," Ryan stated.

"We're working on it together."

"He's the veterinarian, not me."

"We need help."

"I'm busy. Call in partner number two," he said, referring to their AWOL brother, Cole. He'd been Levi's constant companion growing up, but had left almost five years ago. As far as Ryan knew, Cole had an equal share in the family property and was doing absolutely nothing to help.

Levi echoed Ryan's stance, his expression stern, jaw set. Uh-oh. He'd pushed it too far and now he was about to get The Question again. His brother was like a woman who wanted an engagement ring—unrelenting.

"Do you want a stake in this ranch?"

And there it was. Ever since their parents had divorced, and the operation had been turned over to the five sons last June, all

Levi had done was ask what role they wanted to play in running the place, hinting they could walk away.

And leave him with everything? Fat chance.

The problem was that whenever Ryan thought about helping out more, he felt stifled. There was no independence working on the ranch. It was all just following orders, keeping to routines, and being Levi's lackey. And since the flash flood that had swept Ryan downriver at age seven, his eldest brother had been extra vigilant to breathe down his neck at all times. If he wasn't twenty-seven he might not find the protectiveness as oppressing as he currently did.

So if the question was did he want to put on his cowboy boots and hat full-time, the answer was no.

But giving up revenue from the ranching business, as well as his part of the family legacy? That wasn't an easy thing to turn away from.

"Because if you don't want to be involved, I understand."

"I already have a full-time job, and when I asked if we could expand the stables as my way of helping out, you said no."

"We don't need more horses."

"And we don't need to sink everything we've got into cattle. We should diversify. If I end up renting stable space from someone else, I'm charging it to the ranch."

Levi's jaw tightened. "You think I'll authorize something like that?"

"Maybe we should vote on it. You have only one-fifth of the say. I bet if I could find Cole, he'd vote my way. Myles and Brant might, too."

At the table, Myles looked up from his textbook, his spoon halfway to his mouth.

Levi's expression turned hard, his attention fixed on Ryan. "If you don't tell me what you want by December first, I'm going to draw up the papers to buy you out."

"I'm in the middle of football playoffs. If we make it to State, I can't be thinking about the ranch and what you need."

Levi had been happy enough taking charge of the operation, with Myles as his right hand and Brant and Ryan stepping in to help as their jobs allowed. But ever since Levi had started dating Laura Oakes, things had changed. The more serious he got about his relationship, the more he demanded of his brothers.

Little by little, Levi was losing his own independence, Ryan figured. He was giving up pieces of his old, happy life as a quiet cowboy to be with his girlfriend who had a successful modeling career in New York. As nice as Laura was, there was no way things could end well for Levi.

"December first is a few weeks away. You've already had plenty of time to think." Levi's posture stiffened, as though he'd been challenged to a fight.

Myles was suddenly there between them. "How about January first?" he said, arms out as though he expected his brothers to lunge at each other.

Waiting until January would give Ryan about two months to see if some stuff he was working on would pan out or not.

Neither he nor Levi disputed Myles's suggestion, and they silently accepted the new date with a nod.

Ryan headed to the kitchen door, calling over his shoulder, "I'll send you the bill for renting a stable." He grinned when he heard Levi's pained sigh of acceptance.

Carly Clarke had a stable out back of her house. Maybe she'd rent him some space without shooting him. Or having her mysterious, yet-to-be-seen husband do it for her.

"Tell Brant that Carly needs a watchdog," he added as he left the room. Their brother was a gifted matchmaker between dogs and humans, and could find her a protector. Because when he listened to his gut, Ryan would bet his next paycheck the woman was living on the Lucky Horse Ranch alone.

"I'm borrowing the forklift," he called from the hallway, where he lifted the Texas-shaped key ring off a hook. "I'll meet you at Brant's in an hour or two."

"Borrowing it for what?" Levi asked.

"He's going next door to get himself shot," Myles stated, loudly enough for him to hear. "He needs a getaway vehicle he can bleed out in where Mom won't freak out about him ruining the upholstery."

Ryan shook his head with another smile and headed outside, determined to figure out who exactly this beautiful Carly Clarke was and why he couldn't stop thinking about her.

* * *

CARLY HADN'T SLEPT WELL. And not just because she'd done damage to her own property when her cute neighbor, Ryan Wylder, had gotten her exactly where she promised she'd never be around a man again: flappable.

It'd been a long time since anyone had dared drink her in the way he had, and she'd reacted, shooting out her much-needed yard light in order to plunge them into darkness as he returned her goats.

Standing on the dusty ground beside the light pole, she put her hands on her hips and stared up. Beneath her feet were shards of glass. Thankfully, none had landed inside the nearby goat pen. What a careless, dangerous thing she'd done.

And all because a man had been looking at her silhouette. A handsome, challenging man who seemed to see right into her soul in a way that made her feel vulnerable and exposed.

She had a lot to hide, but when it came right down to it, he didn't matter, and neither did his opinion of her.

Really, though, it wasn't just the yard light that had her frustrated, nor was it Ryan's gawking. It was being alone on the ranch. Yes, shooting out the light had been stupid. But so was not throwing a robe over her nightgown before heading out into the yard with her shotgun at one in the morning to see what the ruckus was about.

She needed to think first, then think again. Then act way, way later. Like a week later. Not stomp out into the night all alone on a remote ranch, even if armed. Her US Army Reserves training was one thing, but blindly walking into what could have been an ambush was another.

The gall of him, though. He'd been standing in her yard like he owned it. Just as he did with every patch of ground he tread upon. She'd noticed him around town, as well as at the library fundraiser two weeks ago. It was hard not to, with those bright blue eyes that took in everything, those broad shoulders of his and his confident, commanding presence.

But she was not interested. No, thank you.

She was here on this ranch to learn self-reliance, and she didn't need another man waltzing in and then back out again, leaving her hanging off a cliff with alligators snapping at her feet.

She let out a frustrated sigh and focused on the light again. How was she going to replace the fixture? She'd blown it to pieces, and all that was left was a piece of metal hanging from a few wires.

Electrical work was beyond her skill set. So was dealing with heights. Which meant she'd have to hire someone. And that would cost her a fortune, all because she'd been hotheaded.

Think first, Carly. Always think first.

And why had she immediately become so hotheaded?

Because Ryan Wylder and his intense gaze had stirred up parts of her that would undoubtedly lead to bad decisions and long, dark nights. She'd faced too many of those already in her thirty years.

She patted her ebony curls. "Cool it, hothead."

She didn't have the cash to spend on wild decisions while trying to get her organic farm started. Right now she had nothing but a week of poor decisions behind her, and they seemed to increase by the day. It was time to stop the cycle. And that meant she would be wise to avoid her new terrible-decision trigger, Ryan Wylder.

A small gust of wind tugged at her open jacket, and she tightened the plaid fabric around herself. It was already mid-November, which meant Texas was ready to serve up just about every kind of weather. The days seemed to start cold, grow hot, end cold. Different from Montana, where they tended to start cold, stay cold and end even colder.

In the distance Carly heard the rumbling of machinery, the Sweet Meadows Ranch next door already becoming familiar to her with its predictable morning sounds. The two ranch houses were uncharacteristically close for this part of Texas. She was just a five-minute walk from the Wylders' place, though their ranch-land stretched way back into the hills.

When she heard an unfamiliar engine rev, sounding as though it hadn't been run recently, she couldn't help but wonder what was going on over there, and if anyone knew how to replace a light fixture on the cheap.

As long as it wasn't Ryan.

Making sure her escape-artist goats were still in their pen, she headed back to the house, leaving her yard light problem for later. As she dreamed of her next cup of coffee, she noticed a faded orange, dusty machine rounding a curve in her long drive-way. It disappeared for a moment behind a grove of massive, century-old oaks, before reappearing, the rumbling sound louder. It looked like a 1950s-era truck that had been converted into a forklift.

She hustled to the front yard as the vehicle came closer, and soon recognized the man driving it. Ryan Wylder.

Great. Just great.

It was as if he knew she'd vowed to avoid him, hoping to prevent a wave of bad decisions that would surely follow any interaction with him. And here he was to test her.

She was getting tired of admitting to her family back in Montana that she'd been suckered into trusting the wrong man again, because of another smooth and charming smile. She didn't need to do it a third time.

As she reached the edge of the drive, the forklift came to a stop beside her, the wheels locking and sliding on the loose gravel.

"Get your light fixed?" Ryan asked, adjusting his black cowboy hat. Most times she'd seen him he was wearing a ball cap, and dressed as though he was about to coach his football team. But he looked right at home in the hat, along with the black-and-red checked shirt under a black vest. Dark colors suited him, matching his hair, bringing out the intensity of his blue eyes.

Handsome. That's what he was.

And in Carly's world, handsome spelled T-R-O-U-B-L-E.

"Here you are again." She held up her empty palms. "And me without my shotgun."

To her delight, the man's lips quirked into a slight smile. "I can wait here if you need to retrieve it."

Oh, but she loved a man who didn't take her too seriously. And that light Texas drawl? Mmm. It sounded good with that deep, gravelly voice of his.

What was she thinking? Yes, he was eye candy, but he'd already been established as trouble.

"My goats are accounted for this morning. Why are *you* here?" Her words came out abruptly, but she didn't regret them or the distance they might bring.

"I thought you could use a lift."

She raised her eyebrows and gave the bastardized truck an unimpressed look. There was only one seat and she most certainly didn't need to ride anywhere with Mr. Trouble.

"To fix your yard light."

"Oh!" Her surprise and delight slipped out before she could tamp it down. "That was..." She closed her mouth and instead studied the platform made of pallets and plywood resting on the machine's forks.

"It's mighty neighborly, I know," Ryan said, with a wry smirk that made him look even more devilishly charming. "My parents ingrained it into me, and honestly? Sometimes it's a genuine pain in the butt."

"I see."

"You don't happen to have a replacement bulb for the light, do you?"

"I don't think so." She winced, realizing she needed more than just a bulb. Maybe she could find a cheap solar light she could nail to the pole and call it done. She'd seen a few gnome ones in the hardware store in town. Maybe she could strap up a whole herd of them. However, as amusing as that would look, she didn't think they'd cast enough light to be helpful.

"You're in luck," Ryan said.

"I am?" She hated her growing intrigue, how easily she was drawn into his spell. She didn't want to be. She wanted to keep her status as a self-reliant, independent woman who didn't need a man to save her. Or, help her, in Ryan's case.

"I grabbed a bulb while I was in town." He gestured to a box near his feet.

Carly glanced at her wrist, bare of a watch, then up at the sun. Whatever the time, she was confident it was still too early for any of Sweetheart Creek's stores to be open.

"I have a key for the hardware store," he explained. "I put it on my tab."

"I thought you were a teacher."

"I am. But I used to do inventory at the store while in high school. They never asked for the key back."

And obviously he'd never offered to return it, either.

"You bought a new light bulb?" she asked.

"I picked up a fixture and some wire, too. It looked like you did a thorough job of obliterating that light."

He was too helpful. What was his angle? A man like him had angles. Always. And not just those handsome, sharp ones making his jaw look extra sexy.

"Out of the goodness of your heart?" she asked.

"I can leave it for you and Mr. Clarke to fix, if you prefer."

Hearing someone refer to her late husband brought her back down to earth as that familiar slice of pain jabbed through her heart. She barely even noticed the assessing look Ryan was giving her.

"If you're good with heights," she said, "your help would be appreciated."

"Are you a steady hand with a forklift?"

"I guess we'll see, won't we? How high does this thing go?" She patted the cold metal fender, and it made an odd banging sound as though it was hanging on to the machine by one last bolt.

"Hopefully high enough. Do you know how to drive stick?"

She scoffed. Of course she could drive a standard transmission. She'd grown up on various farms in Montana, where her father had worked as a hired hand. As soon as she and her brother were old enough they were given jobs as well, and their dad had insisted she learn to do all the things Jerome did.

"How much did the fixture cost?"

He shrugged.

How much were yard lights? Carly wondered. A hundred dollars? Less? More?

"I can't accept it unless I know how much it'll set me back."

"Why don't we do a trade?"

And there it was. His angle. She waited for his setup. The one that would surely lead to her second bad decision where Ryan was concerned.

"You have something I need," he said, his voice dropping lower, "and I have something you need."

Carly glared at him. Maybe she should have gotten her shotgun, after all. He was just another cowboy thinking she was an easy and willing mark.

"Do you still have that stable and corral out back?" he asked.

"Yes," she said slowly, her suspicion easing despite her desire to cling to it for safety. The ranch wasn't named the Lucky Horse for nothing. It had originally been a small hobby farm focused on horses, but when the owners retired, the farm had fallen into disuse and the corrals sported thigh-high weeds. When her family had heard the farm was how she was using the inheritance from her recently departed grandmother, they had at first been silent.

Then they'd started asking the inevitable questions about whose idea it was to spend her money, and who she was partnering with. It seemed her relatives were wising up to her pattern of making poor decisions.

But this time it was all her.

She wanted to own something. Something that was *hers*. Something nobody could take away, unlike the farms where she'd grown up, putting her labor into someone else's dreams. Surely her family understood what she was looking for here? And what better place to make a fresh start than on a ranch with the word *lucky* in its name?

"Thinking of renting them out?" Ryan asked, his voice deep and mesmerizing.

"I don't know what condition they're in," she lied. The truth was, she didn't want to fix them up or deal with a demanding and expectant renter, which Ryan would surely be.

She needed that light fixed, though. Not just for her safety when performing chores before dawn or after sunset, but for security, too.

However, the idea of being indebted to Ryan Wylder was like a giant warning alarm going off, blinking and blaring.

But if she didn't accept his neighborly help, she would have to pay someone an exorbitant amount to fix damage she'd caused.

She could accept Ryan's help without causing a wake of problems, couldn't she?

But if she did, then she'd have to rent a stable to him, which would likely ensure that the handsome man would be around a lot more than she could handle.

It looked like either route she chose, she'd be making one more bad decision this week.

2

*R*yan clung to the forklift's pallet platform as Carly hoisted him toward the broken light. All she had to do was keep the forks level while he replaced the fixture.

The power to the pole was turned off, but Ryan didn't feel as though a jolt of electricity would cause him to meet his maker today. It was Carly.

Before turning the machine over to her, he had nestled the lift close to the pole, shown her how to use the levers to hoist him up into the sky, then had climbed onto the platform. So far her caution with the hydraulics was sending him upward in fits and starts. It was giving him a worse case of whiplash than when his brothers had let him tag along while teaching the ranch hand's daughter, April MacFarlane, how to drive a stick shift in a bumpy old cow pasture.

"Almost there," Ryan called down to Carly as she performed another bone-jarring stop. He stayed seated, one hand on his toolbox and the other on the box of supplies beside him. He should have increased his odds of survival by asking Myles to come over and help with this task. However, his brother would have undoubtedly run interference, when all Ryan wanted to do was sort out who Carly was and what she was doing here—alone. Because he was certain she was alone.

She hadn't warmed to his stable rental proposal, and hadn't given him a yes or a no before she'd agreed to let him fix her light. But he didn't peg her as someone who accepted something for nothing, so sensed that if he was patient, he'd leave with a verbal rental agreement.

The forklift lurched again.

"Nearly there," he yelled, stretching his arm out to gauge whether he was close enough to the old fixture. This time the move upward was smoother, but fast. Too fast. "Stop! This is good."

"Is there an emergency brake?" Carly called as he stood up. He could see her looking around at her feet, seeking an extra pedal. She seemed strangely small from his vantage point and he crouched again in case the machine began rolling backward in her distraction to secure it.

"Just keep your feet on the brake and the clutch."

She reached to turn off the engine, the metal Texas key chain flashing in the sun.

"No! Leave the engine on so the hydraulics keep pumping or I'll sink down."

"Okay."

Ryan slowly stood, one hand braced on the light pole as he glanced down. He had to be nearly eighteen feet off the ground. Taking a deep breath, he got out his screwdriver and deftly removed what was left of the broken light fixture, tossing it to the earth below.

Carly let out a squeak as it crashed beside her. Her foot slipped off the clutch, the forklift lurching and butting against the pole as its old truck engine stalled. Ryan tipped forward, his cowboy boots skidding on the precarious platform. His shoulder slammed into the pole as he reached out to hug it, just as the forklift rolled back and his feet swung off into empty air. He wrapped his legs around the pole like a firefighter, keeping his feet high for when the lift inevitably lurched his way again.

"Come back, come back," he called.

He could hear Carly talking to herself in a panicky voice, then the engine started and revved. The forklift's platform crashed against the pole, making everything shake.

Ryan closed his eyes and exhaled.

Was she worth this kind of risk?

"Sorry! This thing has a hair-trigger clutch," she called.

When the platform remained against the pole, Ryan cautiously lowered his feet to it once again. "Please don't kill me," he muttered, loudly enough for her to hear.

"How is it you end up with your life in my hands every time I see you?" she called back, humor lifting her voice, making it sound cheery and melodious. He could have sworn he heard a hint of Jamaican rhythm in her words, highlighting her sheer joy at his predicament.

Ryan shook his head. She was grinning, and he found himself grinning back and wondering once again if she was worth this risk to life and limb. He had a feeling he didn't want an answer to that, because it might not make him happy if she truly had a husband somewhere.

Ryan focused on his task, working quickly to fix the broken wires and attach the new light, securing it to the pole before Carly could send him plummeting to the earth in a heap of broken bones.

"Okay," he finally said, waving his hand as he sat on the platform, his work done. "Let me down. Slowly."

When he reached the ground, he glanced over to find her still smiling. She was pretty when she smiled. No, she was more than that. She was distractingly beautiful, her toffee-colored skin glowing. Her short hair was different today, those tight, finger-length curls kept away from her face with a pink paisley band that somehow emphasized her high cheekbones. Her dark brown eyes sparkled and her wide, pink lips curved upward in an alluring fashion.

"You looked like a monkey clinging to that pole."

He stepped off the platform onto solid ground, experiencing a fresh fear of heights as well as of Carly. "Next time you shoot your own light out because I'm admiring your figure, you're on your own with the repairs."

The smile vanished. "You're reneging on your promise to help fix the goat pen?"

"You sent me home when I offered." Her goats kept winding up in the yard at the Sweet Meadows Ranch, eating whatever was in sight. Including the seat of his pants—while he'd been wearing them. Last night he'd brought her small herd of five back over here and had offered to help fix their pen, but she'd refused.

"There was no light to work by," Carly said.

Broken glass from the old light cracked as he shifted from foot to foot. "Why don't we see if we got this working again? Want to flip the breaker?"

Carly turned off the forklift, slipped from the seat and headed to the house, where the circuit breaker was located. She was wearing jeans, a thick plaid jacket that snapped up the front and worn brown cowboy boots that had seen more action than just on city streets.

Ryan adjusted his hat and craned his neck to look up at the new light. It was crooked thanks to his haste to get back down to solid ground, but otherwise looked good.

While he waited, he picked up shards of glass, tossing them along with the broken fixture into the empty box.

A minute later he heard Carly call, "It works!"

He looked up at the glowing bulb as she joined him, her shoulder nearly touching his as she stopped beside him to admire their work. That was a change he didn't mind, and for a minute it felt as if it was the two of them against the world, not alone. It almost made him feel lonely. Almost.

Carly was single. He'd bet on it.

So why the wedding band? Was it to make men think she was taken?

And what had encouraged her to buy a ranch in the middle of nowhere?

"Good thing you didn't shoot me last night," he said, his voice low as he took in details he hadn't been able to in the weak moonlight. A faint hairline scar down her cheek near her ear; a mole near her upper lip. Those high cheekbones, and the skin around the edges of her lips a gorgeous brown-pink. Long dark lashes devoid of mascara. Natural beauty.

"I'm still debating whether it was a smart decision." She flashed him a grin that lit up her eyes, brightening her entire face and almost taking his breath away.

He reminded himself that he was here for one thing, and it wasn't a girlfriend.

He cleared his throat. "So. About my rental proposal."

"WHAT ABOUT IT?" Carly asked. She was feeling happy with her new light, even though, technically, she found herself in Ryan's debt yet again. First, for returning her goats and now for fixing her light. How self-reliant was she proving to be?

But the light had been his fault. And returning her goats was simply a neighborly thing to do. She could have retrieved them herself had she known they were out.

"Rent some stable space to me," Ryan said, turning to her. The intensity of his gaze was disarming. "You can give me the first week free as a thanks for this." He gestured to the yard light.

She let out an amused laugh. "For fixing something you broke?"

"You pulled the trigger."

"It was your fault that I did."

"This would have cost you several hundred dollars." He tipped his chin toward the pole. "How about we call it even, with you providing the first two weeks rent-free?"

"Now you're up to two weeks free?"

He seemed pleased she'd called him on that.

"Why would I rent out my stable?" she asked.

"What's it earning you right now?"

"How do you know I don't have plans for it?"

His head dropped slightly to the right and his blue eyes studied her like an expert poker player assessing his opponent.

Crap. He had her. She could tell. He had that way of seeing into her. She needed to keep him at bay so she wouldn't end up doing something crazy, like kiss him or rub a hand along his strong jaw to see how it felt under her fingertips.

"You don't," he said, with a confidence that sparked flecks of amber in those blue eyes.

She took a step back, considering her response. He had a determination flickering under the surface that she identified with. He wanted this silly stable, and she knew he wouldn't stop until she said yes. That made her want to keep saying no, no, no. She'd bent for others far too many times and suffered the consequences.

"Maybe I plan on demolishing it so I can put in a garden over there." That wasn't an entirely terrible idea. She planned to create a fully self-sustaining farm with solar and wind power. She was going to grow organic food, raise free-range animals and create her own little Eden. But buildings were always useful, and the stable was in decent shape despite years of neglect. Demolishing it wouldn't be smart.

"It's staying," Ryan said.

His confidence was annoying. Especially since he was correct.

"Why don't you want my horses here?" he pressed.

"Maybe your assumption is wrong," she said sharply. They faced off with crossed arms. She caught a hint of fabric softener and aftershave when the wind shifted. He smelled like promises and hope. *T-R-O-U-B-L-E.*

"I'm never wrong."

"Oh, I doubt that. I bet you've made at least one wrong judgment, especially where people are concerned."

Something fluttered through his eyes before he shifted his stance and dug his heels in a tiny bit more.

There was a wound there. Scarred over, but still making itself felt. It was nice to know she wasn't the only one prone to poor judgments when it came to assessing another person's character. Ryan wasn't infallible despite his bluster, and it made her like him despite not wanting to.

"What's your rental rate?"

They stared at each other for a long minute, and then he quirked his head as if to say he was waiting for an answer.

Okay, okay. She would rent out the stable; she just didn't want it to be easy for him. She also didn't want him to think he was the one determining how this would all work out.

She shifted her hands to her hips. "You want it for horses?"

"Yup."

"And you mentioned the corral?"

He nodded, causing her to sigh. He wasn't going to give up anything without making her work for it.

"Are you planning something illegal?"

Ryan gave her a dry look, his lips pursed.

Of course he wasn't. She might have made some poor character judgments in the past, but she could tell Ryan was trustworthy. Annoying, persistent and challenging in every way, but trustworthy.

"As your potential landlord, it's perfectly reasonable for me to ask your intentions. Especially from a Peeping Tom." Her body heated as she recalled the hungry way he'd gazed at her last night. It had been all she'd been able to do to not return his look with the same intensity and longing.

His eyes swiftly took her in from head to toe, setting her spine tingling again. "You had it on display, sweetheart."

She let out an involuntary huff of indignation at the endearment, which sounded warm and sweet and full of promise, not as a word meant to put her down, hold her in place. She hugged her arms around herself as heat spread through her body. There was something about Ryan Wylder that made her feel alive. Something she hadn't felt since Peter's passing several years ago.

She shook her head. She wasn't ready for this. Wasn't anywhere close to letting herself need someone again. She had to learn to stand on her own two feet before she considered anything like that.

She shouldn't have allowed him to fix her yard light. She should have sent him packing and solved her own problems. Now she was contemplating letting him come onto her property whenever he wanted? Less than an hour ago she'd vowed to avoid him.

She thumbed the wedding band on her finger—one completely unrelated to her former marriage—reminding herself to stay strong. Stay self-reliant. Her full commitment was to herself right now. Just because she'd taken a few steps backward didn't mean she couldn't find her forward motion once again.

"I don't recall sending out invitations for a visual groping," she said, with an edge to her voice. Her arms were still tight around herself, as though the pose would shield her from experiencing her own reaction to that stirring late-night gaze.

"A visual *grope*? If I was going to do that to a woman..." Ryan looked wounded, disgusted, his body shifting away from hers, and she could see she'd crossed a line.

"How many horses?" she blurted.

"Depends how many I can find at auction." He was still giving her a wary look.

"You don't have horses?"

"I have three."

"Where are they?"

"With their original owners."

"What are you planning?"

"Can I count on you, Carly?"

The way he said her name sent tremors down her spine. She wanted to say yes. She needed to say no.

It would be yet another bad decision to turn down the extra income. But it could be even worse to say yes to another business deal when she was still reeling from the last one, which had her lined up to get grilled in court next month.

"I'll think about it." She turned away, glanced up at the light again. The business deal she'd made with her friend Eaton had seemed great. It had served her country and put food on the table. But it had turned out to be something she'd be lucky to stay out of jail for being involved in. Recently she'd been downgraded to a witness, instead of being a member of the accused. As a result, she'd been subpoenaed for the upcoming preliminary hearing, and sometime in the New Year it would all be over. But in the meantime she kept waking up in a sweat, fearing that Eaton would manipulate the courts the same way he had their business's finances, and she would find herself behind bars for something she hadn't knowingly done. She'd worked hard to find the best prices so their food services contract would be renewed each year, but it turned out Eaton had found a way to turn that to his own advantage.

"We can write up a rental agreement, and if I breach any part of it I'm out," Ryan said, his voice rising to carry to the goat pen, where she was bracing herself against the fence, her gaze unfocused. "I'll stay out of your hair. Fix anything that breaks in the stable."

"What would break?"

He shrugged when she turned. "I can give you references."

"Isn't there another stable you can rent?"

"You're next door to the ranch."

"Don't you live in town?" She had taken a few steps toward him and now he made up the distance so neither of them had to raise their voice to be heard.

"How about I pay first and last month's rent up front?"

"If even one check bounces, you're out immediately."

"They won't."

"What's my responsibility to you and the horses?"

"You provide a safe stable and corral."

"It needs work. It hasn't been used in I don't know how long."

"That's fine. Just allow me to use the corrals and stable, and provide access to a well with safe water. You're hands-off."

"Good, because I have a commitment that will take me out of town from time to time. I won't be here to pick up your slack." She couldn't be worrying about things back here when she was being raked over the coals by the United States Army's best lawyers.

"Understood."

"You take proper care of your horses and know that you've rented the stable based on its current condition. You don't get to make demands about changes or repairs, and if I don't like how things are going, you're out of here. No questions asked."

He was smiling. "Fine."

He'd gotten his way, hadn't he? She'd caved somewhere along the line, just like both of them knew she would.

Carly sighed, frustrated by her inability to build a strong wall between herself and this man, then keep it fortified.

"What are the horses for?" she asked. "Are you training them for rodeos or something?"

"I don't need a partner."

"I wasn't offering."

They glowered at each other, neither willing to soften and give in to the other.

"Are you a horse trainer?" she asked, curious despite herself. What was it about him that made her want to learn more? Pry open his hood and take a peek inside to see what made him run? She told herself it was so she'd know what was happening on her own property, so she wouldn't get blindsided.

"No."

"How much traffic should I expect coming through my property?"

"Me and the trainer, daily."

"What kind of training will you be doing?"

"Do you want me to rent the stable or not?"

"You avoid questions like someone's throwing darts at you."

He looked resigned. "You're like my family. Always with the questions."

She reached out and shook his hand, liking the way his grip was gentle yet firm. "When it's ready to sign, I'll drop the rental agreement off at the ranch."

Ryan held her hand for a second too long, his eyes locking on hers. Then his hand was gone and he was placing his toolbox in the forklift's open cab, and she was feeling a sense of loss.

"You're training the horses for rodeo, aren't you?"

He had hopped up onto the forklift's seat and now stared at her. Her heart was beating faster than it should, and she was too aware of everything to do with Ryan Wylder. From his snug jeans to the breadth of his shoulders. From the set of his jaw to the intelligent eyes that gave nothing away regarding his thoughts. She found herself hooked, waiting to see what would happen next.

Then, to her surprise, the planes of his face softened and he said, "Is that going to be a problem?"

His head tipped lower as he propped his right elbow on the steering wheel. She had the sense of him leaning in, the warmth from his body traveling to hers even though over six feet separated them.

She drew a settling breath and peered up at those clear eyes watching her from under the brim of his black hat. He studied her with a care and depth she'd already come to expect from him. She once again had the feeling he saw more of her than she liked to reveal, and yet somehow that was okay.

"I know not everyone approves of rodeos," he said, "but having me on your land while you build a reputation as an organic farmer likely won't be an issue around here. Though if you feel it might, just say the word."

She hadn't even considered that. She'd been more concerned about having this delectable man frequenting her yard. Even now she was having trouble looking away from him.

There was a chance her priorities were slightly scrambled at the moment.

"Do you compete? In rodeo?" she asked. He didn't seem the bull-riding type, although she could possibly see him dominating the cutting events, or possibly acting behind the scenes as a horse breaking expert. There was something about the way he persistently chipped away at her own walls that may have led to that assumption. And the man didn't even seem to try. It was delightful, but also infuriating.

"Are you going to call animal protection services on me?"

"So it is rodeo, but you don't compete."

"Does it matter?"

"I'm trying to figure you out, and training horses for rodeo that you find at an auction is an interesting way to make a living." He had to know what he was doing if he was picking up cheap horses with a plan to train them and somehow profit.

"Who said it's for money or for rodeo?"

She gave him a look, and he had that softening you-win expression again that pleased her more than she figured it should. He made her work for everything and she enjoyed each triumph.

"With rodeo, you know they aren't worth anything unless they have a couple of wins under their belts," she warned. "Unless they're from proven stock."

"I know."

"It's gonna take a lot of work and money to get these horses up to where they're paying for themselves."

"I know."

"Bulls, or other forms of horse training, would be easier to profit off of."

"Yup."

"You already have bulls, don't you?" And maybe did some other form of horse training, too.

He gave a faint smile, something in his expression causing her to take a closer look. As she studied him she was struck by a realization that nearly slackened her jaw. Ryan Wylder was afraid. Afraid of something so familiar it sent a tingle through her nervous system. She could sense his fears: of being broke, of needing others, of not adding up to more than the skin you were in.

She shivered, realizing this tiny insight had made him seem much more human and much more intriguing. And much more dangerous to her plan of keeping him out of her life.

3

As Ryan unloaded his three horses into Carly's stable the next day, he decided it was time to stop thinking about her. Even though nobody could confirm the existence of a husband, she wore a wedding band on her left ring finger. To him that was a blatant Off Limits signal.

And yet the way she looked at him sometimes, her gaze lingering, suggested she might not be married. But what did she think of him, if she'd called his admiring perusal of her silhouetted form "visual groping"? No wonder she'd shot out her own light. He would have, too. Then knocked out his own proverbial lights.

Ryan settled the last horse, unable to help wondering if he would see Carly before he left the Lucky Horse Ranch. She'd slipped into his thoughts yesterday while he'd helped Brant move back to the Sweet Meadows Ranch. Then again when he'd been helping the pregnant teenager, Robyn, move her few belongings into Brant's furnished apartment an hour later. His brothers had found his absentmindedness annoying, and he'd taken a good ribbing for his distraction.

After ensuring his horses had adequate feed and water, he turned toward the open door at the end of the small stable.

Tomorrow Lucinda, his horse-crazy math student, would come over after school to train two of his recent recruits for barrel racing. Her parents, living in town, refused to support her horse addiction. Yet the teen consistently scrounged up enough money to buy riding time at local stables as well as the entrance fee for a few rodeos. So far she'd earned a few ribbons. Lucinda had just about pierced his eardrums with her excited scream when he'd asked if she wanted the use of his horses in exchange for giving them a bit of training.

Some animals would be a gamble, but a winning horse could fetch a higher price than what he'd paid at auction. And its offspring would be potentially valuable, too. He was playing the long game, though, and might not see profit for years.

That was why he'd invested a bit more in purchasing a young American Quarter Horse to develop as a cutting horse. A well-trained cutter was a valuable asset in Hill Country, and he had the patience to get the animal where it needed to be.

Either way, his horses could become part of a passive income stream, hopefully with minor work on his part, in case someone decided to sweep in and take his nest egg again.

Ryan closed the stable doors behind him, double-checking the latch. His eyes naturally turned toward the house, only the roof of which was visible this far back on the property. On his way through the yard earlier he'd noticed a fresh patch of upturned garden behind the house. A rusty old push cultivator had been abandoned after churning up a few rows of soil. Hard work. That's what that job was. Carly needed some serious machinery.

Ryan shook his head, knowing what she'd say if he offered to lend her the cultivator from the ranch. That woman had an independent streak lined with a stubbornness that rivaled his own.

As he secured the horse trailer's doors, he grinned, thinking about how she had refused to let him push his way into getting what he wanted from her. He liked a woman who didn't bend to a smile, give up her plans, her thoughts or beliefs just because he wanted or thought something different.

There was no doubt about it. He might have a growing infatuation for Carly Clarke. Which meant he needed to find out more about the mysterious Mr. Clarke.

No. What was he thinking? He needed to focus on football right now. The team was heading into some big games and he needed to remove all distractions. And Carly definitely had potential to be a big one.

"That's cocky of you," said a hard female voice. *Carly.* He fought the way the corners of his mouth tried to turn upward as he turned to face her.

Man, she was just as stunning today as she had been yesterday.

"Cocky?" he said, trying to hide his amusement. He spread his hands. "But that's how you know it's me."

A massive, shaggy sheepdog that could hardly see past the hair hanging over his eyes came out from around Ryan's truck, planting its feet solidly as it took in Ryan while giving one loud bark of warning. Carly herself looked stern as she stated, "I haven't received a rental check, and yet here you are, putting your horses in my stable."

"I left the check stuck to your front door with an arrow."

Her eyes flashed. "I'm so glad to hear it wasn't Cupid."

"Wrong month for that monkey business." He reached into his back pocket, then held out an envelope. The dog growled. Ryan had planned to wedge the first and last month's payment under the front door when he drove past her house again on his way out.

Carly moved toward him, her shoulders relaxing, her hips swaying—a picture he had to look away from before it drew him in and she verbally lashed him for another "visual groping."

She pushed up the sleeves on her black sweater and opened

the envelope. She glanced at the check before sliding it into her own back pocket. Inhaling, she looked up at him. "So I'm renting to the Sweet Meadows Ranch, not to you?"

"This is an expense that runs through the ranch. They're *my* horses."

The dog, deciding Ryan was okay, came to his side, giving a snuffling inhalation before sitting his giant behind down and looking up expectantly. Ryan patted his head while Carly opened the doors to the stable, one eye on him as though challenging him to stop her.

"My brother brought you a dog?" he asked.

She gave a brief grunt of confirmation.

"What's his name?"

"Sergeant Riggs."

"From *Lethal Weapon*?" Ryan asked, fighting a smile. The name was out of character if Brant had chosen it. His brother always named the dogs based on where or how he'd rescued them. The owner of a local Trader Joe's had found Ryan's dog, Joe. Brant's dog, Dodge, had been abandoned outside a dealership. "How'd he get his name?"

"I liked the movies. More than the TV show," Carly said, walking into the building. Ryan followed, allowing his eyes to adjust from the sunshine to the dark interior. She stopped at the horse pens, looking over his stock. One of the slim quarter horses he'd selected to train for barrel racing ambled up to her, and she reached out to stroke its nose. It huffed and nuzzled in.

"Brant was going to call him Ditch," she said drily.

"Sergeant Riggs is a better name."

She made a humming sound of agreement, then asked, "What makes you think this one will be good for rodeo?" Her tone was testing and Ryan wanted to pass. He felt like he had in the sixth grade, when a new girl had moved to town and all the boys had gone crazy over her. He'd been prepared to do just about anything to stand out from the crowd. And he had, even in his slightly too small hand-me-down clothes from his brothers. The girl had toted him around like a trophy for a week and a half before dumping him in the middle of math class, announcing that he hadn't bought her an ice cream at the lunchtime fundraiser. Greg had. Ryan hadn't even known she'd wanted ice cream. Then she'd told everyone who would listen that he was just a poor farm boy who didn't have enough money for an ice cream cone.

"It's a friendly fellow," Carly said, stroking the horse affectionately.

Ryan leaned over the wood stall door to study the horse. It was his. Bought and paid for. Much better than an ice cream cone for a girl who'd moved away that following summer, her name forgotten.

Marcie.

Her name had been Marcie. If he ever bought a surly, fat mare that's what he'd call her.

But he'd splurged on this fast-looking quarter horse on a whim. Kind of like when you saw a Corvette in the used lot and before you knew it, it was sitting in your garage beside your still perfectly good Jeep.

The horse had seemed like something that might bring him luck, and so when the auctioneer had started his spiel Ryan had raised his hand.

Carly's eyebrows arched as she glanced at him. She seemed amused, but he was too distracted by his own thoughts to figure out why.

"Did you buy this guy on a hunch?" she prompted.

Ryan's attention darted to her, but he didn't answer.

Carly continued to stare at him, her eyes moving over his biceps, then his jaw. It felt as though she was stealing images to savor later.

He liked that idea and allowed his own gaze to trail over her before slowly meeting her eyes again. It wasn't a visual groping, but contained some heat and a lot of smoldering appreciation to let her know he found her attractive.

Her cheeks flushed, and he wondered if she was struggling with a feeling of attraction.

If so, he wasn't sure what that said about Mr. Clarke.

"I bet this guy could make a decent barrel racer," she said, stepping back to admire the caramel-colored horse with the splash of white high on his forehead. "Better than the red roan on the end." She gestured toward the far end of the stable where the chubbier horse—one she hadn't looked over yet—was kept.

"You saw me bring them in?"

"I was out taking soil samples."

And she'd done so while watching him and the horses, and had drawn conclusions. Interesting.

"Well, I guess we'll see what Lucinda, the rodeo trainer, says about Old Red."

Carly sucked her cheeks in, making her face even more angular, like an Egyptian goddess. How was it she looked different with every mood? And always beautiful. He bet she could be covered in mud and as angry as a swarm of hornets and still have the power to take his breath away.

"What?" she demanded.

"Am I ever going to meet Mr. Clarke?" Ryan's eyes drifted to her left hand, which was resting on the stall door. That wedding band was like a wall. A wall to keep others out; he was sure of it. She was skittish, hiding tender wounds under a false front of bravado and confidence.

Who was Carly Clarke, and how had she ended up here? Would she still be at the Lucky Horse Ranch in five years time?

He got the feeling she was hiding out. He could ask, but sensed the details of her life were as off-limits as his own.

"I assume Mr. Clarke is fine with you renting out your stable to a handsome, single man," he said, edging closer when she didn't reply.

Carly didn't look his way, simply moved to the next horse as though he hadn't spoken. She shook the gate that kept the pen secured, testing its strength. "Does Brant know anything about getting goat's milk certified for market?"

"Maybe. Why?" She was edging around something. Ryan guessed she had a project and knew if she shared it with others they might hone in, take it over, shame her, laugh at her or worse.

He'd been there, done that. He knew it was best to keep new projects and dreams close to your chest until everything was established, so the best intentions of others couldn't muck it up.

"I'm going to run an organic farm. Eat local and all that." Her tone was too casual, telling him the idea meant a great deal to her. She ran a hand down the blue nylon lead he'd hung on a hook near the stall.

She'd said "I." Not "we."

This ranch was all Carly. There was no husband at the helm or at her beck and call.

"You might want to move this," she said, referring to the lead.

It was fine where it was, hanging close to where he'd need it should he want to lead a horse somewhere.

"I bet your barrel racer eats it. You're welcome to make use of the tack room at the other end." She drifted away, light on her feet. She wore cowboy boots as though they were slippers, and it served as just one more layer to the mystery of Carly Clarke.

Ryan swiftly hung the lead out of the horse's reach and hurried to catch up with her. "Where did you grow up?"

"Montana."

"Do you know Alexa McTavish?"

"Your cousin?" she asked, her dark eyes turning to meet his.

So she wasn't completely new to the area. Or had Alexa and Carly known each other back in Montana, as they'd both been raised there?

"How long have you been a cowgirl?"

"How long have you been a cowboy?"

He shook his head. She was implying all her life? "No, you haven't." There was something sophisticated about her that spoke of time spent in the city, wearing heels and sharp suits and silk blouses.

Carly glided closer, her eyes meeting his in the dim light of the stable. It smelled like old wood, fresh air, horses and sweet hay. Like home. Like a place that would always be there for him, whether or not he wanted it to be.

"What else have I been doing with my life then?" she asked.

Something. Something that made her want to invent a fake husband and hide away from the world. Something that had toughened her in a way that ranch life wouldn't have.

"Why don't you tell me?"

She ran a finger down the front of his shirt, and it was all he could do not to take her hand, pull her in and give her a searing kiss. She was sexy. Difficult. Combative. A tease. A pain in the butt.

She was everything a man like him might want in a woman.

"I have a feeling you're well on your way to becoming an expert on Carly Clarke," she said, her dark eyes shifting to lock on his.

"I do plan on becoming one very soon."

***

"There is no Mr. Clarke, is there?" Ryan asked as they moved toward the stable entrance, and Carly felt a prick of panic. She hadn't planned to correct anyone's assumption that she had a husband hiding out on the ranch. Having one was the perfect shield against the blast of heat she often found in Ryan's gaze, and the idea of a husband could keep her from tricky moments like this one. Times when she could inhale the scent of hay and animals, and believe she was someone different. When she could allow herself to see what would happen if she let herself experience a delicious cowboy who kept looking at her as though she was at the top of his Most Wanted list.

If the illusion of Mr. Clarke shattered she could be in for a landslide of poor decisions. And where bad decisions were concerned, each new day meant another opportunity to make better choices. She was tired of being left high and dry, crawling back to her family to admit defeat once again. She was getting too old for foolishness, and anything to do with Ryan Wylder would likely be branded with its very essence.

But it was difficult to remain preoccupied with haunting thoughts of her past failures, and all the reasons to remain cautious, when faced with this man's vibrant presence.

"Did he leave you?" Ryan asked. His tone surprised her. It was almost demanding, as though he was planning retribution should she say yes.

"In a way," she admitted slowly. She ran her left hand up and down the sleeve of her sweater and shivered in the November chill that seeped through the stable's open door. Peter had died unexpectedly, leaving her with a stunning amount of debts. She'd been heartbroken and confused. The life they'd built and the future they'd planned had been quickly swept away by bill collectors. She'd been faced with an eviction as well as his angry, grieving mistress, forcing her to face the full depth of Peter's betrayal while in the midst of her own grief. It had taken her weeks to sort out the truth about her husband, his secrets, and their tattered finances.

How could she have loved a man capable of betraying her trust in such a heartrending way?

"He died, didn't he?" Ryan asked.

Carly instantly reacted to the sympathy in his hushed voice, revealing the truth. Ryan inhaled sharply and stepped back, putting space between them. She could see through his pained realization that he felt she was wounded, not as strong as he'd believed.

It was exactly what she didn't want from him. She didn't want pity. She didn't want him to step back or treat her as if she was precious goods. She didn't want him to stop challenging her.

She wanted him to believe she was strong and feisty, someone who could handle him. Someone who could make it through the rest of her life without being blindsided once again by poorly placed trust.

Carly Clarke could stand on her own two feet. Could act on instinct and pursue the things she was most curious about.

And she did just that. She stepped forward, knocking into him as she gripped his face between the palms of her hands and rolled onto her toes, to lock her lips on his.

The man tensed in surprise, grasping her waist to balance them. She continued to kiss him, desperate that he not freak out, but reciprocate. She needed to know he wouldn't change, wouldn't think of her any differently now that he knew she was a widow. She needed him to keep that heat that distracted her from hating herself.

She was a superb kisser. She knew that. She had a generous, soft mouth, and knew Ryan couldn't deny the sparks flaring and exploding between them.

Almost immediately he responded, his mouth sweeping hers, exploring, discovering, and learning the things you can only find out about another person by kissing them.

His arms slowly wrapped around her, holding her as he deepened the contact. The horse beside them released a whinny of approval and Carly broke the kiss that had been meant only as a distraction. She caught Ryan's heated gaze and went in for another one.

Ryan Wylder was most definitely a hitch in Carly's good-decisions-only plan. She also knew that in the moments between now and her inevitable self-destruction she would enjoy every single second.

RYAN WAS HOLDING Carly in his arms, his shock ebbing as a pleasant realization awoke within him. Holding her felt right. Really right. And he didn't want to let go of her until he figured out why she felt so good.

"So there's no Mr. Clarke?" he asked, trying to adjust his thinking, which wasn't an easy feat after being kissed by Carly. Her wide mouth and plump lips had been like a whole other universe, sending him rocketing off to the stars. Thinking straight was not a skill he could rely on at the moment.

She gave a slight shake of her head, not elaborating.

"Why do you wear a ring?"

She had her wrists draped over his shoulders, and now slid her palms down to rest on his chest, her eyes locked on the slender band of gold on her left hand. Her mouth moved silently as though having forgotten how to form words.

Finally she said, her dark eyes meeting his, "I wear it for myself."

Ryan didn't know what that meant, only that her look told him it was something she might never explain.

His mind drifted to his ex-wife, Priscilla, and the feeling of having the entire world yanked out from under him when their marriage ended. He had a powerful reluctance to speak of it, so his family was still unaware he'd eloped during his final year of college. Even now he needed to carry on as though she'd never been a part of his life. He guessed it was the same with Carly and the late Mr. Clarke.

"I understand," he said.

Carly's eyes narrowed in suspicion. "You do?"

He tried to choose the right words, feeling as though two conversations were happening, one verbal and one not. "I understand the ring is something personal. Private."

He felt her body soften against his and she let out a sweet-sounding sigh.

"All I need to know about that ring is that it doesn't commit you to someone who might have a problem with me kissing you," he added.

"I'm single, if that's your question." She seemed edgy as she stepped from his arms, her movements jerky. "But I'm not looking for love."

He nodded to let her know he'd heard the declaration. She was a woman who liked to let him know exactly where her limits and boundaries were.

"Have I ever mentioned how much I like you?" He brushed a knuckle down the side of her cheek. She was vulnerable, yet prickly and difficult, and somehow everything he'd been waiting for.

"So, if neither of us is looking for love, what are we looking for?" she whispered, lowering her lashes as though afraid to meet his eyes in case she saw rejection or judgment there. But she was leaning closer again, and the heat was building. She was tall, almost matching his height.

"Companionship?" he asked, with a touch of irony. He adored the fact that she was bold, willing to lay it out there for him to accept or reject, not bending to what he wanted, and then locking them into something that didn't work.

"I don't expect this to happen, but if we get to a more intimate form of companionship," she murmured, her expression tight with challenge, "I'm an exclusive gal."

"Fine by me." He didn't have the time or inclination to try and juggle more than one woman. In fact, he could argue he didn't have time for one. "So what are you hoping for? Shuffleboard? Darts?"

"I mostly just want to argue with you, then kiss you."

Ryan considered hiding his smile, but figured there was no point. She seemed to do a decent job of seeing right through him and figuring out his intentions. Either that or they were cut from the same cloth and instinctively said what was on their own mind, coincidentally lining up with the other.

He kissed her again, inhaling her sweet scent. The product she used in her hair was unfamiliar, but what he already thought of as wholly Carly.

"You're not going to be my girlfriend," he said, when the kiss ended. He hated the hurt from old wounds that came up with the use of the word. But more so, he hated seeing that flicker of pain in Carly's eyes, even though he was merely stating what they'd both expressed. He gave her a soft, wet kiss to ease the sting of their shared bitter truths. "I don't do relationships."

She smiled against his lips, her body warm against his as her fingers tangled in his hair, knocking his hat to the hay-covered dirt below. She kissed him hard, then said, "Perfect. Neither do I."

He gave her another kiss, this one soon turning frantic.

When they came up for air, he confirmed, "So this is a quiet thing between you and me?"

"That sounds like something I can handle." Her face had lost all traces of tension, and he smoothed a hand down her neck. She was smiling, looking more breathtaking than he'd seen her yet, and she was plenty breathtaking.

"So this is good?" he confirmed, breathing her in, still reveling in gratitude for Carly.

"It's perfect." One of her graceful long fingers pressed against his lips. "Just like this."

And then she kissed him again, illustrating once more how perfect they truly were.

Carly was going stir-crazy on the ranch. She'd spent days stuck with her own thoughts, replaying those kisses with Ryan, while turning over the soil in an old garden plot. She'd flip from trying to sort out her past hurts and failures to wondering if she and Ryan would find more opportunities to kiss. So far, they had. Each day she found an excuse to walk down to the stable, whether to grab an old piece of timber from the stack in one of the broken stalls, or suddenly having an urgent need to ask Ryan a question about his horses.

She was about as transparent as a teenager with a crush.

What she should focus on was getting a winter garden planted. She needed to get a few things sprouted, figure out why her goats weren't producing milk, and finish rebuilding an old chicken coop.

She needed to grow something. Anything. Even just a row of lettuce. Then she'd feel like a farmer, and focus a little less on Ryan.

Unplugging her electric Mini Cooper, Carly climbed in and drove to town. She would stop by the hardware store for some winter produce seeds, such as onions, beets, carrots and lettuce, then grab a coffee at the Longhorn Diner to get some human interaction. She'd barely been off the farm since the library fundraiser dance, and figured spending time around others might help make her kissing relationship with Ryan feel less big and important.

Although this morning's kisses had been worth the wait. That man handled her sharp edges with apparent ease and amusement, and he kissed like nobody she'd ever met. How was it she'd sworn off men, then almost immediately found herself in a kissing relationship with one of Sweetheart Creek's most eligible bachelors?

Carly parked her car in front of the hardware store and shook her head. She never learned, did she? Maybe because it was fun until you had to actually learn the lesson being handed to you.

As she crossed the sidewalk to the store entrance, she inhaled the brisk autumn air and admired the trees lining the street. The town's pride showed with its picturesque downtown, its older buildings well-maintained and charming. Sweetheart Creek felt like the kind of place where parents didn't worry about their kids being on bicycles, out until dark or crossing the road on their own. If she were to have children, she'd want them to grow up here.

In the store, Carly loaded a basket with seeds and headed to the checkout. Minutes later, after explaining that she was starting a produce farm, she walked toward the diner with a full bag of gardening supplies and a giant grin.

She was a few doors from the restaurant when she spotted an armadillo waddling down the sidewalk toward her. As she passed it, swinging her bag merrily, she gave the beast a cheery hello. It turned and hissed, exposing a frightening display of teeth. Startled, Carly let out a shriek, flinging her purchases in the animal's direction while jumping back, landing awkwardly between two pickup trucks. The animal was in her bag faster than she thought possible. It selected the pack of sprouted seed potatoes she'd purchased as an experiment, and trundled off with its prize.

"Hey!" She returned to the sidewalk and stomped her foot, her wallet clutched to her chest. The beast scurried away even faster, the potatoes still locked in its jaws.

Hearing light laughter behind her, Carly turned to see Jackie Moorhouse coming her way.

"You'd best not mess with Bill," she drawled. "He can get a might nasty."

"He stole my seed potatoes," Carly said with a pout. A cowboy who'd just exited the diner stooped to collect her scattered seed packets.

"Thanks, Owen," Jackie chirped.

The man, who was about their age, tipped his hat after depositing Carly's belongings back in her reusable shopping bag.

"Thank you," she murmured.

"He just broke up with his girlfriend," Jackie whispered, after he climbed into an old truck with the Sweet Meadows Ranch logo on the door.

"He works with the Wylders?"

"Yup. Ranch hand."

"I haven't met him yet."

"He's super quiet and shy." Jackie pulled the diner's glass door open. The front windows were plastered with signs supporting the high school football team. "Heading in?"

"Thanks." Carly hurried through the doorway, then hesitated, debating between the tables covered with red-and-white-checked cloths and the row of stools along the back wall near the kitchen. She didn't want to assume she'd sit with Jackie, who had no doubt come to meet someone. And since it was nearly lunchtime, the tables would soon be in high demand.

When Jackie stopped to chat with a group of women hunched over what looked like a bunch of recipes, Carly took a stool at the back, beside a man with flyaway white hair.

"Well, hello. You must be Carly Clarke," he said, as soon as she set her sea foam-green wallet on the countertop beside him and took a seat.

"Yes, I am," she said in surprise.

"Fiona's been telling me all about her smart niece," he said, with a warmth that made her think of her grandfather back home in Montana, even though that was about where the two men's similarities ended.

Carly glanced around for the waitress, Fiona Fisher, a distant relative on her father's side. Almost at once she came sidling up, her bleached hair teased in a true Texas bouffant and her sparkly Western blouse catching the light.

"Carly, dear. Haven't seen you in ages." The older woman gave a tsk. "What can I get for you today?"

Before Carly could reply, Mrs. Fisher said to the man beside her, "This is my great-niece once removed, Carly Clarke." She addressed Carly again. "Hon, this is Garfield Goodwin. The biggest flirt ever to step foot in Sweetheart Creek."

Carly glanced at the man, who was grinning at the waitress. Carly had a feeling he only had eyes for flirting with one woman in town, and she was standing right in front of him.

"Just a coffee, please," Carly said.

"Carly's working on creating an organic farm out on her ranch," Fiona announced.

"Are you now? That sounds like a job and a half," Garfield said.

"It is."

"You have experience with that sort of stuff?" asked a gruff voice on the other side of her.

"Henry, don't be that way," Fiona warned.

"No, that's fine," Carly said. She turned to the man, who was about the same age as Garfield, but more worn looking. "I'm working on it," she told him.

"You can't just grow something without pesticides and call it organic," Henry said, his wrinkled mouth moving as though debating whether to frown.

"I know," she said.

"How's your water?"

"My water?" She looked at the counter in front of her. No water glass. No coffee yet, either.

"In your well. How much can it pump? You don't want to overpump or you'll get bacteria. And if it goes dry from over-pumping, your crop will shrivel right up in the summer heat unless you get enough rain, which is hard to come by when you need it. What's the salt content in your water out at Lucky Horse? What minerals you got in it? Anything your crops need? What are you planning to grow, anyway?"

"Um…" Carly felt as though she'd just been frisked by a dirt devil, one of those twirling dust-filled winds that blew around you, stinging your eyes, temporarily blinding you before it disappeared as suddenly as it had come.

"In time, Henry, in time," Garfield said. "She's just fixin' to get started, and doesn't need to worry about every little thing right here, right now."

"She could lose her shirt if she don't have good water or a well that can keep up with our dry spells. It's not just the obvious, like bugs or soil-borne diseases, that can ruin your crop. Be responsible, Garfield."

The man shut up.

"That's actually good advice," Carly hedged. It was best to know the specifics of what you were getting into, right? She'd run into that problem with Peter, then again with her business partner, Eaton, who'd been caught siphoning money out of their food services military contracts. As a result, she'd been clear and up front with Ryan about what their kissing meant, but she should be just as clear in her business plan, too. She should make a full assessment of what the farmland had going for her as well as against her.

"I've sent soil samples out to be tested," she said. "But I don't know about my well."

"Talk to Tracey down at the town office," Fiona suggested, placing a cup of coffee in front of Carly. "She might have records."

"Profit is a long time coming with ranches and farms. I hope you know that," Henry said, seeding doubt in Carly's mind about whether she could make this idea work for her. Her father had expressed his own doubts, reminding her how hard farming was. Was it wrong of her to want something of her own, something like what she'd had growing up? Land, independence and a feeling of self-sufficiency?

"She doesn't need much," Fiona said. "It's just her own mouth to feed. She's not looking to become a major contender on the world market, Henry."

Carly shot her an appreciative look. Her aunt was right. She didn't want to build a vast conglomerate, just a farm that would sustain her simple lifestyle.

"Your great-nephew knows a bit about that stuff, doesn't he?" Garfield said thoughtfully as he swiveled to face Henry.

"That boy is always messing with some big idea. I can't keep up with them all." He waved his hand as if swatting at a persistent fly, then pushed off his stool, unfolding his wallet to drop a few bills on the counter.

"He took some classes," Fiona said, scooping up the cash as though afraid Henry might take it back if she left it there too long.

"Who took classes?" Carly asked, perking up as she added milk to her coffee. She could use a resident expert to help her start off on the right foot.

"Which of the boys was it?" Garfield asked, as Carly took a trial sip of her coffee. "Why, that was Ryan, wasn't it? Ryan Wylder."

Carly began coughing.

"You've met?" Fiona asked, a mischievous twinkle flashing in her eyes.

"Who's met who?" asked a woman behind Carly. It was Jackie, slipping into Henry's spot, smelling like apples and strawberries.

"Yeah, the youngest whippersnapper," Henry said, turning to leave. "He's got a smart mouth and is too independent for his own good. Stay away from that one."

"Carly's met Ryan," Fiona said to Jackie with a pointed look.

"Oh, the handsome Wylder boys," she exclaimed, pretending to swoon. Henry let out a disgusted grunt and trotted off, while Jackie fanned her face with a hand. Carly laughed despite herself. She'd met Jackie Moorhouse when she'd first moved here, and had thought she was a bit much. And naturally, had taken an instant liking to her.

Ryan was hot, all right. But Jackie's reaction made Carly wonder if he was a player and she'd been caught in his trap of effortless charm.

She took a sip of coffee while considering that idea.

If he was a player, did it matter? They weren't doing anything more than kissing. No relationships. No commitments other than to keep it monogamous if it got more physical than kissing. Come to think of it, that kind of had a whiff of relationship, didn't it?

"Carly, have you met Jackie Moorhouse?" Fiona gestured to her.

"We met at the library fundraiser dance." Jackie turned to Carly. "Are you a football fan?"

She shook her head. Peter had loved football, and since his passing she'd made a habit of avoiding anything he'd liked. But she'd always enjoyed football, and had been a fan long before she'd met Peter. Back in Montana, her family used to drive into the city to watch college football. Then while attending Southern Methodist University in Dallas, she'd go watch the Dallas Cowboys. Now that she thought about it, she missed it.

"I haven't been following it lately," she said truthfully. "I used to be a huge fan and even took player statistics for a college team at one point."

"Our boys are going to State," Jackie said, clamping her hand on Carly's forearm. "They made it through bi-district playoffs and they have area playoffs this Friday."

"Don't go putting your cart before the horse," Mrs. Fisher warned. "The boys still have to win four more games before they make it to the state championship game."

"They'll choke at State. They always do," Henry predicted, reaching between Carly and Jackie to grab his forgotten sunglasses, and making Carly jump.

"They had better not," grumbled another voice from behind her. "This is my son's last year to win."

"They'll win, Davis," Jackie said confidently. "Riverbend's team isn't as strong, so we know the Torpedoes are making it to regionals at the very least."

"They'd better."

She turned to Carly. "The boys are playing their next game in town on Friday. Are you going to come watch?"

"Friday?" Carly repeated.

"You're free?" Jackie said, sliding backward off the stool. "Perfect. I'll pick you up. You're at the ranch by the Wylders? What's it called? Lucky Horse?"

"Yes."

"Great. Wear something cute. Red and white are the team colors. We'll sneak down to the sidelines and help out the team in return for free admission."

"What?" Carly said, but the woman was already scooting out the diner's front door, her pink cowboy boots clacking quickly, like she had somewhere to be. Carly turned to Fiona. "What just happened?"

"Ryan's afraid of Jackie," her aunt replied. "So he's off her list."

"What?" What list? How did that explain things? Suddenly she was going to a football game on Friday and helping the team? What was she even helping with?

And wear something cute? What was that about?

Fiona took in Carly's confusion and nodded knowingly.

"Well, are you going to fill the poor girl in before Jackie changes her life?" Garfield asked.

"I don't think I will," Fiona said with a calm smile, and Carly felt a flicker of anticipation. But she wasn't sure if it was something she welcomed or dreaded.

"No way. There is no way I am going down there and elbowing my way into helping the team," Carly said, as Jackie gave Sheriff Conroy Johnson a little wave as they made their way across the football field. Behind them it seemed as though half the town was sitting in the bleachers, waiting for the game to begin. Jackie was moving like she owned the field, not taking Carly's no for an answer.

"They need someone to keep stats." Jackie shrugged when Carly gave her a stern look. "You said you follow football."

"This is a playoff game." Surely they had an experienced stats-taker who knew the players and was ready to help the coaches figure out who was playing their best tonight and who wasn't, information that could make the difference between a win and a loss. They didn't need two dolled-up women pretending they belonged there.

Carly had been dressed in jeans and a warm jacket, but when Jackie rolled up in her cute sports car, she'd made her change into a denim skirt with leggings underneath.

"Exactly. Playoffs are important," Jackie said, still marching.

"Which means they need someone who has taken stats this century."

"Oh, you're not that old." Jackie laughed. Along the sidelines, she picked up a tablet sitting on top of a medical sports bag and flicked it on, then pushed it into Carly's hands and pointed to an open stats-taking app. The team's players were already listed, along with their numbers. Easy.

"But…" Carly said, as Jackie propelled her from behind, directing her toward the huddle of people along the sidelines as the Torpedoes took to the field for a warm-up. The crowd in the bleachers cheered, and the cheerleaders danced and tumbled along to music.

There was nothing as exciting as Friday night football in a small Texas town. And no better way to get off on the wrong foot with Sweetheart Creek than to butt into the game like she belonged here.

"They have me taking stats, and I get caught up in other things," Jackie explained. "Please help me. You said you've done this before."

Carly hesitated. If Jackie Moorhouse was in charge and actually needed her help, that was different from the two of them honing in as though wanting attention. "Are you sure?"

"Yup." Jackie was propelling her forward again, and Carly focused on the cluster of men ahead. Tall and broad-shouldered, they all looked like ex-football players. Two of them wore red-and-white windbreakers with Coach written across the backs in fat black letters.

"Hey, Ryan," Jackie called.

Carly's feet stopped moving as one of the jacketed men turned.

It was him. Ryan Wylder.

The guy she had been kissing in her stable every single day this week.

Planting the seeds from the hardware store had kept her distracted from thinking about Ryan for about five seconds.

Then again, he seemed to show up on her ranch fairly often. More than the once a day he'd promised. Maybe he was experiencing the same distractions she was.

"Carly's here to take stats for you," Jackie said sweetly. "Have you two met?"

Ryan glanced from the grinning woman to Carly, then back again. He nodded slowly, then inhaled with the same careful patience, eyes drifting shut as though he was bracing himself, before his gaze flicked to the tablet clutched in Carly's hands.

She froze to the spot. Something was up, and she had a feeling it had to do with Garfield's comment in the diner, that Jackie would somehow change her life by bringing her here.

"If I'm taking someone's job," Carly started to say, holding out the tablet, her discomfort growing by the moment, "I can—"

"Nonsense," Jackie stated, grabbing her arm as though afraid she might bolt. "You're my helper."

Ryan and Jackie silently faced off, Ryan stormy, Jackie's long lashes blinking innocently.

Carly kissing Ryan wasn't public knowledge, and while she knew she was just a blip in his life, like he was in hers, seeing him so reserved felt like a blow. Did he not want to be seen with her? Was it a good-old-country-boy thing kicking into gear? In her stable, his kisses were always warm, his caresses gentle and sure. And the way he seemed to peer inside her soul left her on a high for the rest of the day. But seeing him like this proved just how unspecial she was. It hurt, thinking about how certain he'd been when they'd discussed not making their kissing into a thing. He was ashamed of her, wasn't he?

"Really," Carly said in a hushed voice, "I should go."

Ryan nodded in the direction of his brother Myles, the other man in a coach jacket, then turned away as he said, "He'll set you up. I've got to get these players ready."

Jackie had a secure grip on Carly's elbow and began moving toward Myles. As they passed Ryan, Jackie cheerfully called over her shoulder, "You look cute in that jacket, Ryan."

Carly dared to turn to see his reaction. His back was to them, his focus on the field, but she could see his profile, his jaw flexing, his attention fixed with an intensity that caused her to shiver.

What had they told her in the diner? That Ryan was afraid of Jackie? Why? Was it possible this was about Jackie, and not her? And why did she feel such a bright ray of hope at that idea?

"So very cute," Jackie said loudly. "Don't you think so, Carly?" She bumped her shoulder against Carly's in a companionable manner.

Carly frowned as Ryan's jaw tightened even further.

"Did you two used to date?" she asked.

Jackie laughed, not answering.

Myles, hearing Jackie's laughter, turned to face them with a grin.

"Hey, big guy." Jackie gave him a full-watt smile and fluttered her lashes. She looked way too pleased with herself.

Myles shook his head with amusement. "You'll send him to an early grave, you know that, right?"

"Who, me?"

"You're doing stats with Jackie?" Myles asked, taking the tablet from Carly. He slid a finger up and around the screen a few times before handing it back.

"It's been a long time since I've done this," she replied.

"But she knows how," Jackie stated. She added louder, "She used to follow football."

"Yeah?" Myles asked with interest. "Who's your favorite team?"

"The Dallas Cowboys, of course," Carly said with a scoff, as though there was any other team worth cheering for.

Myles chuckled, and she noted that Ryan turned to scowl at them.

She shivered and lowered her voice to ask, "Is he always like this?"

"Only on game day." Myles caught Jackie's eye and there was

that in-cahoots grin of hers again. "Or when Jackie brings a friend to games."

"Should I not be here?"

"Don't worry about it. Just make sure we win," Myles said with another grin, while glancing toward his brother.

Wait. Were they trying to set her up with Ryan? She found her attention drifting his way. He was fully in charge along the edge of the field, calling over players, his focus complete.

"The town will bury these guys alive if they lose," Jackie commented.

"Nobody yells at the stats keeper," Myles said lightly. "Just let us know who drops the ball, who catches it and all that stuff, and we'll love you forever."

Ryan turned to scowl at them again, his dazzling blue eyes stormy, his hands on his hips. "Myles, are you focusing on this warm-up or what?"

"Or what. I'll be there in a jiff." He gave Carly a gentle pat on the back, directing her to chairs set up near the players' bench, where she and Jackie would have an unobstructed view of the field. "Take good care of her, Jackie."

"You know I will."

As Carly sat with the tablet in her lap, listening to the boys shouting terse commands to each other in their deep voices, she felt the familiar thrill of the game.

"Do you want the tablet?" she asked, hoping Jackie would take the lead on collecting stats.

"My job is to look cute. Just keep track of the stuff Myles mentioned."

Carly frowned at her. "Your job is to look cute?"

"So you like Ryan?"

Carly felt her entire being heat at the mention of his name. She reached for the tablet and focused on learning the nuances of the app.

"What's with the wedding band?" Jackie pointed to the ring on her finger.

Carly shifted her hand to hide it under the tablet. She knew the question would come, but hadn't expected it to be so point-blank.

"Are you married?"

"Widowed," Carly murmured.

"I'm sorry."

"I'm not," she said, surprising herself, and causing Jackie to inhale sharply. "Sorry. You just truly learn who a person is after they pass away."

"Really?" Carly could see Jackie was thinking about that. She got the impression the woman liked to play the innocent, slightly ditzy flirt, but underneath she was one of those solid, loyal people who made the best kind of friend.

"Peter didn't leave me in a strong financial position. He hadn't been honest about... a lot of things," Carly said, using a vague umbrella to encompass all the ways her husband had betrayed her.

"That really sucks."

"Yeah."

They were silent for a long moment, Carly tapping the app, testing it, making sure she knew how to account for certain plays as well as delete her stats in case she hit the wrong thing during the excitement of the game.

"You know..." Jackie began thoughtfully, then closed her mouth.

"What?" Carly asked, looking up at her. Jackie had freckles scattered across her nose, giving her a fresh, innocent look, and Carly briefly wondered if she'd ever had her heart broken.

She was frowning in Ryan's direction, and curiosity clawed at Carly. The way he stood there, tall and in command, his arms held loosely at his sides, he seemed every bit the cowboy, coach and quiet fighter she was beginning to know him as. He had a lean, athletic build that was a tighter version of his brother Myles's, who was strong and muscular. In a fight, Myles would win on strength, Ryan on agility and speed.

"Nothing." Jackie gave her head a brief shake, then opened her mouth again, closed it and shook her head once more.

"Well, you have to tell me now," Carly said, feeling annoyed and immensely curious.

"I just get the feeling that Ryan..." She stopped again, seemingly frustrated with her inability to put words to her thoughts and feelings.

Ryan stood in a huddle with two players who, judging by their jersey numbers, were his quarterbacks. He rested his head against their helmets as he murmured to them, and his stance made him seem part parental figure, part confidant and support network. Plotter and schemer. Winner.

"He's a good man," Jackie said, "and he's not quick to show how he feels. Still waters and all that."

Carly got the impression her new friend was bailing out, deciding not to reveal whatever it was she knew about him.

"You feel he has secrets?" Carly suggested. "And that those secrets have changed who he is?"

Jackie turned her head, her eyes meeting Carly's in understanding. "Exactly."

No way. There was no way Ryan was falling for Jackie's plan. Because she surely had one, and he, Ryan Wylder, was in the crosshairs once again. Why else would she appear with the woman Ryan hadn't stopped thinking about all week? And Jackie, who had a history of magical matchmaking skills revolving around football games, hadn't just brought Carly to the game, she had brought her right down onto the field, so she was less than twenty feet away from him.

He was supposed to be coaching, concentrating on his players and the game, not on this breathtaking woman who was now officially part of his team. He wasn't supposed to be worrying about Jackie's legendary status as matchmaker and whether it had merit. Or whether he was about to find himself in a committed relationship because of it.

Ryan glanced over at Dan, his team manager, who was passing out water bottles to the players who'd been subbed off the field. He smiled at Carly as she looked up after recording the latest play in her stats app. Dan gave her a thumbs-up, obviously delighted by her presence. Ryan's heartbeat quickened, and he turned his attention back to the field, clenching his clipboard.

Dan.

What if Jackie had brought Carly here to hook up with Dan?

Ryan rubbed the knot at the base of his neck and rolled his head from side to side. He didn't like that idea any more than getting in deep with Carly himself.

"Did you see that?" Myles asked, his tone incredulous, arms spread wide. "He was open. We need to call a time-out and get their heads back on straight. They're not even trying."

Ryan scanned the field, annoyed that he'd missed whatever had upset Myles. He checked the clock. They were already halfway through the first half and he felt like he'd missed most of it. "You lead the huddle."

Catching one of the official's attention, he signaled for a time-out.

Their players jogged off field, gathering in a circle around the two coaches. Myles, his cheeks flushed, barked out orders, glancing at Ryan every once in a while as though unsure if he should continue taking the lead. Ryan's brother was neck-deep in a coaching course, adding a layer of technical skills to his already natural coaching instincts. Ryan usually led the huddle, but this time he kept his right arm across his stomach, his left fist propping up his chin, remaining silent so the boys would know to listen to Myles.

Partway through Myles's rant, Ryan backed out of the huddle, waving for Carly's tablet. "Stats."

The tablet, warm from her grip, nestled into his hands and he frowned at the screen, trying to focus on the figures in front of him.

He was good at this. Football was his thing. Seeing patterns, sensing opportunities. He did it here on the field and in the class-room. He did it with his investment and business dealings. He even did it with his cockamamie inventions. He hadn't created and sold an app that had netted him almost a quarter million dollars, by allowing some woman to get into his head and keep him distracted. That had happened after the riches poured in.

So what was his deal today? Why couldn't he engage with this important game? Did football no longer matter to him?

He lifted his head and stared at the scoreboard.

Football had always mattered.

"Hernandez has been throwing great," Carly said, her words barely registering even though the surrounding sounds faded, his focus narrowing in on her. "Long passes into the open, but your receivers aren't fast enough to get there." She was standing beside him, the scent of soil, hay and fresh Texas air intensifying as she edged closer. She smelled familiar, like family and childhood. Good times. Good memories. Long before life got complicated. Could his life ever unwind into something so simple once again?

"Which receivers?" he asked, his brain snapping into gear.

"All of them. Except Wiggins. His strength is faking out his blocker and getting to where he needs to be. But his receiving needs work. He hasn't been catching those long passes at gut level. His hands are too far from his body and he's fumbling."

Ryan felt his jaw slacken with admiration and surprise. Not only was Carly the best kisser he'd ever met, the most chal-lenging and invigorating woman to tangle with, she also knew football. That was a quality he wouldn't mind having in a girlfriend.

Not that he wanted one.

Although maybe having a girlfriend who knew football would be nice.

What was he thinking? Priscilla had known football and it hadn't worked out for them. Not at all.

"We've been telling him that all season," Ryan said, blinking twice to get his thoughts back on track again.

Carly had moved closer so they could look at the app together. Her arms were pulled tight to her chest to block the wind coming over the field, her head close to his. He caught Jackie smiling at them.

She hadn't brought Carly for Dan.

"Tell Wiggins again," Carly said. "He could shift things. I mean, you're winning, but…"

"But how we're playing won't get us a win at State." He pivoted to face Carly head-on, taking a moment to drink in her beauty. He lowered his voice so the crew around them wouldn't hear, while glancing at Jackie again, who was still smiling as if she knew something. "You know we aren't doing anything serious. You and I? We're not telling the world about us."

Her jaw slackened for a second or two, then her eyes flared with fire as she said with a hint of disgust, "Get your head in the game, Coach."

He let out a chuckle, reminded once more why he liked Carly so much. "Okay, stats keeper. But I warn you…" He pointed his finger in an attempt to be stern, but was unable to hold back his smile. "…if you continue giving me tips like this, I'm going to keep you."

Carly's chest expanded with a sudden inhale and Ryan froze. He hadn't meant it like that.

"Honestly, I think you should." She gave him a sly wink that was flirtatious, confident and a tiny bit smug. It was the sexiest thing he'd seen in years. "But when you make it official, make sure you spell my name right on the sleeve of my team jacket. Clarke with an E on the end." She winked, taking back the tablet and tucking it into the crook of her arm. "I'll straighten out this team for you in no time."

Ryan laughed as she walked away, until he saw Jackie's grin from her spot in the chair next to Carly's empty one.

He squared his shoulders and pointed at her. "I'm not doing this. You hear me? I am *not* doing this. Your mojo magic doesn't work on me. I'm immune."

Jackie pressed her index finger to her chin, her head tipped to the side as though she was confused. He wanted to march over and strong-arm her out of their home-town stadium and into the next county. Then get her to stay there.

He turned away in frustration, heading back to the huddle.

Jackie wanted to set him up with the one thing he would never give a woman again: marriage.

The whistle blew, the time-out over. Ryan barked out some last-minute orders. "Hernandez, pass to Wiggins. Wiggins, for crying out loud, catch the ball like we told you to in practice. Nice and low." He cupped his hands, body crouched, to demonstrate. "Move your feet. You're fast enough to get into position and catch the ball. If you don't, I'll flatten your truck tires. You hear?"

"Yes, Coach," both Wiggins and Hernandez echoed.

"Hands in," he commanded.

Hernandez, the team captain, led them in the Torpedoes chant, and then the boys were back on the field.

"Think we can win this?" Ryan asked Myles in the last half.

His brother frowned at him as though he'd lost his marbles.

"What?" Ryan asked.

"Have you checked the score recently?"

Ryan thought about it. He had looked, certainly. It was like a nervous tic. Check, check, check. But today he couldn't recall where they were at. He swiveled to face the scoreboard near the end of the field. Okay, so they were ahead by three touchdowns, and there were only twelve minutes left in the game.

Then his team scored another touchdown. Where had that come from?

"Yes!" He felt a fizz of excitement lift him, and gripped Myles's hand after a high five. "We're going all the way to State again this year."

"What's with you?" Myles asked, not releasing Ryan's hand, peering at him intently.

"What do you mean?" About to glance over at Carly, he caught himself and kept his eyes locked on Myles.

"You never say stuff like that. You never call a game until we're off the field and the players are hitting the showers. Then you'll let me celebrate and say that, yes, we won." Myles pointed at the scoreboard. "There's over ten minutes left. Anything can still happen."

"It won't." But Ryan felt the excitement die. His brother was right. You never counted your win in football until the game was good and over. Especially in high school football. He'd seen a sure thing taken away in the last few seconds of a game. Unbelievable plays and twists of fate, taking what seemed like a definite win and turning it on its head.

Plus there was the old superstition of not calling a game or you'd curse it. He didn't believe in that, but adhered to it just in case.

So, yeah. He might be a tad superstitious.

A fresh wave of nervousness tossed his stomach like a small plane gliding through turbulence. He muttered, "Sorry, I got caught up in the moment."

"Is that all you got caught up in?" Myles asked, giving a pointed look over Ryan's shoulder toward where Carly and Jackie were sitting.

"Yeah," he said, crossing his arms over his clipboard. "That's all. Football's my only focus."

And he would do well to remember that for the next month, until the season was over. Too bad the game no longer held quite the same level of appeal as his new stats keeper.

***

"What are you doing for Thanksgiving?" Jackie asked, as they packed up their things at the edge of the football field.

Carly hadn't thought much about the details of next week's holiday other than wondering if the Longhorn Diner would be open for supper. Her parents and brother were still in Montana, and during her last weekly phone call with her mom she'd finally broken the news that she wasn't coming home for the holidays—neither Thanksgiving nor Christmas. The idea of facing the never-ending questions and worries about her newly chosen career didn't hold much joy. Neither did the silent eyes watching her as she walked down the small-town Montana streets, with people wondering how she'd dodged being convicted for Eaton's crooked bookkeeping. There was nothing like having the whole community know your business and make assumptions based on the half-facts they'd heard.

"No plans," she admitted.

"I'm going to the Wylders. You can be my date."

"No, no. I can't intrude." If she crashed Ryan's family event he'd think she was looking for something she wasn't. He'd already felt the need to warn her off thinking they were anything serious. Which was weird, since she was the one who'd told him she wasn't looking for love. Having him feel as though he needed to make sure she adhered to her own rules had hurt.

Was he afraid to be seen with her? She'd felt the reaction brew again and tamped it down. She reminded herself that they were not looking for a relationship, and they were at an age where if they revealed their interest in each other the entire town would start pushing, pushing, pushing. People would expect them to sign up for more than either of them was willing to give.

Myles walked by, hand in hand with the petite, serious-looking librarian who also managed the cheerleading team. Carly had met Karen Hartley when she'd moved to town, using the local library's internet before hers was hooked up at the house. Karen seemed a puzzling match for Myles, but they were obviously smitten with each other. And Carly figured that was what really mattered.

Myles's steps slowed as they came alongside. "Did I hear Jackie suggest you join us for Thanksgiving?"

"I did," Jackie said.

"Everyone's welcome and there'll be lots of food. We're celebrating Thursday night. Pop over at five."

"No, really," Carly protested. "I can't intrude."

"No intrusion." His warmth made her want to accept, and beside him, Karen was nodding.

"Say yes," Jackie commanded, no doubt noticing how Carly was ready to reconsider.

"It's an official invitation," Myles said. "Neighbors should break bread together. We never know when we'll need each other, right?"

"Fine," Carly said with a nervous laugh, unable to avoid seeking out Ryan in the dwindling group of people at the edge of the field. He was accepting handshakes from various members of the community on the team's win, and pointedly avoiding looking at her.

She and Ryan weren't an item. They were neighbors. Joining the Wylders for Thanksgiving wouldn't be presumptuous, right? And anyway, she knew men left, and Ryan would be no different. He was someone who followed ideas and dreams, and soon that would take him away.

"You're sure it's okay?" she asked.

Ryan had broken away from the community members and was wandering their way.

"Hey, Ryan," Myles called. "Carly's joining us for Thanksgiving."

She noticed the hitch in Ryan's step, his normally fluid moves pausing for a millisecond before he continued on with a quick nod, as though everything was fine, normal, not at all unexpected.

"Cool." He beckoned to his brother. "The team's waiting for us."

"Sorry, gals, gotta go have our postgame meeting." Myles gave Karen a kiss filled with such love and devotion that everyone nearby looked away.

Carly couldn't recall ever being kissed like that. Not even by Peter.

She glanced at Ryan. He was a wonderful kisser, but there wasn't that element of love pushing them over the edge. Myles and Karen's kiss had been practically spiritual.

Beside Carly, Jackie sighed. "Those two are so sweet."

Myles, looking as though it was a struggle to tear his gaze away from his girlfriend, said, "Thanks for your help tonight, ladies. See you at the Black Friday game next week?"

"Sure," Jackie said casually.

Myles released Karen's hand and headed toward his brother. "Just three more wins and we're going to State."

"Hey!" Ryan turned, palms raised. "I thought we weren't doing that."

"You know we're winning."

"Yeah, except you just cursed us."

As the brothers walked away Carly could hear their laughter, even after they'd disappeared down the chute that led to the locker rooms. Karen had gone off in a different direction to collect her team's bag of pompoms.

"Are the Wylders a close family?" Carly asked Jackie as they headed across the field toward the stands and parking lot.

"Pretty close." She scrunched her nose, telling Carly there was a "but" to be added to that statement.

As they neared the bleachers, Jackie waved at Maria Wylder and her veterinarian son, Brant, who were talking under the bright field lights. This late in the season, the seven-thirty games started and ended in the dark. Right now it had gotten cold enough that Carly could see her breath.

"Hey, Carly," Brant said, adjusting his red straw cowboy hat. "How's Sergeant Riggs working out?"

"Beautifully. He rounded up my goats when they broke out the other day." She'd been pleased by that. If the dog kept it up, he might earn his keep, considering those hefty bags of food he gobbled up.

"He's a keeper?"

"He is."

Maria nudged her son. "You should find me a dog now that I'm back on the ranch."

"You want another barking beast out there?"

"Why not? The more the merrier."

"Okay, I'll keep an eye out for one that might suit you."

"Brant got you a dog?" Jackie asked Carly.

"Ryan asked me to," Brant replied.

Carly frowned. "He did?" Ryan was not only talking about her, but telling his brother what she needed?

"Living alone on a ranch as you do, he figured it would be good protection."

"Good protection against him returning my goats in the middle of the night?" she said with a laugh, trying to ignore the strange, warm feeling that was growing in her belly. She wasn't sure she'd ever had a man do something so protective for her. At least not someone who wasn't related to her.

Before she could examine what she was feeling, and what Ryan's intentions may have been behind the dog request, she said, "I'm starting to think the goats were a terrible idea. They're becoming the bane of my existence, and they're not even producing milk."

"I don't know a ton about goats," Brant replied, "but I might have some ideas to try."

"All ideas welcome."

"I'll pop by one day soon."

"Carly's joining us for Thanksgiving," Jackie told them.

"Wonderful," Maria said warmly, smiling at her.

"We'll talk then," Brant suggested.

Carly nodded, then asked Maria, "Can I bring anything?"

"I'm sure we'll have plenty of food, but if you have a specialty you want to share that's fine. Or even just a bottle of wine. But don't feel you have to bring anything."

"We're going dancing at the Watering Hole now," Jackie announced, weaving her arm through Carly's. "We'll catch up with y'all later."

"Have fun," Maria said, as Jackie tugged Carly away.

Daisy-Mae Ray came hustling up in an outfit that must have nearly left her frozen while she watched the game. "Did I hear you gals mention dancing?"

Jackie nodded. "Join us! We're meeting Jenny there, too."

"We are?" Carly said in surprise.

"Of course!" She said in an aside to Carly, "She runs the Blue Tumbleweed clothing store beside the diner. Also single."

Jackie looped her other arm through Daisy-Mae's as they walked. "Girl, you're freezing. Are you lookin' to catch your death in that outfit?"

"Just a husband," she replied with a grin.

Jackie giggled, then suddenly ducked her head and steered the trio in a different direction. "Oh, poop."

"What?" Carly said, feeling alarmed.

"It's Henry Wylder. That curmudgeon can bring a black cloud to a sunny day."

"Oh, he's not that bad," Carly said. He'd made her consider things about her farm she hadn't thought of.

"Please tell me you're saying that with irony," Jackie muttered.

"He was actually helpful." A bit of a downer, but a practical one.

"Are you sure you met Henry? Not his brother Carmichael or nephew Roy?" Daisy-Mae asked, as Jackie hustled them along.

"Jackie was there. He gave me some sound advice on starting an organic farm."

"Yeah, by focusing on all the hurdles in your way."

"Well, sort of." She winced. It had been tougher to feel optimistic after chatting with him. But she'd gone to the town office and Tracey had given her some helpful information on her property's water wells. It turned out there were two more than she'd known about, and they all seemed to be in decent shape.

"Carly? Carly Clarke!" Henry called impatiently.

Jackie groaned and slowed her steps. "We were so close to making a getaway."

"Are you still thinking about that organic farm?" Henry asked Carly.

"Yes." She suddenly saw him in the way Jackie did, his frown telling her he was ready to rain down on her dream once again. She said quickly, "You were very helpful the other day. Thank you."

The man hooked his thumbs in his belt loops and rocked back on his boot heels, as though unsure what to do with the compliment. "I was?"

"Yes, you made me consider things I'd overlooked."

He rocked again. "Well, good."

Jackie's eyes widened as the man stood speechless before them.

"If you need help with certification," he said finally, "I might know a man."

"That would be wonderful. Thank you."

"But you need to get all that soil tested and make sure nasty things aren't running off the neighboring land and into your gardens. And get that well checked. You need good water, and lots of it."

"Already done," Carly replied. She began turning away with her friends. "Thank you, Henry. It was nice to see you again."

"And talk to Ryan!"

"Right." She wasn't so sure about that one.

Once they were out of earshot, Jackie giggled, saying gleefully, "Oh, my gosh. I think he likes you. I can't believe it!"

"It's a miracle," Daisy-Mae agreed.

Carly nodded. Once she'd recognized that Henry was a more blatant version of Peter with his your-dream-will-never-work, although without the undertone of you'd-better-let-me-take-care-of-things, she'd known how to deter him from continuing to rain on her parade. And somehow, from her kindness, he'd decided they were on the same team, helping her get further ahead on making her farm a reality.

5

Ryan kept pacing the front porch of the ranch house on Thanksgiving Day, and it wasn't simply because he was trying to sort out how to ensure a profit from his new horse business.

His team had scored a win last week, meaning tomorrow night they played their regional playoff game. And that meant he'd be distracted by Carly's presence as she volunteered as the team stats keeper once again. It hadn't helped that she'd completely nailed which strategy might help ensure a shutout score last week. She was a benefit to the team, that was for certain.

He leaned on the porch railing, looking out over the yard toward the holly hedge that separated his grandfather's home and yard from the main ranch. Beyond Carmichael's was Carly's. Where was she right now? Was she thinking of him?

Ryan mentally scolded himself. He needed to get his thoughts secured and his brain under lockdown. They weren't doing a relationship. Just kisses.

Having her come dine with the family tonight was well-timed, and would surely send a much-needed bucket of ice water over his constant thoughts about her. After all, nothing could cool your jets like having the woman you were secretly kissing come to a family gathering.

There was a flash of color behind the hedge. For a moment Ryan thought maybe Carly was taking the barely-there footpath that led between the properties and joined up with Carmichael's path. Moments later Ryan's seventy-nine-year-old grandfather ambled through the gap in the tall bushes. It wasn't Carly. Why would she take the unlit route when her return trip would be in the dark? Unless she wanted a ride home from a neighborly guy such as himself…

"What are you staring at? Never seen an old man walk before?" Carmichael grumbled as he drew closer.

"Hey, Granddad. Happy Thanksgiving."

"Your mom got her layer dip out yet?" He made his way up the several steps to the porch with a grunt. Judging by how the old cowboy was walking, rain was in the forecast. As if on cue, a cool wind rustled across the yard and Ryan shivered. At this time of the year it wouldn't be long until the sun set and night slipped in around them.

"I think Myles already ate it all," he said to his grandfather.

Carmichael gave him a glare. "I keep waiting for you to outgrow that phase."

"What phase is that?" Ryan asked innocently, holding the door for him.

"I can get it myself." He glowered at Ryan from the doorway before making his way through. His thick plaid jacket, which had not so long ago been filled out by sheer strength, now hung loose on the older man's shoulders. "I'm not dead yet."

"What phase should I grow out of?" Ryan pressed, following him inside. Neither of them took off their hats or boots, the ranch house being a typical working farm home where anything went. Although at the dinner table they'd take off their hats or his mother would have their ears.

Ryan grinned at the thought. His mom could control the men around her as if she'd been born doing it. He'd heard the female teachers in the staff room claiming they needed more from their husbands, as well as me-time, so they could cope. But not Maria. His father had up and left, and she'd carried on, stronger than ever, never seeming to need time away for herself. Ryan wasn't sure if she was, in fact, fully human. Then again, his mom had always seemed to have a bit of superhero steel in her backbone.

"The phase when you stop being a pain in my behind," Carmichael said.

"Boys," Maria scolded, coming around the corner from the kitchen with a tray of appetizers.

"I'm hardly a boy," Carmichael grumbled. "Is that your dip?"

"Take off your hats. It's Thanksgiving," she commanded. Both men obeyed, Carmichael placing his worn gray Stetson on a peg near the door. Ryan did the same with his new felt cowboy hat from Jenny Oliver's shop, Blue Tumbleweed.

Several members of the Wylder clan were already taking up space in the sunken living room and sipping what looked like Ryan's homemade brew.

"There's dip in the kitchen," Maria told Carmichael, as she took the two steps down into the family's midst to place her offerings on the coffee table. "I've been holding it back so you can have first dibs."

Carmichael headed in that direction, moving as fast as the time Ryan had let a bull loose, not realizing his grandfather was still in the pasture. Maybe rain wasn't in the forecast after all.

Ryan stood near the door, feeling unsure about where he should sit. His mother rarely wanted his inefficient help in the kitchen when she put on enormous meals.

Myles and Karen were cozied up together on the love seat whispering to each other, hands intertwined. Ryan knew better than to sit across from them and try to have a conversation. For the first time, he thought that maybe in the future he would not in fact be picking up the pieces of his brother's broken heart, but instead following these two through their milestones as a couple. Engagement, marriage, first child, second child and so on. Myles may have found the exception to the rule that relationships always crumble.

"Hi, Ryan," Laura Oakes said, gliding into the room with a grace likely due to her former career as a fashion model. She came over, a hint of sweet-smelling perfume wafting over him as she gave him a kiss on the cheek.

"Hey, Laura."

Maybe his eldest brother had found an exception, too. Laura had left Levi shortly after they'd gotten together, and man, those had been grim days for his brother. But then she had come back, and the two had been figuring things out like healthy, rational human beings.

If events continued the way they had been lately, Ryan could soon find himself the last bachelor, hanging out alone with Carmichael. Or with Brant. He was still single, too.

"Get that no-good brother of mine to give you a ring yet?" Ryan asked Laura.

Her cheeks flushed, but she laughed. "You and Myles sure give him a hard time about that, don't you?"

"Just want him to make an honest woman of you."

Rings were the litmus test as far as Ryan was concerned. Myles had been smart. He'd given Karen a bracelet. Although she'd given it back, so maybe that wasn't the best plan. But then again, from his vantage point near the door he could see she was wearing it today. What did that mean? They were solid? Or had his recent gut feeling about them been wrong, and they'd bought into an illusion that would soon come crashing down around them?

Laura went and sat beside Levi on the couch, the two of them kissing hello as if they'd been apart for weeks, not minutes.

"Where's Brant?" Ryan asked.

No answer.

It hadn't been like this when they'd all been single. Now, looking around the living room, he felt that familiar need to hustle like he had as the youngest Wylder, always a step behind his big brothers. Although, technically, he had been the first to marry. Not that it had lasted long enough to tell his family.

He headed to the kitchen, along the hall and to the left.

"Need help, Mom?"

Maria was bent over the open oven, poking at the turkey.

"I'm fine, Ryan. Thanks. There's beer in the fridge if you want one."

Ryan took out a bottle of his homemade pale ale and uncapped it. Carmichael was sitting at the long table, which had all its leaves in place, ready to seat twelve.

"You can have some when I'm done," Carmichael said, hunched over the dip. "If there's any left."

"I'm good, thanks." Ryan gazed past his grandfather, movement outside the patio window catching his attention. In the backyard the orange kittens were playing among some black-and-red-headed hens. "When did we get chickens?"

"We didn't," Carmichael said, then shoveled more dip in his mouth.

Did Carly now have chickens on the loose as well as goats? Ryan might have to explain to her that "free-range" still meant keeping the animals in a somewhat confined area and not the neighbor's yard.

He took another sip of his beer, noting the lot number he'd inked on the label. This one was aging nicely and might be a contender for the microbrewery he'd invested in over in River-bend. He offered them recipes, business advice and some financial backing for a 40 percent share in their operation. They hadn't made a profit yet, their startup costs swallowing the first six months of income. But it looked as though by month eight they might make a nickel or two, and after that, if things continued the way they had been, it wouldn't be long until they had a nice steady stream of revenue.

Smiling to himself, Ryan looked at his beer. It would be all right. Life was looking good for this single man.

Feeling the need to move, he left the kitchen, taking the hallway that overlooked the sunken living room. He heard a knock and the front door open, and when he rounded the corner from the kitchen, he stopped as though he'd hit a wall. Standing in the entry was a woman who took his breath away. She noticed him, her head of black curls lifting, her eyes meeting his. She smiled, and it was all he could do to hold his beer and not rush to her, pull her into his arms and kiss her.

Yes, life was good. The only question for his current life plan was how he could fit more of Carly Clarke into it.

***

CARLY STOOD in the entrance to the ranch house, feeling slightly out of place until she saw Ryan. He had rounded the corner from another room and then stopped short. The hitch that often seized his shoulders melted and his expression, before he tamped it down, was one of joy. It shot to her chest, lifting her. And then she caught herself, realizing she was in his family home, surrounded by the most important people in his life, for a big holiday dinner. It immediately felt too intimate, too meaningful.

She took a small step back toward the door, shyness overtaking her. She forced herself to look away from Ryan's probing, sea-colored eyes and appear nonchalant as Maria pushed past her son to come fuss over Carly's pecan pie and potted geranium.

"I hope you don't have too much dessert already," Carly said, having to clear her throat twice to get the words out. "And the flowers are just because."

"My boys are bottomless pits, which means food is always welcome here. As are flowers." She pointedly raised her voice on the last sentence, while casting a glance toward her sons. "You'd think with this many men kicking around I'd get flowers more often."

"Sorry, Mom," Levi called. "We'll try harder."

"You know everyone?" Maria asked Carly, gesturing to those seated in the living room. It was a big home with a warm, welcoming feel. A fire was crackling in the fireplace and two couples were cuddling on the couches.

She nodded, recognizing Levi and Laura, Myles and Karen. There was no Jackie to be seen. She hoped the woman hadn't invited her to the family event and then gone and ditched.

"Your goats haven't been around much lately," the old patriarch, Carmichael, said, entering the room from the direction Maria disappeared with the pie and flowers.

She leaned back around the corner, calling, "Ryan, take Carly's coat, please."

Ryan jolted, taking an awkward step forward as though someone had broken a layer of ice that had frozen him to the ground.

"Ryan helped me fix the goat pen," Carly told Carmichael, in reply to his earlier question. Her eyes were drawn toward the man in question. Ryan was wearing a crisp white shirt and dark jeans. He looked handsome, capable and very kissable. When he slipped her coat off her shoulders, his breath dancing across her bare neck, his fingers grazing her arms, she felt a spark of awareness.

"Looks like you might need to fix your chicken coop, too," Carmichael announced.

Carly's shoulders dropped. "Are they out?"

"They were here a bit ago," Ryan said, his voice feeling like a caress. She turned to take her coat, but he held it to him in both hands as though it could prevent him from kissing her. Or her him.

She shivered. It seemed any time she was close to Ryan she

wanted to lock herself in his embrace and forget about everything else in the world. She lowered her eyes and turned away, unsure how to break the tension that was rapidly growing between them.

She had learned to handle the aloof, cool version of Ryan she'd met on the football field, and she'd come to expect the open physical affection of the man she met up with in her stable. But this version was different. A layer with emotion and something else burning deep that could get them into trouble.

"Ryan was fixin' to cook one for supper," Carmichael said, a twinkle in his eye to let her know he was joking. He'd hobbled down the two steps to the living room, telling Levi to shove over and make some room on the couch for an old fella.

"Ryan!" Carly said, putting her hands on her hips and pretending to be aghast. "I can't believe you would eat my chickens."

She was getting a poor reputation with all her livestock breakouts. Not that she blamed her animals. The grass was greener over here, and not just figuratively.

"Isn't that why they're free-range?" Ryan teased. "So they'll taste better?"

She bit her bottom lip, trying to fight the smile as she gave his shoulder a playful shove. A solid wall of muscle, he didn't budge.

"They're egg layers, actually," she said haughtily. "Not for eating."

"Do you have any for sale?" Maria asked, reentering the room. "I love fresh farm eggs. Does everyone have enough to drink?"

"Only one egg so far," Carly said.

"They likely just need to settle in," Ryan said. "When did you get them? Yesterday?"

"The day before."

"Keeping tabs on her, are you?" Carmichael teased, causing Myles to smirk.

Ryan was adding Carly's coat to the line of jackets hanging by the door. The bottom hooks were filled with work attire and a range of cowboy hats occupied the pegs above.

"Ryan, put Carly's coat in the spare room," Maria called to him, heading back toward the kitchen. "That rack is full of dirty farm coats. Then be sure to offer her a drink."

"Yes, Mom," Ryan said gently, as though he was used to being bossed around by her.

Maria's voice changed from one of command to something softer. "Let me know when you have eggs for sale, Carly. I go through dozens every week."

"Okay. Hopefully soon."

Ryan jerked his chin toward the hallway behind the living room where doors opened into bedrooms. "I'll show you where I'll put your coat in case we chase you off by being too over-bearing and nosy."

"We wouldn't do that," Carmichael said with a wry tone.

"Sure we would," Myles said cheerfully, munching on some chips.

Carly followed Ryan around the living room and to the third door along the back wall. Ryan disappeared inside, and not sure what else to do, Carly followed. As she rounded the doorway, she felt hands grasp her waist, pulling her against a warm, hard body. Ryan's lips landed on hers, firm and demanding. She returned his kiss with an urgency that rocked her further against his chest. He pivoted, backing her against a wall as his hands roamed up her sides, their kiss deepening. Her palms slipped up his chest, her fingers dipping into his hair as their lips met again and again. Kissing Ryan was like unleashing a tornado, but she wasn't sure if it was inside herself, or him.

Ryan finally pulled away, the two of them breathing hard. "Happy Thanksgiving."

"Gobble, gobble," she whispered, yanking him back for another consuming kiss.

When they broke apart again Ryan smiled, then stole one

more kiss before exiting the room. Carly, propped against the wall, drew a deep breath to calm the rush of desire that had left her shaking. She took a few more seconds to compose herself, smoothing her outfit, before joining Ryan, who was standing casually in the hallway.

"You two are a couple?" Carmichael asked. "Since when?"

Carly felt her eyes widen in alarm. She glanced at Ryan, who gave his grandfather a bored, unimpressed look. "Not everyone is hooking up, Granddad."

"Yeah, I'm not," he said. "And neither is your mother. But you boys sure have been. You'd think there was a war coming and you US Army Reserve lads had only a few more weeks of freedom left." He nodded thoughtfully, as though verifying the accuracy of his statement. "Making up for lost time, like the late bloomers you are."

Carly held back a giggle while making a quick visual sweep of the family, curious what their take was on Carmichael's pronouncement. There were a few curious glances shot her way, and she made a point of looking indifferent, and hopefully not as though she'd just been consumed by a dozen hungry kisses.

"You're in the reserves?" Carly asked. She edged closer to Ryan as though he might save her from any further awkward exchanges, before realizing she might be acting like his date.

"We all are." He sized her up. "How long have you been in?"

She didn't hide her surprise. "I no longer am, but how did you know I was?"

He shrugged, giving her one of those looks of his that hinted that he saw a lot more than she typically allowed anyone to see. She wondered if he could tell that she'd been asked to leave the reserves.

The front door opened and Brant, the middle Wylder brother, entered. "Happy Thanksgiving. Hey, Carly, Karen, Laura." He gave each of them a nod.

"What? I don't rate a hello?" Ryan asked, arms out in protest.

"No, you get a hug." Brant grinned and opened his arms, but Ryan waved him off.

"Levi," Brant said, as he hung up his coat by the door, "did Ryan convince you to get chickens? Weren't those useless sheep enough of a lesson when it comes to Ryan's cockamamie ideas?"

"They're not useless," Ryan said with a smirk.

"You told me there were benefits, so I bought some," Levi grumbled.

"I was just thinking out loud."

Carly had forgotten all about her chickens, and she ducked back into the room to retrieve her coat so she could round them up before the coyotes got them.

"What's up, Granddad?" Brant asked, stepping down into the living room as Carly returned with her coat.

"I already ate all the layer dip," Carmichael announced. "So you may as well go home."

Brant grinned. "I asked Mom to make double. I bet she hid some away for me."

Carmichael seemed affronted. "Now why would she go choosing favorites?" He eased himself off the couch and hustled toward the kitchen.

"Are the chickens still out in the yard?" Carly asked, sliding into her coat.

"About a dozen Australorps," Brant confirmed.

"I'd better go round them up."

"They're yours?"

She nodded, heading toward the door as Ryan said, "I'm sure they'll be fine."

"I heard coyotes the other night," she stated. "I don't want them having their own Thanksgiving meal."

"I'll see if my dog knows how to round up chickens." Levi's long-legged strides took him across the living room in a matter of seconds. He chose a hat and jacket as Brant opened the door.

"I guess we'd better train Sergeant Riggs how to work with chickens and not just goats," Brant said.

Before Carly could fully realize or protest what was happening, everyone except Maria and Carmichael was rounding up her beautiful black-and-red chickens.

"Do we have time before supper?" she asked, horrified that her problem might delay the meal Maria was preparing.

"Don't worry about it. Mom understands," Ryan said. "She's a ranch woman through and through."

"But I can't make all of us late. She's worked so hard on the meal."

"It's not as important as livestock on the loose," Brant declared.

"Tell me about it," Laura said with a groan, earning a chuckle from Levi. "And anyway, she kicked us all out of the kitchen a while ago, saying to go keep ourselves busy." Laura checked her watch. "We probably have close to an hour."

The group worked seamlessly, creating an arc that gently herded the chickens back toward the Lucky Horse Ranch. Ironically, Lupe, Levi's dog, refused to take part in the efforts.

Back in Carly's yard, the brothers found the problem. An enterprising chicken had pecked at a loose piece of netting she'd thought was secure enough, creating an escape hatch.

"I had no idea they would do that. I mean eventually, sure. But that was fast."

"There's some lumber in the stable," Ryan said. "Can we use it?"

Carly nodded, and soon enough wood, wire and tools were rounded up. The sounds of sawing and drilling filled the quiet November evening. Ryan was in the thick of it, taking measurements and giving orders with a confidence Carly found appealing.

"He must be hungry. He's not usually this helpful," Levi said, jabbing a thumb in his brother's direction.

Carly felt an apology almost make it to her lips before realizing he was just teasing his brother.

"I really appreciate everyone's help," she said, kneeling beside Ryan, who was securing a board. She held one end, trying to be helpful as the group fixed her problem, no questions asked. Her sheepdog, Sergeant Riggs, wandered over and sat beside her, panting his warm wet breath in her ear. The drill was near her right knee, and she picked it up, ready to fasten the board into place once given the command.

"Where did the drill go?" Ryan demanded. He glanced at her and his sternness melted. "Oh. Hey, want to secure that end?"

She drilled in a screw, then shuffled toward him and attached his end as well.

"I didn't know you were handy with power tools."

His sentence started as though he was going to make a playful dig at her about her goat pen, but then his tone changed, an awareness building between them as the silence stretched.

"There's a lot about me you don't know."

He had been staring at her lips and now his gaze darted to hers as though asking her just how much was yet to be discovered. And maybe also asking how much they wanted to reveal to each other, how deep they wanted to go.

And right now? The answer, as scary as it was to her, was everything. She wanted to share every sad and sordid detail of her life, as well as explore every bit of his.

Behind them someone cleared a throat and Ryan quickly stood. "I think that'll keep your chickens in place. Let's go eat before we all wind up on Mom's bad side."

As THEY WALKED from the chicken coop to the stable, to return the tools and lumber they hadn't used, Ryan caught himself moving closer to Carly, and at one point almost reaching out to take her hand. In front of them Myles and Karen were holding hands, as were Levi and Laura, the dusk growing around them as the last of the sun's rays continued to fade. It felt natural to reach out to the woman he'd been thinking about, as well as sneaking in moments with all week.

Instead he moved a step to his right and quickened his pace to help Brant, who had the extra lumber, even though Ryan was already carrying a toolbox.

"I heard you'll be at the regionals game to take stats," Myles said to Carly. "Are you coming to State, too?"

She lifted her head from watching her steps through the dry grass and immediately glanced at Ryan, who shrugged. She didn't need to check with him, even though he was the head coach and she was a major distraction anytime she came near him.

So, yeah, maybe it was good to check in with him first.

Not that he could say no. She was an asset.

"There's room on the bus," he said.

"Such a lovely invitation," Brant muttered. "Sorry, Carly. Seems I got Ryan's share of the Wylder charm."

She released a light laugh.

"It's called working out logistics," Ryan barked at his brother.

"So, as a spectator, if you need a ride to State Ryan has you covered." Brant's tone was teasing but amicable, making Ryan feel like a heel. He was used to giving women his back-off vibe to the point that he no longer recalled how to give them the come-on-over one. Or at least the come-a-little-closer-but-don't-go-expecting-too-much vibe, if there was such a thing.

"A ride would be lovely," Carly said, giving Sergeant Riggs a quick scratch behind the ears as they walked. "Even if I don't know if I'll be working as a stats keeper or not."

They were playing him. Ryan knew it. They were baiting him as if he didn't know any better.

He would not rise to their bait. He would not bite. If Carly wanted to come with the team, then fine, but he wasn't putting his heart out there.

"Maybe I could talk to the head coach on your behalf," Brant said. "He's my brother, you know. He usually brings a stats keeper or two and often puts them up in the team hotel." Brant placed a hand on his chin as though deep in thought.

"Sorry, Brant," Ryan said with a hint of sarcasm. "Was I supposed to say we appreciated Carly's invaluable input? Maybe wax on about how she saw a unique perspective that helped us add a few more plays to our repertoire? Or that it would benefit the team if she came along to help? Maybe I was supposed to say she's already the best stats person I've had in my five years of coaching, and she could make the difference between us winning or losing State, if we make it that far. And that my only concern is how distracting I find her when she's on the sidelines, because it makes it difficult to focus on football?"

Everyone had gone silent, their footsteps slowing as they neared the stable. Ryan could feel their eyes on him while they pretended to look at the tall oaks that lined the edge of the property behind him.

He let out a disgusted sigh.

He'd taken their bait, and now Carly knew how dependent he was on her insights, and she'd lord it over him. Then, when he was most invested, she would vanish, leaving him high and dry.

Or, because they weren't doing the relationship thing, his brothers would tease him about his soft spot for Carly and scare her off.

He knew the deal. Not a couple. No feelings. No obligations between them. Just independence and freedom.

"The position pays," Myles said, breaking the silence.

"A pittance," Ryan said pointedly.

"And it covers staying in a hotel?" Carly asked. The yard light he'd helped install came on as they walked past it. Her dark skin seemed darker, no doubt a hint she was blushing over how he'd broken their rule. He'd just made it obvious to all that something was going on.

If Carly came to State, there was no way she could stay in the same hotel as him. There wasn't enough self-control in a man like him. Not with her being his dream woman on the field, taking stats and suggesting smart plays.

Doomed. He'd be a doomed man.

He was already.

"You can room with me," Karen said. "The two cheer coaches are rooming together, and Jackie's staying at her brother's."

"Yes! That's a great idea," Ryan said, too enthusiastically. The cheerleaders stayed in a different hotel than the players, meaning Carly would be blocks away if the team made it as far as State. He'd only see her on the field and at any potluck meals the parents put on.

"I don't think I can leave my animals," Carly said, setting down a spool of chicken wire and using both hands to open the large stable doors. "And there's a chance I'll be in Montana that week—the Tuesday for sure. I might not be able to get to Dallas by Friday."

"I'm sticking around," Brant interjected. "I can come over and feed your animals. I'm already filling in for Myles and Ryan next door."

"You don't go to the game?" Carly asked.

"I'll drive to Dallas after I do chores."

"That seems like a lot. Dallas is a long way from here."

"Putting out a bit of dog kibble, chicken scratch and goat feed is nothing compared to what these guys have me doing." Brant jabbed a thumb toward his brothers.

Ryan could tell Carly wanted to go.

He wanted her to come, too.

"If you can mange it, we'd love it," Myles said.

Still she hesitated.

"I'll buy you supper if you come," Ryan said, instantly regretting it. "You know, as a thank-you for taking stats."

Levi shot Ryan a questioning frown.

"Like a date?" Carly teased, causing Ryan's brothers to laugh.

"No," he said firmly.

"Ryan doesn't date," Levi said, heading inside the stable. Sergeant Riggs trotted in ahead of the rest of them, sat in front of one of the horse stalls and gave a low woof.

"His kiss-and-tell adventures up at Devil's Horn aren't dates?" Myles joked from the doorway, where he'd found the switch for the overhead lights.

"I doubt he even sees any of those women again," Levi said, organizing the return of Carly's supplies into the empty stall at the end. He stacked the boards and tools the way they'd found them and then started ushering everyone out of the stable.

"That's the dream," Ryan muttered, then he shook his head and sighed. Why had he told his brothers he was with women, when in fact he went out to the Devil's Horn lookout to think?

Because they would think he was cool, that's why. And wouldn't ask questions, like they would if he told them he needed a quiet place to think that was far from everything. No cell phones, no distractions.

Anyway, what did it matter what Carly thought? She wasn't going to become anything serious or permanent in his life.

"I'm sure most of the female population of Sweetheart Creek has seen the view from that lookout," Levi said with a laugh as he reached the stable doors, holding them open for everyone as if he owned the place.

Ryan expected Brant to join in with the ribbing, but when he turned to check his brother's expression, he found him standing near one of the stalls, next to Sergeant Riggs. Savoring the way the stable held the heat from the day, warmer than outdoors, Ryan headed back to them.

Brant was frowning at a horse, arms folded over the chest-high stall gate.

"What do you think?" Ryan asked.

His brother straightened, his focus still on the quarter horse Ryan had bought for barrel racing. "Why did you buy these guys, anyway?"

"Training."

"This one needs help."

"What kind of help?"

Brant ran a hand down the snout of the animal, a serious, focused look on his face.

"Why is there feed coming out her nose?" Ryan asked, noting the fact with sudden alarm.

"It's okay," Brant said in a soothing tone. Ryan wasn't sure if that was for him or the horse as the vet let himself into Blackberry's stall. He made hushed, reassuring sounds as he checked her over. Every once in a while the horse would jerk her head upward. Lucinda thought this sweet beast could be a winner. She couldn't get sick.

"Everyone's gone back to the ranch to wash up," Carly announced, reentering the stable. "What's up?" Her presence drew Ryan's attention, and he noted how good she smelled. There was something about her and the stable that just felt so right.

"Brant says there's something wrong with Blackberry." The horse stretched her neck and made a strange hacking sound, causing Ryan to step back, his alarm increasing. Riggs let out another soft, deep woof.

"Oh, no," Carly said, her voice hushed as she joined Brant in the stall. "Choke?"

He nodded.

"She's choking? Help her!" Ryan tried to figure out how you could give a horse the Heimlich maneuver. He'd never encountered this on the ranch and didn't know what to do.

His brother exited the stall, saying to Ryan as he walked past, "I'll get my bag."

"But Blackberry's choking! She can't wait." He didn't know where Brant's vet bag was, but it definitely wasn't nearby. How much time did the horse have?

"She can wait," Brant said, his steps steady, not rushed.

Ryan turned back to Blackberry. She was breathing, but her discomfort was clear. There were bits of green mucous and saliva, the color of feed, coating her nostrils and possibly her throat. Should he have chopped up her feed, like he saw their friend April doing with hot dogs for her young son?

No. You didn't have to chop up food for horses.

Ryan took a step back, bumping against a warm body as the stable doors closed behind his brother.

"It's okay," Carly said, wrapping her arms around his middle from behind. She reached past his open jacket, placing her palms against his chest. The heat from her touch ate through the fabric between them and he absently placed a hand over hers, accepting the comfort, letting her know she should stay exactly where she was.

Long moments later she pivoted so she faced him, her hands loose on his waist. Her brown eyes held concern—for him as well as the animal.

The horse stretched and retched, looking as though she was trying to vomit. Ryan's tension coiled tight again.

"How long does a horse have—" He wasn't able to finish the sentence.

"It's a minor esophageal obstruction. There's time. She'll be right as rain once Brant flushes it out." When Carly slipped her arms around his waist and laid her head against his chest, he wrapped her in an embrace, unsure what else to do.

It was so soothing, having her run her hands up and down his back as they stood there in silence. No expectations, no complications. Just them together in a crisis.

He could get used to this. Having somebody.

Eventually, Carly stirred, taking his chin and forcing him to look at her. "I know we're just casual, but what's the deal with taking all those local gals to the lookout?"

<hr>

CARLY TIPPED her head back to watch Ryan's face when she asked about the women at the lookout. His smile was sad, almost haunted, so she let the question go, instinctively knowing there was more to his supposed escapades, and that it was a private struggle beyond the realm of their relationship.

She used to be glad for the boundary they'd set between their lives, but lately she'd come to despise it. It was a barrier preventing them from making what was already good between them even better. If they trusted each other a bit more they could share so much, forge a connection that was deeper than a few heated embraces.

But that wasn't what they'd agreed to, and she had a feeling neither of them would ever renege.

Ryan wound one of her curls around his finger, saying, "If you want to head to the ranch and enjoy supper, go ahead. I'll wait here for Brant."

"You might need an extra set of hands."

He hugged her tighter, resting his cheek against her forehead.

Carly had dealt with choke before, her barrel riding horse in high school having dealt with it once. She knew how alarming it could be, but she hadn't expected Ryan, who took everything in stride, to be so tense about it. Sure, he hid it well, but the way he was holding her so close, rubbing her back while they waited for Brant to return, was telling. The horses meant more to him than an income stream, and this man, who seemed to take her jabs and teasing like he was made of solid oak, had a well-hidden sensitive side.

When they heard a truck approach the stable minutes later, headlights temporarily brightening the cracks between the closed doors, they broke apart, Ryan striding to the doorway to greet Brant.

Like most rural vets Carly had met, Brant had his truck equipped with a large vet box that took up the entire back box, turning it into a mobile veterinarian clinic. She was surprised to see a woman pop out of the passenger seat and Brant lift a small boy out behind him.

"Hey, guys," said the woman. "I heard you have a horse in distress. Thought maybe you could use some extra hands."

"How many hands does it take?" Ryan muttered, just before Carly introduced herself to the newcomers. April MacFarlane was cute, had dimples when she smiled and an aura of an able-handed ranch gal.

Brant took his bag to the stall as the others trailed behind.

"Did you used to barrel race?" Carly asked April.

She flashed a grin. "Yup. You?" She squinted in thought. "You did, didn't you? I think I remember you on a high-strung thoroughbred? Um, from out west. No. Up north?"

"Montana. Man, Terror was fast," Carly said, grinning at the flood of memories. The horse had been difficult, but a perfect partner. They'd taken home a lot of hardware in their four years of rodeo.

"Tell me about it," April muttered wryly. "You smoked me and my horse Cookies a few times."

Ryan was looking at Carly, eyebrows raised. She gave a shrug and mouthed *"What?"* It wasn't as though they asked each other about their pasts. And as for the horses, he'd made it clear he was training them his way. He didn't want a partner or input, and she was smart enough to butt out.

"Hold this," Brant said, handing Ryan a length of clear medical hose.

"You were good," April said, appraising Carly.

"You, too."

"You two remember each other?" Ryan asked.

Carly smiled politely. As one of the few women of color in rodeo, she knew she was memorable. More memorable than someone like April might be—that was if she hadn't always left a wake of fighting cowboys everywhere she went.

"And now look at us," April said with a laugh.

"I'm sure you still have it," Carly stated. April had been strong and sure on top of a horse, and that wasn't a skill she would have lost.

"The rodeo world is small," Brant remarked, handing Carly a bucket. "Can you fill this with water?"

"Sure." She turned to the little boy, Kurt, asking, "Want to see where the tap is for watering horses?"

"Okay."

Together they filled the bucket, then returned to Brant's side. He had several large needleless syringes lined up to flush water through the horse's mouth to remove the obstruction. Ryan was standing nearby, frown in place, the coiled hose loose in his hands. Flushing the obstruction wouldn't be pleasant for the animal, but the relief it brought would be worth the discomfort.

"Your daddy will help Ryan's horse feel better," Carly said to Kurt.

"My daddy isn't here," he replied.

April shook her head. "Brant's an old family friend." She reached out and gave him an affectionate push, and he looked at her in a way that left Carly with a sting of longing. There was obvious affection, trust and comfort between the two of them.

"I'm sorry," Carly said, referring to her assumption.

"That's fine," April said. "We were raised like siblings." She tipped Brant's hat, knocking it off his head with a smirk. "Weren't we?"

In retaliation he grabbed a handful of straw from the floor of the stall and tossed it at April's legs, before returning his focus to the lined-up tools once again.

Soon everyone was helping Blackberry, eventually clearing

the obstruction. As soon as that happened the horse went right to her feed and began eating again.

Ryan stared at her, shaking his head.

"That horse is just like you Wylder boys," April said, patting him on the shoulder. "Always with your head in the feed bag." She laughed and Brant gave her a warm smile.

"I can't believe she's already eating," Ryan said. "She totally okay now?"

His brother nodded.

"I hear you're starting an organic farm," April said, pulling Kurt off a ladder that led to a small hayloft above. She gave him the empty bucket and sent him to Brant's truck, reminding him to be helpful.

"That's the idea." Carly refrained from glancing over at Ryan, who was still in the stall with Brant. Apparently Ryan knew a fair bit about organic farming, according to his great-uncle Henry.

Carly knew some guidance could add efficiency to her current plan, but she didn't quite have the courage to ask him, worried he'd think she was expecting more than he was willing to give.

"I'll likely start with some sell-direct locally grown veggies. Maybe some organic goat's milk and free-range eggs. Casual, small orders to deal with the unpredictable supply in the first few years as I figure things out."

"Well?" April asked, her voice rising with authority, her hands settling on her rounded hips in a way that reminded Carly of Maria Wylder. "Are you going to help her or what?" She was gazing at Ryan, who lifted his head at her tone.

"With what?" he asked.

"You learned all about permaculture." She turned to Carly. "That's where you plant the right things and then those plants all help each other grow without the aid of fertilizers or something like that, right?"

Carly nodded.

"It sounds like the stuff you're going to do," April said.

"You don't need me interfering." Ryan scratched his ear as he stepped out of the stall, looking mildly uncomfortable. "You have your own plan."

"Yes, and Henry Wylder pointed out a few pitfalls. Now I'm unsure what else I may have overlooked," she said, before she could catch herself.

"Ugh. Henry," April said with an eye roll. "Is he over there tonight?" She pointed toward the neighboring ranch.

"Don't think so. At least not yet," Brant said, guiding April back toward his truck where, giggling, Kurt was letting Sergeant Riggs lick his face.

"Only twelve places were set," Ryan said. "I don't think he's coming."

"Speaking of dinner," Brant said, "we should head back. You two want a ride?"

"I'm going to stay another five," Ryan said, from in front of Blackberry's stall.

"She'll be fine, Ryan," his brother assured him. "See you over there?"

Carly nodded, feeling as though she'd just revealed her worst fears for the farm to April and then left them hanging in the air. But she knew she could do this. And yeah, sometimes she was scared, but she already had a few things sprouting in her little garden and Brant would give her ideas about her goats and milk. It would all work out, and the day this place fed her an entire meal would feel amazing.

April called from the door, "Ryan, help her figure out a plan. A woman can't do everything on her own, even though we say we can. And let her give you some advice on this ragtag herd of rejects you've collected."

Carly hid her laugh before Ryan turned her way, saying, "I'm sure you have everything under control around here."

"Uh, sure. Just like I'm certain you have everything under

control every moment of every day with your horses."

Hearing the amusement in her voice, he gave her a questioning look.

"It's fine, really," she said. "I was just venting. This start-a-farm thing is difficult, but I'll get there."

"It takes time."

"I happen to be an impatient woman."

He laughed, turning to his horse. "Yeah, I sensed that."

Carly stood beside him, patting Blackberry's nose when she stuck her head over the gate to see what food they might have to offer. "It's probably why we get along so well. I don't see you as the type to sit around and wait for life to reach you, either."

He gave a small nod of agreement.

"And sure, sometimes I wonder why I think spending fourteen hours a day collecting eggs, milking goats and weeding vegetable gardens just to keep my head above water is wise. But then the sun sets and I hear my goats bleat and it feels good. It's mine."

Ryan was watching her from under the brim of his hat. "Exactly."

"Exactly," she echoed, dusting her hands together as though settling something.

"This is where most people give up," he murmured.

"Because they're smart," she answered with a laugh, reaching over to give him a nudge. "The doubt gets big, doesn't it?"

He let out a long breath, pushing his cowboy hat farther back on his forehead. They were both facing the horse they'd just helped to cure. Carly was used to being able to read Ryan's expression, but this was one she couldn't quite figure out.

Maybe his horse-training plan was as fraught with potential hazards as her farm plan was. The red roan in the end pen had potential, based on his build, though he seemed to be a heavy eater who resisted exercise. The young quarter horse might be good for cutting, but he needed to be trained soon. And this sweet animal in front of them was kind and gentle, reminding her of Ryan's softer side. Carly didn't doubt he'd bought the mare because she had walked up to him, fluttered her long lashes, given him a nuzzle and promised to always be there with unconditional acceptance and support. A man like Ryan needed that, even though he'd never admit it.

But would Blackberry make a good barrel racer? Carly wasn't sure. She'd seen Lucinda working with her and there was potential, but maybe not enough for what Ryan was looking for.

"You still going to go for supper?" she asked, taking a few steps toward the still-open stable doors.

Ryan continued watching his mare. "Are you certain she's okay?"

"She's fine."

"Maybe I should have Brant send a scope down to make sure her throat's okay."

Carly remained silent as Ryan reached over the stall door, stroking the horse's long white nose stripe. There was something in his quiet expression that made her shiver.

"What if my gut's wrong?" he said, his voice even and low. He had an intense look when he turned to her, his bright blue eyes alight with questions. They stared at each other for a long moment, tension arcing like a live wire between them.

How much did they dare become entangled in each other's lives? How much were they willing to risk?

Carly swallowed, taking a step closer. "What if your gut is right?"

They closed the distance between them, and he twisted one of her curls around his index finger in a move that was beginning to feel as familiar as his kisses.

"I thought you were a team of one," she whispered, taking a risk with her words.

"Maybe we both are, and that's why we're so good together." He lowered his lips for a soft, tender kiss.

6

As Ryan walked back to Sweet Meadows Ranch with Carly in the deepening dusk, he grew quiet, trying to sort out his tangle of thoughts. He knew what he wanted in life and he had a plan. No detours. No pit stops. Full speed ahead. Alone.

But when he took inventory of his current rules for living, his thoughts and plans somehow seemed less important than they once had.

What if he and Carly tried being a team of two? Nothing big, just two teams of one working together. What could be the harm in that?

"Do you want help with your plans for the farm?"

Carly tensed, her normally fluid movements tightening, just like his quarterback Hernandez's out on the field, when he got caught playing favorites.

"I'm sure you're busy with other things," Carly said. "You don't need to take this on."

He paused at her words. "I don't want to take it on. I want to help. Help you."

Her lips twisted in a skeptical frown. "Men have an inborn

need for control though. They take over. I wouldn't be calling the shots for very long if I involved you."

"That's not fair."

"Is it unfair?" She stopped on the path through the tall grass they had taken earlier as they'd herded the chickens—a path no doubt initially created by her wandering goats. Carly's dark eyes were flashing, analyzing him as she stood with her arms crossed, hip out.

"Darn right it's unfair. We're both independent and—"

"Exactly! We're independent. You won't want to answer to me. Your idea or approach will become The Plan. My thoughts on how to run my farm will be discarded." She swung an arm through the air with a flourish.

Ryan caught her elbow, trying to calm the storm he'd inadvertently created. "Hey, I think you're forgetting something important here. It'll always be your farm. It's your name on the deed."

There was still anger in the set of her jaw.

"Do you really think I could march in here and tell your independent bossy side what to do?" He let out a laugh at the thought, but could see she wasn't convinced. "What did you do the first time you saw me and thought I was interfering with your farm?"

Her anger ebbed and she almost giggled. "I threatened to shoot you."

"See? And what did you do when I brought my horses over before I'd officially paid the rent?"

"I threatened you? I can't recall the details."

"You're strong enough to handle me, Carly. You won't let me run you over." He paused to let that sink in, and for her to believe it. "If you want help and advice, I can provide that. Yes, I'm opinionated, but so are you. We'll have some good fights, and you'll decide what's right for you and your farm. I have faith in that."

She gave a slow nod, letting him know she'd heard him.

"Do you have faith in yourself?" he asked.

The earlier tension returned full force. Her defiant fighter side wanted to say yes. But, for whatever reason, she wasn't there yet, and that broke his heart. She reminded him of his students, not yet confident in their strength and ability. But for Carly it wasn't because of inexperience, and he'd hazard a bet it was experience that had her doubting herself.

"You're amazing, Carly Clarke."

She rolled her eyes with impatience.

"Seriously. You know how many women I've kissed lately?"

She shifted away from him, that tension building in her graceful, strong spine, her eyes like daggers once again. "I told you I'm a one-at-a-time kind of woman."

"You," he said, before she could assume the worst. "Just you. That whole Devil's Horn lookout thing my brothers joke about? I have never taken a woman up there. That's *my* spot. I tell them I'm taking a lady up there so they'll leave me alone with my thoughts."

Carly was watching him out of the corner of her eye and he grasped her left hand, toying with her wedding band for a moment. "If you want my help, you have it. Just say the word."

"Okay."

Was that an okay to the offer of help? Or an okay meaning she'd heard him? He got the impression she didn't want to be someone in need of help. She wanted to be a capable lone ranger.

So did he. But he also knew he needed her, just like she needed him.

"I honestly want you to come to the rest of the season's games and help me with the team as a stats keeper."

"So this is tit for tat?" she asked. "I'm helping you, so now you have to even things out by helping me?"

"No."

She stared at him for a moment that stretched out to the point of discomfort. He was recalling several of the reasons he preferred to fly solo.

"Fine." She began walking again, crossing the spot where the remnants of an old fence marked the property line between the two ranches. "Yes to helping with stats. Yes to help with the farm." Before he could say anything her voice rose. "I'll be there at tomorrow night's game, but you need to know there's a very good chance I won't be able to make all of them."

"Okay."

"Stop interrupting me." She had grown agitated, a fear coming off her he wasn't sure how to alleviate. "And I want to tell you that when my business went under—"

"Carly, it's fine. I don't need to know the details. This farm is a fresh start, right? We'll come up with a plan that's as flawless as possible, and I promise that every decision will be yours to make."

She didn't need to relive the embarrassment and shame from her past. He got it. Mistakes were made. No need to dwell or talk it out. Live, learn, move on.

"I feel you should know the details if we're going to work together."

"Carly, I trust you. We've both lived, learned, and moved on with life. We are who we are, right here, right now." His tone was firm. "Let's talk about your farm."

She wrinkled her nose as though fighting with herself, and he waited for her to argue, to insist that they bond by sharing their past slip-ups with each other.

"I know what I want to accomplish with the farm," she said finally. "But getting there will take a long time, and I'm not sure my plans are as efficient as they could be."

"What are your plans? Do you have something written down?"

She shook her head as they passed Carmichael's small house, where a string of lights hanging from the trees lit the way to the main ranch house. Those were new. Ryan wondered who'd put them up. Likely Levi, looking out for their grandfather.

"It might help you focus on what needs to happen to get your farm certified organic. As you work toward that you can start spreading the word and line up future orders."

"But I'm not certified, and my first garden has barely sprouted."

"So?"

"I'm going to run my business by the book."

"Leave room for life to happen, Carly. You'll get certified and your garden will grow. Get the word out now so you're ready."

"You want me to lie? Mislead my future customers?"

"Is there something you feel will prevent you from getting certification?"

Carly slowed her steps, and not because they were heading through the narrow break in the holly hedge. He could see she was deep in thought, arguing with him in her head.

She was thinking too linearly. She needed to shoot threads out ahead so things would be lined up when she got there. You didn't grow a garden, then try to find customers once it was harvested.

"Working inside the box is going to take longer. You'll suffer a lot of waste."

"Yeah, but I might still have a business by the end. I don't need some grand financial adventure. I want a simple life, to be independent and save a bit for retirement." A shadow crossed her face.

"Farming might not be the easiest way to do that," he said with a chuckle. "You're at the mercy of Mother Nature so much of the time."

"I can control everything else. I can learn all aspects of this business." Her voice was firm, illustrating her determination. "I can choose which crops, plan what I put on them to help them grow organically, do my own accounting, watch my cash flow."

There were plenty of other businesses that were less fraught with risk. "Why did you buy a ranch?"

She inhaled audibly. "It's a long story."

They had stopped walking and Ryan stooped to pet his brothers' dogs, Lupe, Buckey and Dodge, as they wound their way around him to see what was happening. The string of bright lights ended here, with the yard light illuminating the rest of the way.

"I have time for long stories," he said.

Just then, the dinner bell rang, no doubt by Maria who would be leaning out the patio door off the kitchen.

"Well, maybe not a ton of time." They began moving toward the house again.

"The quick version was that I wanted out of the city," Carly said, "and a way to be independent. Self-sufficient. Not relying on someone else for anything. So a farm like the ones I grew up on seemed like a good idea."

Ryan gave her an appraising look. There were a lot of reasons to love this woman, and what she'd stated was another thing to add to the growing list.

"I can respect that," he said, as they climbed the steps to the porch.

"What's your story?" she asked, stopping at the door, gaze pinned on him.

"Nothing exciting." He reached to open it but she stepped in front of him.

"You're so full of it."

He felt his eyebrows jump in surprise. "Okay, fine. I don't want to rely on others, either. I like being independent. Although maybe that makes little sense, seeing as I'm a coach who depends on his players, and I work in a school and depend on a school district. Plus I'm part owner in this ranch and depend on my brothers to take care of the bulk of its problems."

"So? I depend on seed suppliers and buyers."

"Is there a way to be entirely independent?"

"I'm sure there is. It's just a lot of work." She leaned her head to the side, studying him. "Why are you so intent on training some fat horses for rodeo?"

There was a hint of amusement in her tone and Ryan narrowed his eyes, waiting for her to make fun of the idea. She didn't.

"The roan will get in shape."

She was silent, waiting for him to tell her more.

"I believe in financial diversification. I'm also part owner in a local brewery." As well as a few other things.

"Building your retirement fund?"

The walls went up. He didn't want to talk about money. That was a swift way to make yourself a target. And even though Carly seemed more interested in him than in his finances, he'd also believed that about Priscilla.

"I made a poor investment once," he said. "I have some rebuilding to do." Her lips parted, and he assured her, "Don't worry. I'll never make that mistake again." He shifted, hoping she'd move from in front of the door so they could go inside.

"Obviously," Carly said with an air of authority, "she wasn't worth your affection."

His gaze snapped to hers. "How do you know that?"

At his harsh tone, Carly backed into the closed door and lifted her hands to show she was unarmed. "It's easy to see," she whispered, "based on the way you talk and act."

He rolled his eyes upward in frustration. There was that connection between them that kept popping up, bringing them closer, revealing things he didn't want to have seen. He wasn't ready for this. He liked having her at a distance.

"Nobody else has figured that out," he said.

Had he been leaving hints for ages, hoping someone would do so? See his pain, then come fix him? He didn't think so. He'd successfully kept the truth about Priscilla to himself for many long years. And as far as he knew, nobody had noticed, nobody cared that he carried that giant chip on his shoulder or where it had come from. Go figure that Carly had spotted it and was taking aim with her sledgehammer.

She watched him for a long moment, her expression somber. "Maybe it takes someone who's been burned straight to their soul to recognize it in someone else."

This time when the flare of connection threatened to rise within him, he gave up trying to tamp it down.

"We're talking about someone who takes your love for granted and abuses your trust?" he confirmed.

Carly inhaled slowly, as though bracing herself against familiar hurts, and without thinking Ryan pulled her into a hug. He sighed, holding her close. How sad was it he found relief in discovering someone else was holding on to the same shards of pain that he was?

When Carly hugged him back, he wasn't certain if the reassuring embrace was for her or for himself. All he knew was that it felt good having someone finally understand.

Carly sat at the large, bustling table beside Ryan clutching her sides, which hurt from laughing so hard. The Wylders and their significant others were welcoming, boisterous, honest and fun. Even Carmichael, seated at the end of the table to her left, was letting out a few chuckles, his weathered face crinkled in mirth.

Laura and Levi had been telling the story of how a few weeks ago her little dog, Target, had sent a stampede straight through the middle of his birthday barbecue. Laura was obviously embarrassed, but she told the tale with such gusto that Carly couldn't help but admire the woman. Especially since she seemed to be recounting it for the sole purpose of making Carly feel better about delaying the meal by a few minutes because of her chickens, followed by Ryan's horse issue.

There was a knock on the front door, then footsteps sounded

in the entryway. Moments later Jackie Moorhouse hurried into the room, a pan in her hands, her hair swept up in a loose bun. "Hey, sorry I'm late! I hope I didn't miss dessert, because I brought something!"

"There's no such thing as late around here," Maria assured her, getting up to give her a hug, then take the pan, while Myles offered Jackie the vacant chair between himself and Ryan.

"Is that your broken custard pie?" Myles asked as he seated her.

"Sure is. Where's Uncle Grumpy Pants?"

"Henry is having issues with his kidney stones," Maria said.

"That's too bad," Jackie said, seeming to truly mean it.

"Dr. Aldridge is taking good care of him."

Ryan winced. "Today?"

"Do you miss everything?" Brant asked.

Ryan leaned back, shrugging. "I haven't missed how you pretend to be someone's boyfriend to help get their ex off their back."

He smirked when Brant scowled. "I haven't done that in years."

Myles cleared his throat and lifted his brows as though disagreeing.

"I'll take Henry a plate of food after supper, as I'm sure he'll be home by then," Maria said.

"Careful, cranky old dogs tend to bite the hand that feeds them," Levi muttered.

"Hey, Ryan." Jackie gave his forearm a friendly squeeze.

He shifted his chair closer to Carly, and Jackie smirked. "What did I miss?" she asked, heaping her plate with food as everyone passed dishes her way.

"They were telling me the story of Levi's birthday party," Carly said.

Jackie rolled her head back with a groan. "That was so awful. I can't believe you won't let it go, Levi." She gave him a chastising look across the table. "It could have happened to anyone."

"I told the story," Laura said.

"It was pretty funny," Carly admitted.

Jackie pointed a serving spoon at Ryan, then Carly. "So? Are you two an item yet?"

Carly had been taking a sip of her punch and spit it back into her glass as she began coughing. She didn't think anyone knew the two of them had been enjoying kissing on the side. She loved how Ryan saw her as independent, strong and determined enough to deal with his own strong-willed personality. She was growing and changing, just like she'd hoped she would by moving out here, but a relationship wasn't what either of them was looking for. And if the family figured out what they were doing, they would likely expect something to come of it.

April shook her head. "Come on, Jackie. Let up already."

"Just asking," she protested. "I took Carly to the football game, you know. I should take you, Brant."

Across the table the man stiffened.

"It's time you said yes to one of those numerous women bringing their pets in for random, unneeded checkups."

"What does it take to get a dog around here, anyway?" April asked with a wink, while passing the hot buttered biscuits Jackie's way. She was wearing a green Western blouse that made the amber flecks in her eyes sparkle.

"I want a dog!" Kurt said.

"I know, sweetie."

Ignoring the questioning glance April gave Brant, Carly asked, "What's significant about taking me to the game? Garfield implied it would change my life."

Meaningful looks darted around the table, but Laura spoke first. "The local lore is that when Jackie takes a girlfriend to the football game, she soon hooks up with someone in a serious way." Levi leaned closer, placing a light kiss on her cheek, causing her to light up. Carly turned away and caught Karen gazing at Myles.

Was Jackie responsible for the two smiling couples?

Ryan rolled his eyes and said in a dry tone, "Carly and I were already an item, so don't worry about it. We're exempt."

"Really?" Jackie squealed, clasping her hands together.

"No," Carly said firmly. "We are not an item."

All eyes turned their way. That the two of them were sitting shoulder to shoulder likely didn't aid their argument.

"We're just helping each other," Ryan said patiently. "We're not looking for romance or love or anything like that, Jackie."

"You're working together?" Maria asked, her interest piqued.

"Ryan's renting Carly's stable," Levi stated.

"And he has some ideas for my farm," Carly said.

"You two would make a good couple." Karen rested an elbow on the table so she could lean forward to see Carly.

"You're both direct in a way that scares people," Myles said with a wink.

"Ryan's cute and all," Carly stated, "but like he said, neither of us is looking for love."

"You don't have to be looking," Brant said, and beside him, April's cheeks grew pink. "Sometimes it just comes along."

"Thankfully," Levi said, giving Laura another kiss, this time on the lips.

Beside Carly, Carmichael had nodded off, his plate long ago scraped clean.

"Speaking of the stampede," Maria said, bringing the topic back to Laura's story. "How is Target doing with his lessons on becoming a proper ranch dog?"

"His training is almost done."

"Have you changed your mind about moving out to the ranch?" Brant asked. He leaned forward to say across Laura, "Levi, this gal needs a ring."

"They're on sale right now over in Riverbend," Jackie said, and Carly winced at her friend's blunt approach.

"Do you need your house back?" Laura asked Brant.

The brothers eyed April, then glanced away. She was studiously cutting up a piece of turkey for her son, although he seemed to be doing an adequate job of it himself.

Carly gave Ryan a questioning look, but he just shrugged.

"I thought maybe you and Levi were ready to take the next step," Brant said. He popped a forkful of mashed potatoes in his mouth, chewed and swallowed, then added, "But yes, if you're ready to move the house could be put to use."

Laura set her utensils down as the table went silent. "When?"

Brant looked uncomfortable. "We'll figure something out later."

"Who did you buy the house for?" Maria asked casually, one eye on him while dishing more green bean casserole onto her plate.

When he didn't answer his mom set down the bowl and rested her right arm on the table, watching him closely.

"He bought it for me," April stated, her voice calm.

Jackie inhaled audibly. "I knew it."

April glanced pointedly at her son, warning the group not to dig into the topic. But Carly was even more confused now. April was married, but Brant had bought her a house? And Laura was living in it?

Nobody spoke as everyone processed the implications.

"We have a house," Kurt said, his high voice laced with confusion.

"We do, honey. But this one will be closer to our family." April looked out over the table, daring anyone to argue with her.

"You're all related?" Carly asked Ryan.

He gave a slight shake of his head, and April said, "I grew up on the ranch with the Wylder boys. My dad was one of their hired hands. So they're family to me. These guys are like brothers."

"Except she used to date Cole," Jackie blurted. Laura's eyebrows shot up in surprise as she glanced to Levi for confirmation.

"Who's Cole?" Carly asked.

There was a beat of silence.

"Our brother," Ryan said. "Second born."

"He's in Colorado last we heard," Maria said, picking up the platter of honey-baked ham. "Carmichael?" The elderly man awoke with a start. "More ham or cornbread stuffing?" He frowned and shook his head, but she passed the two dishes down to him anyway, and he added a few more bites to his plate.

Jackie whispered across the table to Brant, "Maybe I don't need to take you to a game. Seems to me you're doing fine on your own."

His cheeks reddened. "I'm helping family. Don't read into it."

April immediately ducked her head again. Not at all like that wild and lively rodeo queen Carly remembered from her youth. It was clear that life had taken its boots to April's heart at some point, but that she and Brant Wylder felt deeply for each other. Whether things were romantic between them, Carly wasn't sure, but it looked as though the road ahead might be a tricky one.

"I'll find a place to rent," Laura said.

"You can move in here," Levi offered.

"I don't want to oust you," April protested.

"I already know of a place that's available, and I can be out in a matter of days. It was always clear that when the time was right, I'd move out. The time is right." Laura gave her a look as if daring April to argue with her. She turned to Levi and unspoken words passed between them, as though they'd known each other for years rather than a few months. "I'm not sure I'm ready to move in with you, but thank you," she finally said.

"Too fast?" Levi asked.

"A bit."

"Good," Myles said. "As I've said before, I don't think I could handle being under the same roof as you two." The brothers laughed.

"Like you and Karen are much better," Jackie joked, elbowing him and receiving a grin in response.

As the brothers continued to joke, Maria asked April, "Are you doing all right?"

She nodded, but her lips were drawn together.

"If you need anything, anything at all…"

April nodded again, her gaze sliding to Brant, who had his shoulders pushed back, a self-assigned protector.

"Please don't tell anyone about the house," Brant said, loudly enough to break through the chatter and joking.

The group fell silent, then nodded as one, with Carly following along, unsure why the house was a secret.

"That means you, too, Kurt."

"Why is creamed corn so gross?" he asked, smacking his fork into the yellow mush.

Myles laughed.

"Everything will be out in the open soon," April said to the gathering, rubbing Kurt's back. "There'll be a clean break before Christmas."

"When is Santa coming?" Kurt asked, his face lit up.

"Soon," April murmured.

"What are we doing for Christmas this year?" Brant asked. "Mom? Are you and Dad doing separate family events?"

"We'll see," she said, an uncharacteristic tension tightening the lines of her face. From what Carly understood the couple had split up last year and Roy had already remarried.

"Henry was asking if you're both planning to come to his party," Brant said casually, and Maria's brows lowered.

Levi cringed. "Is that a no, Mom?"

"Good luck getting out of the party," Brant muttered. "He's already roped me into going."

"Just so everyone knows…" Jackie paused until she had everyone's full attention. "I'll be saving some seats at the state championship game." A slight smile was growing despite her obvious efforts to hide it.

She received a few chuckles in response, the mood around the table growing lighter.

"Saving one for yourself?" Myles teased.

"I might."

"Who will the other seats be for?" Levi asked his gaze on Ryan. "I know a brother who's single."

Ryan tossed his napkin down beside his almost-cleared plate and glared at him.

Carly shifted in her chair, the fingers of her right hand automatically moving to cover the ring on her left.

"Just get married already and butt out," Ryan grumbled to his eldest brother.

"How about you get married first?" Levi said, challenging him from the opposite corner of the table. "I heard Old Man Lovely is planning to do another of his quickie New Year's Eve weddings for anyone looking to elope."

Ryan's expression was stony as he forked some sweet potato into his mouth. When his brother continued to wait for a reply, he said, "How about I keep living my independent life so I don't have to relearn the basics?"

"Which basics would those be?"

"Namely, marriage never works, because women up and leave."

Maria was shaking her head as though unable to stop. From what Carly had heard, it didn't sound as though she had been the one to leave her marriage, shooting a hole in Ryan's theory.

"Who's ever left you?" Levi asked Ryan with a chuckle. "They can't even catch you."

"That's true," Jackie said with an authoritative nod.

Levi's eyes had narrowed as though he was closing in on something. "In fact, after we started asking if you were going to marry Priscilla back in college, you two were suddenly no longer even speaking to each other."

"We all thought you would pop the question," Myles said.

The whole family was eyeing Ryan now, and Carly saw his hands flexing under the table.

"Kind of glad you didn't, though," Levi commented, when Ryan refused to speak. "Not to be a jerk, but there was something about her I never fully trusted."

"What?" Ryan's voice was dangerously low. The table went silent.

Levi shrugged, while Brant and Myles nodded. Maria didn't appear as though she was enjoying the conversation, but was watching it unfold as though she had a stake in it.

"You kept asking if I was going to marry her."

"I was trying to be supportive," Levi explained. "Open the conversation to see where you were at. When it seemed like you weren't going to pop the question, I let it go." He shrugged as if to say no harm, no foul.

Ryan pushed away from the table. "You know, it would've been nice to know you didn't trust her."

"It didn't seem important," Brant said gently.

Ryan stood, taking in his brothers with a steely-eyed sweep. "I listen to your opinions way more often than I should, and it's always been to my detriment. I listened when I was seven about where to cross the river during the flood, and I just about drowned." He leaned forward. "Everyone was wrong. And I took your probing about marrying Priscilla as approval." He shook his head and left the room, the air around him crackling like a thunderstorm.

Everyone was speechless, their jaws unhinged. Even Jackie was quiet.

"He married her, didn't he?" Carly asked on a held breath, trying to sort out what had just been revealed about this man she found herself drawn to.

Ryan had married Priscilla, and she had been untrustworthy.

Some things burned you to your soul.

"What was all of that?" Maria asked. She was pale, looking almost shell-shocked.

Nobody answered.

"Maybe I'm wrong," Carly said, as she took in the expressions of stunned disbelief. She had to be wrong. How could she, a newcomer, know Ryan better than his family did?

Yet her gut was telling her she was dead on.

RYAN SAT on the front porch swing, trying to sort out his next move. Storming out of the house like that had no doubt blown open his biggest secret. He sighed, trying to decide if it mattered or not. For a long time it had, but right now the humiliation of being such a poor judge of character felt moot, buried under the fresh new anger at his brothers for not speaking up, for not protecting him from what they'd seen in Priscilla.

The screen door opened with a slight creak, drawing Lupe from his post at the top of the steps as Carly came out, sliding her arms into the sleeves of her coat. She gave his head a pat on her way by, and the Australian shepherd wagged his tail, then flopped back onto the porch. Brant's dog, Dodge, tottered up the steps, slowing as he approached Carly, tongue out and tail wagging. His hopeful look was met with a quick scratch behind the ears.

"Hey," Ryan said, shifting to make room for her on the swing. For some reason he didn't mind sharing his misery and humiliation with her. Maybe because she wasn't perfect either, and therefore reserved judgment.

"You okay?" She smoothed her hands down her jeans after

sitting beside him. It was cool enough that he could feel her welcoming warmth radiating against his left side. He hadn't bothered to grab his hat or coat on the way out, eager to outrun the hard bubble that had been growing in his chest, pressing against his lungs and ribs.

"Yeah."

"You married Priscilla, didn't you?"

Ryan blinked, not knowing what to say. If he admitted to that fatal mistake everything would come out. But keeping it a secret would be like trying to juggle flaming torches on a unicycle. And he wasn't so great on the unicycle. He also wasn't wearing flame-resistant pants.

"Because it felt like you had, and so I asked your family."

Ryan winced. "What did they say?"

"They just kind of stared at me with their mouths open."

Ryan let out an amused huff. He bet they hadn't been blind-sided like that in a long time. He felt a spark of pride for keeping Priscilla a secret not only from his family, but in a small town, too.

"I take it she was a piece of work?" Carly asked.

"You could say that."

There were so many ways Priscilla had betrayed him, and still so many unanswered questions as to why. He hadn't seen her once since their honeymoon. Not even while he'd successfully petitioned for an annulment.

"I listened to my family," Ryan said, shaking his head at the irony of it all. "They seemed to think Priscilla was great even though I had my doubts. They started asking if we were going to get married when I was about halfway through my last year of college. And since we'd been dating for a year and a half, it seemed like it was the next logical step. I trusted their judgment, and she seemed game. We eloped on a Friday night, and by Monday she was gone."

He still remembered trying to let himself into her apartment on Monday morning after their whirlwind weekend honeymoon. He'd arrived with a box of possessions under his arm after his morning class. He'd told the college he was moving out of the dorm and in with his new wife. But when he got to the apartment, the key he'd had for over a year no longer fit the lock, and someone new had already moved in. Priscilla was long gone, proving she'd been planning to leave him long before their whirlwind weekend.

"What did you do?" Carly asked.

Myles's dog, Buckey, came onto the porch and placed her large black head in Ryan's lap and he absently rubbed her soft ears.

"I went to the pub to try to think my way through what was happening. She refused to answer my calls or texts. It was when I tried to pay for my drink that I discovered my account had been emptied. All the money I'd earned from developing an app had been cleaned out. At least I'd already paid my last semester's tuition, but I had nothing to live on for the next three months."

"You sold an app?" Carly asked. "What was it for?"

Ryan gave her a blank look. Seriously? He'd just poured out his deepest darkest secret, and she wanted to know about the app? An app he'd told no one about because it had never felt quite real, even after the money had been deposited into his account the month before Priscilla took it all.

The fact was, he'd been swayed by his brothers' opinions yet again, and this time it had been over Priscilla.

"Okay, then tell me about this woman," Carly said, giving him a hint of that attitude he admired.

Ryan put an arm around her shoulders, strangely happy she was there, pulling secrets from him. With her at his side, those painful and humiliating moments where his judgment had failed him no longer felt as traumatic. He didn't even care if his family came outside and saw them cuddling.

"This is nice," Carly said, snuggling closer. "But don't kid yourself that it'll distract me from needling you for the full story."

"I'm just cold," he protested lamely. "I stormed out and didn't grab my jacket, and now I'm too afraid to go back in."

"You're such a liar."

He smiled and pulled her closer, planting a kiss in her hair, inhaling her scent.

"It was a dating app," he said, feeling the slap of irony once again.

"Did you meet through it?" Carly asked.

"In creating it, yes."

"Sometimes life is just too perfect, isn't it?" Carly twisted in his arms to look up at him.

"That's not my definition of perfect," he grumbled.

"So you met because of the app, fell in love, married, then she ran away with all the app money."

"Yup."

"And you didn't tell your family because you were ashamed and embarrassed for trusting someone you shouldn't have? Because you thought they believed she was wonderful, but it turns out they had their reservations about her the whole time?"

"Apparently."

"Did she drop out? Was she a student, too?"

"She graduated the year before me. I met her the first month of school and let it slip I was working on an app. Turns out she knew a guy up in Canada who could help me. Connor MacKenzie. He was a great partner. And no, he doesn't know where she went, either. He offered to have his buddy Evander de la Fosse who has people-tracking skills do a search for her. But I just wanted a clean break and to walk away."

The swing's chain creaked as they swung idly, looking out over the darkened yard.

"Want to hear the full story about why I moved out to the ranch?" she asked.

"Is it as wretched as mine? Because I don't want you stealing my thunder."

"It shares a similar theme."

"How very English studies of you."

"Do you teach English?"

"I did for a semester. Mostly just math and sciences, though."

"Well, after my husband passed away, I found myself up to my eyeballs in debt. He'd mortgaged everything to the hilt, but hadn't insured a thing, including himself. So when he died I found myself in a situation that was not cool." Her voice had grown thick, and she sat up, no longer cuddling against him. "There was other stuff, too. We weren't true partners, that was for sure."

She inhaled audibly, pulling herself back together. "I managed to sort myself out, but what did I do? I walked right into a terrible business deal. For seven years I ran a company with someone I believed was a friend. I thought it was great because I didn't need start-up money, but it turned out he was shady. And this time I lost my reputation, which in some ways hurt even more."

"Shoot. That's worse than my story," Ryan said, wincing. To be taken twice? "No wonder you want to be independent."

"Yeah. See? Same theme."

"Same scars on our soul."

"I came out to Sweetheart Creek determined to figure out how to take care of myself without getting taken advantage of again. There's so much more to learn about farming than I thought, though. I grew up on a farm and believed I knew what it took, and how to do it. Put seeds in the ground, hope for rain and sunshine in the right patterns, harvest your crop, rest and repeat. But organic vegetable gardening on a small scale is much more than sticking seeds in the ground, avoiding commercial fertilizers and pesticides, and living happily ever after."

"Are you passionate about it?"

"I love being outside. I love having my hands in the dirt."

"But?"

"It feels like your horse idea."

Ryan shifted to look at her better, making the swing's chain creak once again. "What's wrong with my horse idea?"

"Really?"

"Yeah. Tell me."

"Fine. The roan will always be too slow for rodeo."

"Too slow?"

"You can change fat and out of shape, but you can't change short legs."

"You think he'll be slow? I thought he'd be nice and compact. He has good bursts of speed." Ryan had seen him in full gallop before he'd bought him.

"He's a nice horse, and might win a ribbon or two for a rodeo kid, but he won't fetch the price you're looking for if profits are the name of the game."

"Right. You used to ride rodeo." April had recognized her right away. "Why didn't you tell me?"

"You didn't ask. You were too busy kissing me," she said with a sly wink, and he realized it had been at least an hour since he'd kissed her last.

"That sounds like it could be true." He nuzzled closer, leaving a trail of kisses across her cheek until his lips landed on her warm and welcoming mouth.

"Besides," she said, when they'd finished kissing, "we weren't going to open the vault."

"The vault?"

"Share our deepest, darkest secrets. We promised to remain independent and… you know. Teams of one."

He thought about that for a second. That had been the plan, but now that they'd shared a bit of themselves he didn't want to go back to just kissing. He didn't want to lose this feeling of being close to Carly.

"Are we no longer good? Now that we've shared?" He gave her

a long, slow kiss. Every intimate moment with her felt different, and this one felt just as powerful. And yet it somehow felt more personal and like something he couldn't get from anyone but Carly Clarke.

He opened his eyes and gazed at her, catching a glint of her ring as her hand drifted down from where it had rested against his cheek during the kiss. He placed his palm over her ring finger. He had a feeling the ring's presence was still an item for her personal vault, despite what they'd shared today. It would be simple if she was wearing it to honor her dead husband, but it didn't mesh with her story of betrayal.

All he knew was that when she took the ring off her finger, she'd be ready for someone like Ryan to enter her life in a serious way.

The screen door opened and Ryan eased away from Carly, bringing the arm that had been around her shoulders back to his side.

"Hey, that red roan I bought?" he asked Brant, pressing his feet on the porch floor to set the swing rocking again. "Would it make a good rodeo horse? Barrel racing or a cutter? We're talking full-out winner."

Brant stared at him for a moment, his obvious doubt sending a rush of determination through Ryan to prove it wrong.

"No."

"No," Ryan repeated, feeling deflated. "Next time, I'm not listening to the auctioneer."

"Or you could have a few of us come along," Brant suggested.

Carly laughed before Ryan could.

A decision by committee? Not going to happen. It was his project, his decisions.

"Would asking for a little help kill you?" Brant leaned back against the porch's white railing, arms folded.

"Probably," both Ryan and Carly said at the same time. Ryan chuckled. So many things to like about this woman.

"Seriously, I could come with you to the next auction," his brother offered.

"I'm fine, thanks," Ryan said automatically.

Brant sighed, his head shaking slightly as he pushed himself off the railing. "Why don't you just develop another app? Seems like an easier way to make cash if you're feeling broke."

"How do you know about the app?"

"I was standing inside the doorway waiting for the right moment to come out."

"Maybe I need to start eavesdropping," Ryan said, feeling peeved. "That way I'd know you'd bought a house for April. A house her son isn't supposed to know about. And I presume her husband, too."

"Mom's about to serve dessert," Brant said, turning away. "You want to finish your plates or should we add your leftovers to the bin of scraps for the sheep?" He headed inside before Ryan could answer or drill him any further about April and the house.

"Come on, Mr. Independent," Carly said, pulling him to his feet. "Let's go get fat on your mom's cooking before we reveal the rest of our deep dark secrets to each other."

"You have more?" he asked.

"There's always more."

7

The week after Thanksgiving, Carly sat near the back of the bus heading for the high school football quarterfinals. As predicted by most of Sweetheart Creek, the Torpedoes had won last week's Black Friday regionals game by a landslide. Carly sat across the aisle from Ryan and three rows behind. From her vantage point, he looked exhausted.

He'd been spending hours each morning before school helping with her farm plan. Then after school working on the family ranch, with his horses or with his team prepping for their next game. Despite her gratitude for his willingness to bounce ideas and brainstorm ways to bring her dreams to fruition faster, Carly had told him her farm could wait. He'd refused to listen, determined to help. But he'd been burning the candle at both ends, not even getting a good night's rest, since he'd spent the first few nights after Thanksgiving in the stable at her ranch, worried about Blackberry. Finally convinced the horse was well, he was sleeping at home again, and Carly missed how she'd find Ryan wrapped in a straw-covered saddle blanket in the stable each morning. He'd be nestled between a hay bale and his dog, his hat pulled low, after spending the night on watch like a worried father.

She'd made a habit of coming out in the morning with a cup of coffee before inviting him in for bacon and eggs to warm up, a routine she adored.

The red roan Brant had declared not built for rodeo star status had gone to one of the special needs kids enrolled in the Sweet Meadows Ranch riding program, for less than a song. For a man eager to make money, Ryan had likely taken a large loss with that horse, and his cheerful acceptance of the situation endeared him to Carly even further. In every way Ryan proved he was different from Peter, revealing his scars and caring for others in a way her husband never had.

In the bus, Ryan looked up from the stack of homework papers he'd been marking, and stretched his neck, tipping his head from side to side. It seemed as if nearly everyone on the bus had checked in with him during the almost-two-hour ride, seeking advice, and interrupting his work.

Carly got up and moved down the narrow aisle toward the empty seat across from him. The man had to be under tremendous pressure from the community, the school, parents, players, and most of all himself, when it came to each game. She figured if nothing else, she could let him know she was here for him to lean on. But before she reached him, quarterback Blake Hernandez shot into the vacant seat. Carly ended up dropping into Blake's seat, just behind Ryan.

"Trust your gut," he was saying to the athlete when she leaned forward, accidentally eavesdropping.

"If it's telling you something different from what I'm saying, trust it. Experts, family, coaches, parents—we all believe we know best. But listen to your gut and it'll get you to the place you're meant to be." Ryan reached over and gripped Blake's shoulder. "In life and on the field. If your gut's saying you can make a pass, and Wiggins can get his wheels there in time, do it, even if I'm over on the sidelines hollering at you not to. You hear me?" He gave the player a small shake, and the boy nodded even though he looked conflicted.

"I'll be mad," Ryan said with an easy smile, releasing the young man's shoulder. "I always believe I know what's best, but I'm not the one out on the field. I'm not the one in the game, feeling it, making eye contact with my players and knowing what they can endure. These last three games are your moments to shine."

Blake grinned, a flash of cocky, unflappable confidence common to teenage boys.

"No. We don't do that," Ryan said immediately, shaking his head.

"What?"

"Don't let your ego take the wheel. It's ruined a lot of scholarship opportunities for a lot of players. Stay humble. Stay in the game. Stay grounded with your team."

"And trust my gut." The teen nodded, his voice serious.

"And trust your gut." Ryan held out his fist and Blake tapped it with his own. The quarterback pointed his index fingers at Ryan and he echoed the pose.

"Huzzah!" the two said in an undertone, lifting their arms.

"This is your moment," Ryan said. "You know what to do."

Carly wondered what would be different in her own life if she'd listened to her gut rather than the people around her.

She couldn't help but wonder if Ryan was following his gut where she was concerned. Was it whispering to him that maybe this time he'd found someone who wasn't looking to use him, but rather someone who might complement his already full life?

Carly leaned out into the aisle, to find Ryan looking down at his papers, signaling he was done talking to Hernandez. She lifted her hand to the back of the seat, ready to swap places with the quarterback, but stopped when the teenager bent close to the coach.

"I'm afraid I'll lose her," he said, his voice cracking with worry.

Ryan turned to him, watching him silently. His eyes cut to Carly, who was half out of her seat, and she edged back, casting her gaze out the window at the rolling Texas scenery.

"What if everything changes after she has the baby?" Blake asked, his voice laced with fear, and Carly immediately knew he was talking about his girlfriend. "What if I get into a good college and make the team?"

"Things will change no matter what happens over the next few months. That's part of finishing high school."

"I love her."

"Good."

"But what if she leaves me?"

Carly held her breath as she waited for Ryan's reply.

Finally he said, "Blake, here's the thing."

The teen swallowed hard, his Adam's apple bobbing.

"You know what I said about your gut? Listen to it. And when you listen, ignore everyone and everything else, and especially what you *think* they're saying."

Priscilla. Peter, too. She'd ignored that niggling feeling of doubt she had whenever he'd change the subject. When she'd asked where he'd been, how their finances were, why he smelled of perfume... What would she have done if she'd discovered the truth before he'd died? How different would her life be now if she'd allowed herself to trust her instincts instead of his smooth words?

With Ryan, her gut told her the only thing he was hiding was his old scars. But she'd also seen him airing those old wounds. He was healing and recovering, just as she was every time she stuck her shovel in the ground at her farm, every time she shared bits of her past with Ryan and built a stronger plan for her future.

"If you're true to yourself, then what will happen will happen," Ryan said, his voice soft. "And always remember there's no stopping what feels right in someone else's heart. That's not you, it's them."

"But what if I stay in Sweetheart Creek? What if I just keep working on the ranch and don't take any scholarships?"

"You need to live your life, Blake. If Robyn truly loves you, and not just what she can take from you, she won't want you to stop growing and expanding. She won't sabotage you when you're following your dreams."

"And?" the teen asked, as if sensing there might be more.

"And if all else fails..." Ryan let out a sigh, palms raised in surrender "...enjoy what you have for as long as you can."

FROM HIS SPOT on the sidelines, Ryan turned, looking out at the crowd. It was reasonably mild for the first week in December and the weather shouldn't be a problem in tonight's game to determine the quarterfinal winner for their little chunk of Texas. The Torpedoes were officially in the top eight of all high school teams their size, and they'd taken to the field for their warm-up with an energy that could carry them right on into the top four. Fans were waving their homemade signs, and on the sidelines the cheerleaders were performing what looked like a new routine.

All members of the Torpedoes were present, and things were as they should be. And yet Ryan felt as though he was in a giant bubble, with everything around him not quite real.

"I saved seats for April and Brant," Jackie said excitedly, grasping his arm to get his attention.

"She only left Heath a few days ago."

Jackie shrugged. She was decked out in the team's colors, with a red Torpedoes T-shirt squeezed over a white sweatshirt, white leggings under a denim miniskirt, and white cowboy boots. She looked more like one of the cheerleaders than a stats keeper. Ryan noted Carly was wearing a similar outfit, and his heart lifted, knowing she was here for him and the team. She wasn't family, but she supported him, no questions asked, as though she was bound by blood. Which meant she truly cared. Because if she didn't, Carly Clarke would have surely stalked off to do her own thing by now.

Either that or she had a deep-seated agenda, like Priscilla had.

Ryan shook off his unwelcomed paranoia. During the long bus ride to the game, he'd told Blake to follow his gut. He'd told the teen to enjoy his life as it was, and that was what Ryan planned on doing with Carly. Enjoy it while it lasted.

As though sensing his thoughts were on her, Carly turned his way and smiled. Without thinking, he smiled back. Yeah, his gut said she was okay. Maybe even more than okay.

Beside him, Jackie was still nattering on, as Dan, the team manager, came to join them.

"Carly a permanent thing?"

Ryan did a double take.

"With the team. Henry was asking if we ran a criminal check on all of our volunteers."

Ryan caught Dan looking toward Carly in question. "Oh. Uh, no. She's not supervising students or in direct contact without one of us present." He hadn't even thought to run her through the school's volunteer paperwork. Where was his head? "I'll check with the principal on Monday."

Dan nodded and went to help a player wrap his wrist.

"What's with the twin stuff?" Ryan asked, gesturing to Jackie's outfit.

"Jenny ordered them in for us. Laura's wearing hers, too, but Karen said no. She has to wear her cheer manager stuff. Laura looks super hot in her outfit, and I think Levi's going to propose to her this weekend—" She broke off abruptly, her eyes going wide. "I'm sorry. You probably don't want to hear about stuff like that." She squeezed his arm again, and he looked at her strangely while pulling free from her grip.

"Why not?" Just because he was the black sheep of the family didn't mean he didn't want to know what was going on in everyone's lives.

"Well, after that thing with Priscilla…" Jackie's voice was hushed, as though that might make him less susceptible to any lingering pain. "You must have been heartbroken."

"Mostly just ticked off." He adjusted the headset that allowed him to talk to his quarterback during the game, as well as to Myles if he went into the bleachers to get a different view of the action. Ryan hoped that would give Jackie the hint it was game time, not gossip time.

He glanced at Carly, hoping she needed Jackie's help. But she was holding up the stats-taking tablet, snapping photos that would likely end up in the school's yearbook or on Sweetheart Creek's town news website. She pivoted in her folding chair, sending Ryan a bright, happy look that lifted Ryan's mood.

"Say cheese," she called out.

"Feta," he said, refusing to smile.

She frowned at the screen and shook her head. "It looks like you're about to swear. Don't say feta."

Jackie put her arm around Myles, bringing him closer so she could squeeze between him and Ryan for the next photo. She beamed at Carly. "Cheese!"

Ryan was sure Carly got a picture of him rolling his eyes. He disentangled himself and turned his focus back to his players. Right now he needed to know which guys were spooked by how far they'd made it in the playoffs and which ones were channeling the energy. He didn't need to get distracted by photos or how gorgeous Carly looked in red. Although he liked the idea of her wanting a picture of him.

He stood beside Myles and watched Hernandez finish leading the team through their warm-up movements, then some ball tossing and practice tackles, as well as a few pranks and jokes to take the edge off. A throw came too close to the sidelines and

Myles jumped, knocking the ball out of the air before it could hit either of them.

"They're jittery," he remarked.

Ryan nodded, then gestured to his brother and the direction of the save he'd just made. "Maybe I should find you a jersey and put you in."

"I do miss it."

"Hey, how did that course go?" Myles, who had hated every single second of school and acted like a tortured POW when it came to homework, had recently enrolled in an online coaching course to increase his credentials, as well as move him up the coaching pay grid. Ryan admired the fact that his brother, who was challenged by dyslexia, was giving it his all. "When's your final?"

"I took it on the weekend."

"You did? When do you hear back?"

"I already did."

"And?" Ryan asked, surprised he'd said nothing. Which meant it couldn't be good. Myles tended to not talk about stuff like school or reading, or anything else that made him feel incompetent or stupid.

"I made Karen read the email, but not tell me what it said."

"What did her expression say?"

Myles shrugged. "I couldn't tell."

"You couldn't tell?" The couple had been joined at the hip for what felt like months now. How could Myles not read her expression? Sure, Karen kept things close to the chest, but Ryan could already tell what Carly was feeling just by glancing at her expression, and the two of them weren't anywhere near official.

Ryan held out his hand. "Give me your phone. I'll read the email and tell you."

Myles took a step back. "I don't want to know. Not until after State."

"That's weird. You know that, right?"

"Go away," he said, his tone flat as he began walking off. He moved in among the players, offering words of encouragement, reminding them of little tips, and generally being a brilliant coach. Whether or not his brother passed was of little consequence as far as Ryan was concerned. Myles did all this naturally, correcting technique flaws before Ryan often recognized they existed. Myles liked to tell the world Ryan was the technical coach, but it was Myles who picked up on the nuances of technique and form without even realizing it. The two worked well together and Ryan hoped they could coach together for a long time. Maybe even when they had their own sons to coach.

Surprised by the thought, Ryan cast another glance in Carly's direction. She had a pen between her lips and was chewing thoughtfully on its cap. She was adorable. Smart. Trustworthy. Somehow, she had pulled more secrets out of him in the last few weeks than his entire family had over the past half decade.

Something hard hit Ryan and he landed on the turf with a harsh exhale as the wind was knocked out of him.

"Sorry, Coach!" Hernandez said, jumping to his feet beside him. He grabbed Ryan's arms and pulled him up. "Are you okay? I thought you saw me coming."

Ryan wheezed, willing air back into his lungs. Shaken, he bent over to dust off his legs, even though they didn't need it, trying to hide that he couldn't yet breathe. Slowly his ability to draw air returned, and he straightened, waving off Blake's apologies. "Sorry. My fault."

What on earth? He never got taken out while standing on the sidelines, and he'd just been flattened by his quarterback, because he'd been thinking about Carly.

That woman was a danger to life as he knew it, for sure.

He looked around to see if anyone else had noticed the incident. About ten feet away, Myles was smirking, his eyes sliding to where Carly was sitting.

Please, let her have missed that photo opportunity.

Ryan stared at Carly for a long moment to see if she was hiding amusement. She didn't once smile, her thoughtful gaze focused on the opposing team as they warmed up. He realized that even if she'd seen him, she wasn't the type to laugh. She would have come running over, her soft hands pressing into his back and stomach, her sweet, fresh scent filling his nostrils as she worried over him. It almost made him want to get hit all over again, but this time to catch her attention before impact.

He felt his chest expand with happiness. The only reason Carly Clarke spent time around him was because she liked him. He let out a soft chuckle, turning away. Him. Of all the men to choose from, she liked him. Beautiful Carly, whose red shirt brought out the different browns and pinks of her darker skin tone, liked him. Serious and aloof Ryan.

"Did I tell you I like that woman?" Myles murmured, walking by.

"Just because she's my girlfriend, it doesn't mean I'm going to lose my independence," Ryan said, instantly defensive.

Myles leaned in with a grin. "She makes you let your guard down and say stuff you don't intend to."

***

THEY WON their quarterfinal game by a narrow margin, meaning the Torpedoes would carry on to the semifinal game next Saturday afternoon. And if they won that one, move on to compete in the state championship game. They were officially a top-four team in their division. Scouts would look at his boys and scholarships might be offered, changing lives. Ryan hoped Karen was still willing to help tutor his academically struggling players toward the grades they'd need to move on to college.

His adrenaline waned as he sat in the high school gymnasium of the opposing team. Their hosts had set up tables for the team and cheerleaders to enjoy their potluck meal before they headed home.

By the time they finished eating and climbed aboard the bus, another hour would have gone by, and they wouldn't get home until well after midnight. Ryan would have preferred to eat before the game, but most of the players were too nervous to down much, and it was a tradition to eat afterward. At least it wasn't a school night.

The room was buzzing, with likely at least a hundred people present, from players and cheerleaders to their parents and coaches, and extended family. It was Sweetheart Creek's hospitality all wrapped up into one big room miles away from home. And as always, the hometown support had been fabulous.

While Ryan welcomed the distraction of the gentle thumps on the back and general camaraderie of the community, he also wished everyone would go their own way so he could focus on what they needed to do to win next week's game. He had to sit down with Myles, Carly and Jackie to look over the day's stats and finesse a plan for beating next week's opponents, which would be even more difficult.

But everyone wanted to celebrate, which meant right now he had to exercise one of his weaker skills—being patient.

Ryan pulled a chair to where Myles, Karen, Levi, Laura, Jackie, Brant, April, Kurt and his mother were already sitting. The round table was made for eight, but as per tradition, he knew his family would all squeeze in, adding more and more chairs until nobody could reach to set down their plate.

"Good game tonight," his mom said, addressing both him and Myles.

"I heard the team we'll meet in semifinals has a similar win-loss ratio. It might be tough to proceed," Ryan said.

"Be positive," Jackie told him.

"I am positive. Positive we need to have a sound strategy in place as well as work hard." Ryan turned in his chair, scanning the room for a familiar head of curls. "Where's Carly? She said she wouldn't be long."

He'd introduced her to Honorée Smith, a woman he'd met in one of his permaculture classes, and the two had started talking about seeds and organic fertilizers. Ryan checked his watch, then scanned the room again in case he'd missed Carly. A quick glance said she had either sat somewhere else or was still outside talking. Surely she knew to squeeze in with him?

"She's a great gal," his mom said. She'd taken the saltshaker from the middle of the table and was attacking her fried chicken. "Smart, too. I like her."

"Did her chickens start laying?" Brant asked, handing April a biscuit from his plate. She thanked him and broke it in two, offering half to her son.

"She said she got three the other day," Maria said. "Maybe it's the feed. If they don't like it or its poor quality, then forget about eggs."

"She's already changed it once," Brant said.

The table was silent for a moment as everyone focused on eating. From the next table over, Davis Davies, the Sweetheart Creek radio station DJ and father of one of the players, said, "Good game today, boys."

"Thanks," Myles said, then turned back to his plate.

"You gonna take it all the way this year? Bring home the championship?"

"Of course," Ryan said mildly.

"Looks like Hernandez has his head back on straight. Don't muck it up."

To Ryan's surprise, his mom tossed down her paper napkin. "Davis, enough. We all know you want your son to have this win. Everyone's working hard. If it's meant to be it's meant to be. Let it rest. I don't see you out there coaching."

"Hey!" The man raised his hands, leaning back in his chair. "I was just saying. I'm not as football-crazed as some parents."

The Wylder brothers shared a look. Davis had more ejections

from the stands by game officials than any other spectator because of his erratic behavior.

"What's with the new girl on the sidelines?" Davis asked.

"Girl?" Ryan said, bristling.

"Yeah, the dark chick. Why's she there all of a sudden? She some secret weapon?"

Almost everyone at Ryan's table seemed to stiffen as one.

"You mean Carly Clarke," Myles growled, before Ryan could. "She's an expert stats keeper and her skin color is irrelevant."

Davis raised his hands again. "Just describing her. Don't freak out." He turned back to his meal, his face red with embarrassment.

"Thanks," Ryan said, lifting his chin in Myles's direction.

"No problem. Besides, I like how your girlfriend gets in your head." He grinned and winked, immediately lightening the mood around the table. Maria, however, pivoted her full attention on him.

"She's not in my head," Ryan muttered. "Or my girlfriend."

"Don't tease your poor brother," Karen scolded Myles, and he smiled at her, his face softening. The man had nothing but respect and affection for his librarian girlfriend. She pushed her glasses farther up her nose as Myles leaned in, and when he placed a kiss against her temple, she beamed and shut her eyes.

If Ryan wasn't so happy for Myles, he'd be disgusted or jealous.

"You need to keep Carly around, Ryan," Jackie said. "She rocks with the stats."

"Yeah, she's good," he said, rubbing his nose.

"Probably because she pays attention to the players rather than who she can flirt with," Myles teased. Jackie laughed good-naturedly.

"That probably helps," Maria said, still watching Ryan.

"Probably." Jackie giggled. "Not nearly as much fun though, right, Myles?"

His brother offered a raised palm so Jackie could high-five it. Kurt, wanting one, too, stood on his chair and leaned across the table, teetering until Brant caught him and helped him reach Myles, then Jackie, before placing him back in his seat.

Ryan shook his head. Myles never seemed to take Jackie's quest for a Wylder like the serious threat it was and instead seemed to think it was amusing.

"So? Are you going to ask Carly out?" Karen asked Ryan. Her cheeks flushed immediately and she blurted, "Sorry. I didn't mean to go all Sweetheart Creek on you, but it seems like the two of you are well suited for each other."

"Yeah, they're on the same wavelength," Myles agreed. He was leaning back in his chair, grinning at Ryan.

"This again?" Ryan complained.

"What did you call her on the field today?"

"What do you mean?"

"I'm pretty sure it started with a *G*," Myles teased, eyebrows waggling. "You can deny it, but I heard."

Girlfriend? Yeah, right. He started to laugh, then froze, bits of a conversation coming back to him. He *had* referred to Carly as his girlfriend, hadn't he?

"She seems like a good match for you," Levi said.

"Are you just saying that to get a gauge on my thoughts, or do you mean it?" Ryan asked, narrowing his eyes. He still felt the sting of how he'd believed his family supported his relationship with Priscilla, not noticing their hidden reservations.

If he'd known how they felt, he likely wouldn't have eloped with her. Back then he'd respected and listened to their opinions almost as much as he had as a kid, even though he'd often acted as if he didn't want their input.

"I mean it," Levi said, meeting his gaze. "I don't know her well, but it appears the two of you have more in common than you and Priscilla ever did. I like that Carly's independent and ready to fight you. You're a match in that regard."

"She's really nice," Jackie said. "Smart, too."

"I know."

Ryan felt a change in the air around him, and he sat straighter, trying to figure out what was different. He scanned the room, and there was Carly, a few feet away, her cheeks flushed from being outdoors. The sun had set hours ago, and it was chilly out there. He stood up as she approached the table.

"Are you cold?"

She shook her head, placing a hand on Ryan's bicep. "I'm sorry. Am I late?" She was watching him for the answer, even though the other eight people at the table were happy enough to offer a reply.

"Not at all," he said. "Why don't you grab yourself a plate, and I'll scare up a chair for you."

As one, his family all started scooting their chairs over, making room beside him for Carly.

Approval. A chill ran through Ryan as he thought about all the ways things could go wrong.

8

When Carly returned from the food tables with a filled plate, she discovered a spot had been saved for her beside Ryan. She squeezed in, her chair legs hitting Karen's, who was on her right. Ryan's knee pressed against Carly's left, then moved away before she could figure out how to make it a permanent condition.

As conversations took place around them, Ryan asked, "Was talking with Honorée helpful?"

She grinned, thankful for the introduction. "I learned so much. She invited me to join an online group where people share what they know about Texas soil and its unique growing seasons, pests… everything!"

Carly had taken out her phone and joined the group during the conversation. It had been energizing, and she wanted to kiss Ryan in appreciation for sending her, once again, in the right direction.

"Are you happy with how today's game went?" she asked.

"Yeah, I think so," he said thoughtfully, taking the last of the meat off a chicken leg before discarding the bone onto his empty plate. "I'm hoping the four of us can look over the stats and discuss what you saw."

Carly hadn't been prepared for how busy Ryan would be after the game. As soon as the field began to clear after the win, the media had descended like locusts on a particularly tasty crop.

During the game Ryan had been in charge, as usual, barking commands, but calmer than normal. It was as though he'd shifted, trading emotions with the players. Back home the games had been easy, and the boys had been relaxed, needing Ryan's energy and determination to stay engaged. But here, Ryan had become serene, giving them what they lacked as they fought through what was likely their toughest game of the season thus far. She had found it sexy, watching him stride up and down, talking into his headset, in command and control. There was something so honest and raw about him she couldn't help being drawn closer.

"Has Ryan always been so independent?" she asked the table at large during a break in the chatter.

Jackie rolled her eyes. "He's the hardest man to get your hands on in all of Sweetheart Creek."

Carly placed a hand against her chest and said innocently, "I haven't found him to be like that at all. He's always asking me out on dates."

Everyone laughed uproariously, and Ryan tried to crease his face into a frown, though his eyebrows and lips didn't seem to want to cooperate. His leg pressed against hers, warm and sure.

"Come on, Ryan. It's okay to smile," she said sweetly. "It'll only hurt the first few times." His family laughed again and Ryan shook his head, casting his eyes to the sky as though needing to summon patience.

"She's tough on you, man," Brant said. "I like her." Carly's heart warmed at the approval.

"Listen to your family, Ryan," Jackie said. "Let this one catch you." She winked at Carly, who felt her face heat. She hadn't intended to cause his family and friends to gang up on him about their relationship status.

"We're fine. Really," Carly insisted.

"Ryan used to listen to us," Myles said thoughtfully.

"The last time he listened to us was when we told him where to cross the flooding river," Brant said.

Maria's face paled. "That drive from the farmhouse to the creek was the longest of my life."

Brant rubbed his head. "I can't count how many times my head hit the cab ceiling on that ride across the pastures. I'm lucky I didn't get a concussion."

"I told you to put on your seat belt," Maria chided mildly.

"Y'all know why I no longer listen to you," Ryan said, an edge to his voice that caught Carly's attention. He leaned back in his chair, one arm draped behind Carly's shoulders and his free hand on his hip. "You know if I'd crossed where I'd wanted to, along the top near the outcropping, I would've been fine." He said to Carly, his expression solemn, "I almost drowned, thanks to listening to these guys."

She held his gaze until he looked away, trying to piece together what must be another puzzle as to why Ryan was so fiercely independent. And why she found him so intriguing.

AFTER SUPPER, Carly stepped outside the school gym to stretch her back, walking up and down the hallway. Through the window in the outer door she could see a few people out by the bus in the parking lot, preparing for the ride home.

The Wylders didn't seem to have any reservations about suggesting she and Ryan should get together. Their banter was light and fun, but it was also a nod of approval, and she'd noted a glimmer in Ryan's eyes as his gaze had lingered on hers a few times.

He was thinking about it.

And so was she.

Despite their pledge not to get serious, it felt right to take things a step further. Their friendship and trust had grown naturally in such a brief period. Did she actually need to be stronger before she entered a real relationship?

Her gut told her she could be a work in progress with Ryan, and that things would still turn out okay. He wouldn't take advantage of her, and he wasn't going to sweet-talk her into something she didn't want. Ryan Wylder was much more likely to walk away than to manipulate her into choosing something that wasn't good for her.

She toyed with her gold wedding band, circling it around her finger as she gazed out at the blustery evening. She'd put it on after the failed business deal as a reminder to stay strong and independent, but now it felt like a barrier preventing her from moving into her new life. It was a reminder to be distrustful, to close a circle around herself. And the more time she spent around the Wylders, the more she realized that wasn't what she wanted or needed.

She'd also seen the way people's eyes sometimes caught and lingered on the ring, before darting to Ryan. They thought he was getting close with a married woman.

She tested the ring to see if it would still glide over her knuckle, and felt the air stir as someone approached her from behind. She slid the ring back into place, knowing without turning that it was Ryan. His fingers brushed against her hip as he moved past and opened the door. His Torpedoes ball cap shadowed his face under the entry light as he tipped his head and murmured, "Let's go for a walk."

"Aren't we leaving soon?" A gust entered the warm hallway, bringing with it a brisk, damp cold suggesting it might rain tonight.

"I could use a distraction," Ryan said, those lips of his curving into a sweet smile.

She automatically followed him as he moved through the doorway. "What kind of distraction?" All that hinting about the two of them getting together had kissing on her mind.

"Where are we going?" she added moments later as he led her across the parking lot toward a green space with a walking path lit up by small lights.

"I just need a few minutes to think," he finally told her, his hand slipping into hers.

Her heart lifted at the implication that she was part of his safety zone, someone he could walk and think with. She gave his warm hand a squeeze. The wind was brisk, and while her coat was cozy, her ears were being nipped as the two of them made their way toward the trees.

"Have you ever assumed something, but then doubted yourself?" Ryan asked.

"Well, I assumed I'd never want to date you, and yet here I am," she teased.

Ryan blinked once, as though processing her joke.

"I was kidding. We're not dating."

"We're not?" He glanced down at their linked hands.

"Are we?"

"I'm not sure anymore."

"Don't think what everyone was saying in there matters to me." She waved her free hand toward the school, where his family was still gathered. "We made an agreement and I'm fine with it."

"What if I'm not?" He'd stopped walking, pausing under a gigantic oak, its broad trunk protecting them from the wind. Their hidden spot was sheltered and private.

"I almost drowned in the creek behind our ranches." Ryan's eyes held a faraway look, and he shivered as though reliving the moment. "Myles jumped in and saved me. He could've drowned.

I would have if he hadn't come in after me, and then Cole fished us out downstream. I wanted to cross the creek along a ledge of rocks we'd built before the flood. We'd crossed there many times, and even with the floodwaters rushing over the rocks, I knew I could do it. They convinced me to take a muddier route, but I slipped and got swept downstream.

"My brothers were wrong about the creek, but they were right about Priscilla." Ryan turned to her, his light blue eyes almost navy in the near darkness. "And I think they're probably right about other things." He gazed down at her, his face hidden in the shadows.

"About me?"

"Yeah."

Unlike Ryan, she didn't have family telling her he was the real deal, but her heart and mind were certainly rooting for him.

"And what does your gut say?" she asked, thinking about the conversation she'd overheard him have with Blake during the bus ride.

"It says you're all right."

"Just all right, huh?" she joked. "So, does that mean we're dating?"

"We're doing something here, and if you don't want to hide it any longer..." He shrugged.

"You're very romantic, you know that?"

He let out a chuckle. "I'm sorry. That wasn't romantic at all, was it?"

"Yeah, but I get it. Remember?" She shifted so her body was snug against his. "I don't need flowery prose to tell me what you're feeling. I just need your refreshing, brutal honesty."

"That's about all I have."

"Then we're perfect." She slid her arms around his neck, her mouth close to his. "And since we're adults, we can do whatever we want."

9

*D*uring the afternoon semifinals game Ryan felt someone grab his sleeve, pulling him aside as he headed to the locker room for the halftime chat with the team.

"I've got to talk to the boys," he said to Carly. Since it was halftime and players weren't changing, females could enter the room. He gestured impatiently toward the closed door. They were behind by a touchdown and if they lost today that was it for the season. He wanted to go all the way to the end.

"I only need a minute, and what I have to say might affect what you tell the team." Her eyes were bright with excitement as she held up the stats tablet for him to see. She was wearing the same outfit as she had at the quarterfinals, and looked so beautiful she stole his breath away.

Ryan nodded to Myles, who closed the locker room door, giving Ryan and Carly a minute alone in the concrete chute that led off the football field. She began tapping on the tablet and Ryan stood behind her, looking over her shoulder. As he leaned closer, he wondered how, miles from home, she still smelled like hay and fresh air. She smelled like her ranch, like his, like home. She smelled like the place he'd fought against for so long due to his fears and his need to be self-sufficient. The place he knew he could always turn to if he needed to. A place filled with people who loved him.

Was his family right about Carly? And if they were, where did the two of them go from here?

He was thinking about it too much. Carly was happy to take things one step at a time, and so was he. He needed to get out of his head and just live and watch what unfolded.

"You see what I mean?" she asked, pointing to the tablet. She had switched from the usual stats application to one where she could draw with her finger. The screen was covered with X's and O's, circles and lines as she presented a possible new strategy.

"You think Hernandez should toss short and take the field ten yards at a time?" The other team would catch on, but the Torpedoes might make it farther than they were with their long passes, which gave their opponents enough time to intercept. Despite their training, his boys just weren't fast enough to outpace this team. Carly knew it, saw it and didn't have the ego and pride invested like he did. She was willing to consider a strategy he'd discarded as not being complex enough for a game this late in the season.

"Hernandez is good at bluffing the other team into thinking he's going to pass one direction," Carly said, switching back to the stats app. "They also know he prefers the long glory throws. Meanwhile, we have that short player who acts like he's afraid of the other players—what's his name?" Not finding what she was looking for in the stats application, she tapped back to her drawing, pointing at a position on the field where a quick pass could be received by whoever happened to be there.

Mix it up. Be unpredictable.

He liked it. A lot. And it would use the diversity of strengths he and Myles had focused on building into their team.

"Deitz. He could catch it," Ryan said, getting excited, then lowering his voice in case anyone was eavesdropping. "Deitz isn't fast and hates being tackled, so they won't expect it. But he can spin his way out of a block or a tackle like nobody. What if Hernandez throws right, toward the sidelines? Deitz is left-handed, and his blocker probably isn't. He could reach out, curl his body around it and even step out-of-bounds if need be. Or he could run. I'd be happy with any yards we can beg for at this point."

Carly gave him a smile so warm it made his entire body feel good as they stepped into the locker room. Unable to resist, and not caring who might see, he cupped her jaw and tugged her in for a quick kiss. At least he intended it to be quick, but as her generous lips touched his, their mouths softened and he found himself in a long, sensual kiss. The catcalls from the team began, but he didn't stop kissing her. And she didn't stop, either.

When they finally broke free, Carly's eyes were wide with surprise. "What was that?"

"Nothing."

"What happened to being open and honest with each other to the point of brutality?" she said under her breath, staying close to him near the doorway, as though afraid they might get bombarded if they moved any farther into the locker room.

"Okay, so it was *something*. Did that embarrass you?" Her fierceness and the annoyance in her steady stare amused him.

She gave him a firm look.

"Sorry. I couldn't resist kissing you. I love it when you talk football." He released her, raising his hands in surrender. "We're still ourselves. We're not getting married. You have your life, I have mine, but now we're public."

She slowly released a puff of air, still looking uncertain, so he lowered his voice to an intimate level. "Maybe I want to kiss you whenever and wherever I like." He linked her hand with his and held it up between them, admiring the contrast of light and dark as their fingers entwined. "And anyway, we are dating, right?"

She studied him with those serious brown eyes for what felt like the longest moment of his life.

They'd never come to a real conclusion about dating, had they? Was a kiss like that unfair?

"I think I can live with that, but next time, maybe refrain from kissing me in front of the team," she said finally. She was trying unsuccessfully to school her happy expression.

Ryan shook his head when he realized she'd been yanking his chain the whole time. She didn't mind taking their relationship public, and maybe his bad-luck go-round with Priscilla had simply been so he'd recognize it when something good like Carly came his way. He liked that idea.

Carly made her way over to Jackie, who was standing near Myles. He was struggling to keep the team's focus on him, and Jackie's nose kept crinkling with glee whenever she looked at Ryan or Carly.

When Ryan went to join his brother in front of the team, he caught Carly's grin. He wanted to eat the distance between them with large strides and kiss her again.

Jackie, unable to contain herself, yelled, "I'm three for three with matching up Wylder brothers."

Ryan sighed and rolled his eyes, while Myles struggled to hush the team again.

Wait. Ryan frowned in thought. Just because he and Carly weren't hiding their kisses any longer didn't mean they would be a serious couple like Laura and Levi, or Karen and Myles. This wasn't even Jackie's doing. How could she take credit for their relationship? They had been kissing before Jackie had brought Carly onto the field under the pretence of helping with player statistics so she could work her matchmaking magic.

"Coach!" Blake called. "Did you see the signs?"

"The signs?" He glanced at Carly.

"In the stands."

"Oh, right! Yeah. Cool, huh?" Sweetheart Creek had turned

out for today's game in droves, and right at field level a long line of white T-shirts with red letters spelled out Sweetheart Creek Torpedoes. It had to have taken a fair amount of coordination to claim those twenty-six seats in a row.

Ryan checked his watch. "Okay, listen up. Carly noticed some things out there that I want you to try." He glanced at Myles, hoping he wouldn't mind a mix-up.

He gestured for him to continue, and Ryan wondered how he could ever doubt that his brother would have his back.

"Coach? What is it?" Hernandez called out.

Ryan leaned in, his focus back on his team. "We'll play like we've never played before. Literally."

As he outlined the plan, his brother listened thoughtfully. "I think that could work," Myles finally said, admiration in his gaze as he nodded at Carly.

"Should we try it?" Ryan asked his team.

"Yes!" they yelled back, and he grinned. They were sweaty and exhilarated. They had the right energy to catch up with the other team and maybe even surpass them.

"Let's go show them the best game we can give them," Ryan said.

"We've got this, Coach," his quarterback called. "And nice choice on the babe."

"Babe?" Ryan asked in an unimpressed tone, eyebrows raised.

"She's hot and she knows football. Totally perfect for you." Hernandez aimed his pointer fingers, waiting for him to do the same. With a reluctant sigh, Ryan mimicked the gesture and carried through with a "Huzzah!"

He had a feeling that sharing that one simple kiss with Carly had just altered some major things in his life.

And he felt ready for it.

"YOU AND RYAN?" Jackie practically jumped on Carly in her excitement as they left the field after the Torpedoes won the game. They were officially heading for the state championship final game in Dallas next week. Well, the team was. Carly might not be able to make it due to that stupid court case. Her business partnership with Eaton just kept messing up her life, didn't it? She'd be in Montana on Tuesday for the preliminary hearing, but hopefully be released in plenty of time to get back for Friday's game.

Jackie was nattering on to herself about how she'd known it, and how right Carly and Ryan were for each other.

"Man, that game," Carly said on an exhale, breaking her friend's stream of chatter. She was still reeling from the stress of trying to play it cool and not get sucked into what had almost turned into a tie-breaker. A crazy play had led to their last-minute win. Carly had nearly thrown the tablet in the air as she'd jumped out of her chair in excitement.

She'd glanced over, ready to share the moment with Ryan, but he'd looked so solemn she'd sat again, aware she might break a sidelines superstition with her enthusiastic cheering.

"Are you trying to change the subject?" Jackie asked.

"Maybe a bit," she admitted.

It hadn't taken the other team long to figure out what the Torpedoes were doing with their mix-up à la Carly, but it had been key to evening the score. And that's all the Torpedoes had needed, their unpredictability unhinging their opponents enough that they could slip past and win. And it felt great. Really great. She'd earned her spot on the sidelines, and nobody could argue that she'd been placed there for any reason other than she was good. Carly hadn't realized how much the possibility of people thinking she was there for anything other than her merit had been stressing her out.

Her life was finally becoming hers, and she was becoming the person she'd always wanted to be. And strangely enough, that was in part due to Ryan and their "casual" relationship, not from being alone.

Maybe wearing a reminder ring hadn't been what she'd needed. Maybe she'd needed to surround herself with people who cared enough not to take over her life and dreams. Kind people who wouldn't crush them into the ground as they used her as a stepping stone for their own lives. If she'd realized there were people like Ryan who wanted to help her get to the spot she'd marked on the map for herself, she would have sought them out ages ago.

"How long have you two been together?" Jackie demanded. She'd tried to ask that when they'd returned to the field for the second half, but Carly had shut her down, needing to call on intense focus to pull herself together after that hot kiss in the locker room. "Was that the first time you kissed? Because that was seriously steamy, and if that was your first—" She stopped abruptly. "That wasn't your first, was it? Y'all have been telling us the truth, but saying it sarcastically or ironically so we'd run right past it."

They had been walking toward the parking lot where the bus was waiting, but now Jackie turned, hands on her hips. "How long have you two been sneaking around?"

"About three weeks."

"Three weeks!"

"Depends how you count." Carly pulled her hands inside the sleeves of her jacket to shield them from the December wind.

Her friend's eyes grew enormous. "You have got to be kidding me." Then she froze. "Wait. Were you together before we started this stats thing?"

Carly smiled.

"No." Jackie clutched her head. "That means this one doesn't count."

"What are you talking about?"

She was spinning in slow circles as though she'd lost her way, and Carly began directing her toward the bus. "Are you okay?"

"Three weeks?" Jackie let out a lengthy sigh.

"Hey," called Levi. He was with Laura, Brant and April. Kurt was riding on Brant's shoulders and wearing the man's red game hat.

Carly and Jackie waved back and waited for them to catch up. The team was already mostly on the bus, with Ryan and Myles waylaid by yet more press outside the field.

"I can't break the chain," Jackie moaned.

"The chain?" Carly stared at her.

"If you don't count, then what about Brant?" Her voice hitched as she added, "What about Cole?"

"Who's Cole again?"

Jackie stared at her, crestfallen.

"Hey, what's wrong?" Brant asked her. "Didn't you hear we won?"

"Carly and Ryan were a thing before I took her to the game," she said glumly.

"Oh, that means…" Laura paused, her expression falling like Jackie's had. She caught herself and closed her mouth.

"Is this a superstition?" Carly asked.

"Jackie believes that if she can get the four brothers—" Laura began.

"Hush! It sounds stupid if you say it out loud." Jackie clapped her hands over her ears and turned away.

"You've heard of Jackie's thing about taking friends to football games, and they end up in a relationship?" Laura asked, ignoring her pleas to remain quiet.

Carly nodded.

"Well, she was two-for-two this season, and was hoping for a higher number. Specifically, in the Wylder family."

"I was three-for-three," Jackie said with a deep frown, then a glare at Carly. "But she went and kissed Ryan before I could take her to a game."

"You're taking credit for Karen and Myles?" April asked. "They're always on the field together, with her and cheer, and him and football."

"Yes," Jackie said with exaggerated patience. "It's complicated, April, but yes."

"Then why can't you count Ryan and me? They were just kisses." Although they were more than that now. Ryan was officially her boyfriend.

"Is that why you saved me a seat today?" Brant asked Jackie, cutting his eyes to April, who turned red.

"Jackie likes Cole," April revealed quietly, and Jackie refused to meet anyone's eyes.

"And so she figured if she hooked up all four brothers at games this season, then maybe..." Laura cast a glance at Levi, who had the grace to look sad that Jackie's plan seemed to have been foiled.

"Then maybe he'd come back?" Levi said softly, draping an arm across Jackie's shoulders.

"Yeah. Yup. And I only like him as a friend," Jackie said, shrugging off the gentle embrace. "Who's hungry?" She began marching away. "Let's tell the bus driver to get moving to the hall so we can have our potluck supper."

"That was awkward," April said, looking at Brant with pink cheeks. He shrugged, his expression unreadable as he shifted Kurt on his shoulders, making the boy laugh. He begged him to do it again, so Brant shuffled around in circles, making horse sounds as he went.

"So? You and Ryan?" Levi asked Carly, as they began moving toward the bus. "You're a thing, huh?"

"We are," she said. Admitting it out loud caused her chest to expand with happiness. She glanced down at her chilly hands. The familiar wedding band that had once given her a sense of security now felt so wrong. It was no longer a reminder to focus on herself, but an old habit that no longer served her. It was time to make a change.

"He can be a royal pain in the butt," Levi warned.

"It's okay. So can I," she murmured, knowing that she and Ryan were a good match. In fact, they might even be perfect.

<hr>

AFTER THE POTLUCK SUPPER, Ryan snagged Carly to go out for a quick walk before they got on the bus to return to Sweetheart Creek. Only one more week on the field with her, then taking what he thought of as their postgame walk. It was like when he'd slept in the stable, monitoring Blackberry, and each morning Carly would come out, her face still soft from sleep, a cup of coffee in each hand. They'd sit on a bale outside the door, a thick blanket wrapped around their shoulders, chatting, sipping coffee and enjoying the sunrise with their dogs sleeping on their feet. It had felt like this. Private, intimate. It was something he'd miss when their routine changed. But maybe they'd find a new routine, new habits.

It was almost mid-December and soon he'd be off for Christmas break. Maybe they could go on an official date. They could drive over to Riverbend to see a movie, or work on her farm, go for a trail ride on their ranches, attend a barn dance or enjoy a backyard fire and some of his home brew.

"Do you drink beer?" he asked, his hand tucked in hers as night set in around them.

"I do. Hey. So what's with April and Brant?"

Ryan shrugged, then realized he could tell Carly anything. It didn't matter if he knew the answer or not.

"I think something's up," he admitted.

"You think?" She laughed, then, catching his expression, apologized. "Something romantic?"

"He bought her a house."

"So you think it's serious?"

"They've always been close." Ryan shook his head, thinking of the predicament April had gotten herself into with Heath. "Her husband's a bit of a jerk."

"I think I remember him from rodeo. A bull rider who liked to end conversations by using his fists?"

"That sounds like him. April always had an interest in making life lively." Although it appeared she'd finally tired of it.

Ryan had been about twenty-three when she married Heath Thompson, and preoccupied with other things at the time, such as getting over what was supposed to have been a one-year anniversary with Priscilla. He had paid little attention to April's life until recently.

"I don't know why she married Heath and not Cole," he mused. "Maybe Heath was ready to settle down or something."

"So she dated Cole?"

Ryan tucked their joined hands between his arm and ribs to keep them warm. "They were always on again, off again."

"That's awkward if Cole comes back and Brant's playing house with April, don't you think?"

Ryan paused, then nodded.

"But Jackie likes Cole and wants him to come home for her?" Carly pressed.

Ryan slowed near a park bench in the grassy area behind the hall. Why were they talking about his brothers when they could be kissing?

"We all want him to come home. Jackie just wants anyone with the last name Wylder."

"Is Henry available?" Carly asked with a giggle.

Ryan released her hand and slid his arms around her waist. "Funny."

"Why did Cole leave?"

"Not sure."

Carly let out a long, slow exhale, her concern for April and Brant clear when she said, "April's still married."

"Things are going to get messy," he agreed.

"I hope Brant's a good fighter."

"He was the one who broke up the fights when we were kids and forced us to talk it out."

Carly grimaced, and Ryan snuggled her closer. "I'm sure it'll all work out."

"If not, hopefully April's first aid certification is up-to-date. Life gets so complicated sometimes when we follow the wrong path, doesn't it?" she added, a wrinkle forming between her brows.

Ryan finally stole a sweet kiss from the woman in his arms. She ended it before he was ready to, her mind obviously too busy to focus on kissing right now. "You know that business deal I was involved in that ended poorly?" she asked.

"Yeah."

"There's more to it than the business just falling apart."

He could sense her hesitation, and that old feeling of shame and the need to push his feelings aside reared up inside him again. They'd both had big failings, and when she talked about her past it always reminded him of his own. Trusting people when he shouldn't have. Being blindsided by deceit. It all made him feel stupid, and he just wanted to ignore it all and move on with his life. He didn't want to hash it out. Not even with Carly. They'd connected over their past errors in judgment, and that was enough for him.

"There are still some loose ends I need to take care of in Montana. On Tuesday," she stated.

"You'll be back for State?"

She nodded.

"Okay. Thanks for letting me know." He snuggled his arms around her.

"I feel you should know the details about where I'm going and what I'm doing."

"We're independent, remember? It's not necessary to check in with me." He trusted her, and didn't need her ETA or a list of who she was going to be meeting with. "Your life is your life. Mine is mine. I'm not planning on judging you for your past mistakes. I understand, remember? We're moving forward. Fresh start."

She sighed at his light tone. Finally, she said, "I want you to know I'll be here for you when I can. You're important to me."

"You're important to me, too." He couldn't imagine what his days would be like if she wasn't around.

Her voice was forced, like she was pushing through something based on sheer willpower, and his heart broke for her as she said, "I don't want you to lose faith in me because I was stupid and naive and allowed my business partner to ruin everything."

She choked up, her eyes filled with pain and regret, and Ryan could see her fear. She feared he didn't care enough to be able to overlook her past mistakes. If only she knew that her imperfections made her even more precious to him.

He clasped her cheeks with his hands, bringing her forehead to his. "I would hate to be with someone who made no mistakes. I like being with someone who understands how turning a blind eye can mess up a person's life. It allows them to appreciate it when something great comes along. That's who you are to me, Carly. I won't ever think you're stupid. We've both been hoodwinked by others. That's part of our past. It's not part of our future."

She gave him a ghost of a smile, then opened her mouth to say more. He shushed her. "Remember? We're a thing, and that thing is good. Forget the past, Carly. All we have is the future. I trust you."

CARLY CONTINUED to walk with Ryan, mulling over why she'd yet again given up on telling him the details of how she'd been blindsided by her former business partner, and how she had been subpoenaed to attend a preliminary hearing before the trial. They considered her a witness, but she didn't trust the lawyers, the courts, or the decisions that had already been made. Things could get twisted. She could be thrown in the line of fire once again. It could still be her on the stand getting ripped apart.

She would fight with everything she had to ensure it didn't happen, and that Eaton got what was coming to him, not her.

She needed to believe in the system. And that was not an easy thing to do.

But Ryan was right. She needed to focus on the future. A future bright with opportunities. One that would differ from her past.

The problem was that the trouble from her past could change Ryan's perception of her. She'd tried to tell him. And yet the way he'd looked at her so tenderly, his words, his trust… It had all combined in a power she'd been unable to overcome, and she'd lost the courage to confess everything.

He was right. They were great as they were. Independent. It was becoming a relationship, but it wasn't like they were looking for love and forever, right? He still wanted distance, and he didn't want the gory details of her past. Was it wrong that she didn't insist on telling him, even though she wanted to share that part— all parts—of her life with him?

Thankfully, her Montana court appearance wouldn't affect her ability to take stats at State. She'd fly out on Monday night for Tuesday's court date and be back in time for Friday's morning game in Dallas. She wouldn't have to experience letting Ryan down.

As though sensing her mood, he gave her hand a squeeze

before pointing at a fox squirrel nibbling on a stale piece of bread just off the path. They took a few steps, sending the squirrel scampering, before Ryan paused, a thoughtful look in his blue eyes. He lifted her hand, linked with his, and stared at her bare ring finger for a long moment.

Carly's doubts about what she'd done earlier in the day ate at her. Maybe it had been too soon to remove the ring. Maybe it had represented something to him that had felt safe.

But she wanted to be fully free to enter this relationship with Ryan. She didn't want to hide behind that ring any longer.

Just like she didn't want to hide her legal issues. But one thing at a time, right? She'd find a way to tell him before she left on Monday.

"You took it off?" he said, blinking at her.

She looked at her bare finger, then up at him, unable to mask her hope. She could see him thinking. He didn't believe he could be the man she needed. He didn't know how far he could trust her. He worried she was trapping him. What if his gut was leading him astray?

Ryan looked away, his jaw so tight she could practically feel the tension radiating through his temples.

She pushed on his arm, wishing he'd look at her and see that she wasn't asking for more than he could offer. The ring was about her. "What's wrong?"

"Nothing."

"I thought we were going to be open and honest with each other. To the point of brutality."

"I am being honest."

"Haven't you noticed we can tell when the other person isn't speaking the truth? I've freaked you out."

Ryan rolled his shoulders as if trying to dispel the urge to run. She was pressing him, crossing lines, but she didn't care. This was important. If she let it go, it might hover between them forever.

"This is bugging you?" She pointed to her finger.

"I'm not ready to replace that piece of jewelry."

"Who asked you to?" She crossed her arms, feeling very much like the woman who'd fired a shotgun into the sky last month.

"Taking that ring off means you're ready for something that was never part of our bargain."

"Maybe I took it off because I'm ready to take it off."

He shook his head. "I swore I'd never be here again."

"Where?"

"Looking at marriage."

She laughed, her chest aching with the harshness of the sound that creaked out of her. "Well, you do whatever you want, but if you were to ask me to marry you, I'd send you packing. Just so you know."

His eyes caught hers, that assessing look that probed deep within her. She spread her arms, showing she had nothing to hide, no ulterior motives.

"Nothing has changed," she said. "And just so you know, maybe I swore I'd never be here again, either."

"And where are you?"

"Offering more of my heart than is likely wise."

He had moved away from her, until several feet stretched between them. "I made it clear—"

"This isn't about you!" She pointed to her finger, feeling the tears well up despite her wish that they'd dry up. "Why do men always want to make my life about them? Like my actions are some big earthquake about to upset the balance in their world? It's my life. My dreams. My thoughts. My healing. Not yours. So back it up a step!"

He inhaled as though bracing himself for a blow.

She couldn't meet his gaze for a moment, knowing she wasn't being fully up-front. It hadn't just been for her. It had also been for him, for his reputation.

"Carly, this isn't a great time for me to be dealing with this."

She shook her head, realizing he was talking about the championship. And that whatever they were dealing with as a couple wasn't important enough to be on his radar, wasn't worth dealing with right now.

Her expression must have shown how she felt, because he closed the distance between them and took her in his arms. "I'm sorry. I didn't mean to discount you, or us, or this."

She remained stiff in his embrace, not wanting to care as much as she did.

When she didn't relax, Ryan gently tipped her face upward. "Are you okay?"

"This ring is about me, Ryan. I didn't put it on or take it off because I'm playing games or expect things or am jealous of the attention and focus you need to place on the game and your players. It just felt like it was the right time in my life to remove it."

His brow furrowed. "You didn't wear it for Peter, did you?"

He was quiet, close to her, his body warm and tight to hers, refusing to let her go until she softened against him. It was the first time he hadn't shied away from asking for more about her past, and she allowed herself a moment to let that sink in.

"It's not Peter's, but people assume it is. I pawned that ring. I didn't want to see it again, and I figured it owed me something. It wasn't worth much, sadly."

"Where did this one come from?"

"It was my father's."

"Is he gone?"

She shook her head. "It doesn't fit him any longer, and he never wore it on the farm, anyway. He gave it to me when Peter and I got engaged, but it never felt right giving it to Peter. I put it on after I got burned in that business deal, as a reminder that I need to come first in my life."

She waited for Ryan to ask for details about the deal so she could finally confess.

"I don't need to be alone to heal and move on," she finally said, when he didn't speak. "It seems I just need the right people in my life." The roar of fear caused ringing in her ears as she spoke the truth, worried Ryan might react again, might assume she was expecting more than he was offering.

With resolve, she looked up at him, locking her gaze on his. She was going to put it all out there. If he didn't like it, he could walk away.

"Everything works out if you have good people in your life," she said.

arly and Jackie walked the few blocks from their Dallas hotel to the one where Ryan and the football team had stayed. The team would play a morning game in the Cowboys' stadium, since another high school playoff, for a larger division, was slated for that afternoon. After today's win or loss, the team would take the long drive home. Hopefully in triumph.

The cheerleaders had their own bus to take them to the stadium, but being part of the football team, Carly and Jackie would ride with the athletes.

The team and various supporters were already gathered around the charter bus that had been arranged for the occasion. Jackie, spotting Maria Wylder, who'd just flown in from a quick vacation in Indigo Bay, South Carolina went over to chat. The mayor of Sweetheart Creek, Travis Nestner, and his wife, Donna, were talking to Daisy-Mae, who was fixing the red and white ribbons in Mrs. Fisher's hairdo.

Carly mingled, chatting with people and wishing the boys luck as they climbed into the bus. They weren't due to pull out for another twenty minutes, but people were congregating, eager for the day's game. Even Maverick Blades, Ryan and Myles's old friend who played in the NHL, was there signing autographs and wishing the team luck.

Everything was perfect. Carly had been worried when Tuesday's preliminary hearing in Montana had been postponed, due to the judge being under the weather. She'd waited, certain Murphy's Law would have the hearing rescheduled for the same day as the state championship match. But the call hadn't come, giving her a chance to attend the last game of the season.

Carly felt a familiar tingle of anticipation and turned around, spotting Ryan. He was striding toward her in his red coaching jacket and a black cowboy hat. The hat was an interesting touch, and she wondered why he'd chosen it instead of a Torpedoes ball cap like usual. He briefly gripped the brim of his hat, dipping his head as he approached her.

"Mighty formal of you," she teased.

"How's this for formal?" He snagged her hand and pulled her to the far side of the bus, where it was more private, before gliding his arms around her waist and tugging her against his chest for a kiss. His mouth angled over hers, drawing her in like he always did.

The kiss left her breathless and giddy, as did the idea of no longer having to hide their kisses or how they felt about each other.

"I love it when you kiss me like that," she whispered.

"And I love you," he said, playfully tapping the end of her nose. He froze as he realized what he'd said. The two of them stared at each other for a long moment.

"You know," Ryan said, after clearing his throat, "in an independent way."

Carly laughed, happiness welling up inside her as she placed her cool hands on his warm cheeks, drinking him in. Her boyfriend. Her boyfriend who had just let it slip that he loved her.

He had shaved recently, his skin smooth and soft as she pulled his lips to hers for another kiss.

"It's okay," she said, when they broke apart. "I happen to love you in an independent way, as well." She rested her forehead against his, knocking his hat farther back on his head.

A chilly December breeze whisked across the parking lot, wrapping itself around them. In her bubble of happiness, Carly barely noticed the cold or the gloomy clouds brewing to the west. She had everything she needed right here with this man, and he would keep her safe and warm in any storm.

"Have I told you how cute you look in your stats-keeper outfit?" Ryan asked, looking at her legging-clad legs.

"It must've slipped your mind."

"Well, I'm telling you now it looks good. And if you want to sit beside me on the bus, that seat will be vacant."

"You're kicking Myles out of his seat?"

"It's for a worthy cause." He gave her a crooked grin, looking slightly mischievous in his black hat. With his hands around her waist, he pulled her in for another kiss.

"I think a seat reassignment could be arranged then."

"There's a condition," he warned.

"What's that?" Would he need her to kiss him again? Or refrain from doing so around his players?

"Don't distract me when I get into game mode." His eyes were bright with a hint of heat and longing as his grip tightened on her waist. He gave a rusty-sounding sigh before releasing her with what looked like regret.

"Who, me? Distract you?" She pressed a hand against her chest as though surprised by the claim.

Ryan's eyes traced her movements, his pupils widening. "I have a feeling it's something you do without even realizing it." He slipped her another kiss and she wrapped her arms around him. "Maybe I should arrange for you to ride with the cheer team."

"You couldn't handle being that far from me for that long."

Ryan plunked his hat on her curls and steered her around to the other side of the bus where the crowd of fans, families and players had grown. He whisked her up the bus's steps while she held the precariously perched hat. She claimed a seat for them near the front, and Ryan continued past, doing a roll call of players. She watched him retreat down the aisle, enjoying the view of her cowboy.

Smiling, she fished her phone from her pocket when it rang.

"Carly Clarke?"

"Speaking."

"Thank goodness. I was worried we'd have to charge you for being in contempt of court."

"What?" The air rushed from her lungs.

The clerk rattled off Carly's landline number. "Sorry I forgot to try your cell until now. But I've been calling that other number since yesterday to inform you that your preliminary hearing will proceed this afternoon."

"Today?" Her heart dropped. It would take her hours to get to Montana, and that was if she could get a flight.

"The judge has scheduled you for three thirty this afternoon."

Three thirty? She was still in Texas!

"I…"

"I trust you're staying in Montana as recommended?"

Carly uttered something unintelligible. With the courts not giving her a timeline, she hadn't known what day to reschedule her flight for, and had left her ticket open. She'd received the impression that the court's rescheduling could take days—which it had.

"Please check in, then proceed to Courtroom One when you arrive."

Carly dropped the phone back in her purse, her spirits plummeting.

Dallas had a huge airport. There had to be lots of direct flights from here. Maybe she could help at today's game and still make it to court on time.

She pulled out her phone again and scrolled through an online booking system. Flight after flight was marked as full. She furiously checked again. There was one flight available and the timing was tight.

She needed about thirty minutes to get to the airport from the stadium. The flight itself was about three hours. There was a one-hour time zone difference in her favor, meaning if everything, including the game, went flawlessly she could miraculously squeak in on time. But she had to tell Ryan.

As the bus driver shifted into gear, heading toward the stadium, Carly felt the pressure under her ribs increasing.

Ryan fell into the seat beside her, his expression relaxed. "I think today's game's going to be great. Everything's in that flow state, you know?" He glanced over at her and she pasted a bright smile on her face even though inside she was panicking.

She couldn't tell him. Not now. It would break his flow state, but so would taking off before the game ended.

He glanced around for onlookers before leaning in for a quick, soft kiss, looking like a man whose entire life was falling into place.

"Ryan... I..."

His expression was tender as he tucked one of her curls behind her ear. "Don't distract me with those big eyes of yours and that beautiful mouth." He turned to face the front of the bus, his focus returning to business. "We need this win. This is what I've been working toward. I've missed it in the past, but this year... This year we're getting it!" He turned with a grin and kissed her again.

She fought the tears that wanted to come. She needed to tell him. Now.

"Hey, Ryan?" Myles leaned across the aisle to ask something about one of their plays, and the two brothers began strategizing.

She'd left Ryan in the dark for too long, taking the easy way out and using his wish to leave their pasts behind them as an excuse. But their lives were interconnected enough for her court appearance to matter. This would never become the real relationship they were rocketing toward if she continued to keep it from him.

She had to take that flight. But if she didn't tell Ryan, she would be sprinting into the parking lot as the game ended with a quick "Have to be in court in Montana. Explain later. Love you! Bye!" And that was seriously uncool.

But she also needed to protect him. If she tugged on his sleeve right now and spilled it all, she might distract him from important mental game prep. And if they lost because of her, she'd never forgive herself.

Anyway, it was her problem, her past, her life. She was being independent while also being there when Ryan needed her. Just like he wanted.

Her heart sank as the truth elbowed its way in. Her justifications were weak. Everything about her omission reeked of being a deal breaker.

She'd painted herself into this corner and her only valid plan was to keep Ryan in the dark until the last moment, and hope for the best.

***

RYAN PACED the hall outside the locker room designated for the Sweetheart Creek Torpedoes. The game started in less than an hour. By noon, this season's fate would be sealed.

Absolutely no pressure.

He was calmer than he'd expected. Maybe it was because he'd come this far before and faced the worst—a loss. But this year, with Carly on their side, they'd win. He could feel it.

He'd nearly lost his mind when he noticed she'd removed her

ring. He'd made it about him, and what she might want from him. It had quickly become clear the ring was a tool she'd used as part of her healing process. A good boyfriend would have known that and been happy for her.

He'd caught himself, though. But not until after she'd given him heck.

He chuckled at the memory. Maybe it was the ring's removal coinciding with him picking up a Christmas gift for her the day before that had sent him for that mental loop. He'd spotted a cute shovel charm bracelet and had bought it for her. He'd planned to simply give it to her, but so soon after their first fight it had felt like a significant peace offering for what had simply been a minor freakout moment.

Still, he worried that her removing the ring might mean she expected more of him. And as it was, he already had moments where the proverbial torrent of muddy floodwaters seemed to be swirling around him, swallowing him like it had when he was a child, unrelenting as it pushed him toward a serious relationship. In other moments, he smiled just thinking about her.

He entered the bustling locker room, where, earlier, a clean jersey had been hung at each locker. Now they were on the players, the final countdown to the season's last game underway.

It was time to focus on what mattered: the game. Carly was here, helping, and wasn't about to leave or upend his life. She wanted nothing more serious than he did. Other than the ring blip, they seemed to be totally in step, and she'd proved she was someone he could trust.

He spotted her mass of curls almost immediately across the crowded room, where she was bent over the stats tablet with Jackie. Ryan took a moment to drink her in, the floodwaters of fear receding.

MYLES WAS AMPED UP, serving as the perfect counter for Ryan's quiet demeanor. In life the two brothers often balanced each other, and game day was no different.

As the players moved into their pre-game warm-up, Ryan paused to watch part of Karen's cheerleaders' routine before he went to chat with the opposing team's coaches. It was tradition for him to say hello, shake their hands, as well as the officials'.

Myles said he preferred to avoid looking their competition in the eye until he was victorious. But Ryan found if he chatted with the other coaches it gave him insight into their attitudes and personalities, which often translated into something useful. And speaking to the officials? It showed he was human, and while it didn't lend a specific bias, it sometimes felt as though the benefit of the doubt was granted where it might not have been otherwise.

Ryan inhaled the stadium air, rolling his shoulders. It was growing louder inside, with fans filtering in from their early morning parking lot tailgate parties. The sky above was gray, the translucent panels in the stadium's retractable roof murky. Inside, they were protected, allowing the weather to do what it wanted. There would be no game delays, nothing unpredictable to mess with the flow of positive energy he was feeling.

He waved as he caught an image of himself on the massive screen hanging above the field. Some of his players freaked out at the enormity of the stadium and being the focus of everyone's attention. Others reveled in it, promising him they would work hard and make the Cowboys' team someday. None had so far.

As Ryan moved along the sidelines toward the opposing team he spotted Carly standing near her stats chair, wearing the same red, white and denim outfit as Jackie. Like a superstition, they'd worn it for each of the playoff games.

Ryan inhaled again, steadying himself. He'd told Carly he loved her, and she'd said it back. He'd fumbled the ball with his awkward words, but she'd caught it, made the touchdown.

He was in love.

He shook his head, marveling that after all the potholes he'd hit so far in his life he should suddenly seem to have it all. He and Carly were solid. They were independent, but also together. So perfect.

She had game nerves, though. He'd felt the shift in her on the bus ride over. He couldn't blame her, as he knew how unnerving today could be.

Carly was talking to a slight-figured person wearing the opposing team's colors, Carly's face lit up in a large smile. She was beautiful, and at one point she reached out to touch the person in the coaching jacket as she laughed, obviously happy to be where she was. The coach had a ponytail, her back to Ryan.

Based on his research, this team had male coaches and he couldn't shake the feeling that something was off, and that there was something familiar about the woman Carly was chatting with. Female coaches weren't common in football, and he tried to place where he may have seen her. Maybe during last year's play-offs, when they'd battled teams from other areas of Texas?

Ryan readied his smile as he approached the duo, weaving among the players already gathered on the sidelines. Carly caught his eye and her grin grew a little larger, a little happier, and made him feel special. He was her number one, even with that lingering haunted look in her gaze. One he planned to put to rest right here and now with a giant kiss.

He picked up his pace, glancing left as movement caught his attention. He faltered. Myles was staring at Carly and the coach, his expression closed, his mouth pressed into an uncharacteristically stern line. Ryan, a few feet from the women, heard a laugh he would know anywhere. It was high, a tinkling sound tainted by a hint of condescension, and it cut through him as if the woman was saying, "Can you believe it? How pathetic!"

His blood ran cold, and he found himself rooted to the fake turf under his shoes.

"Here's our coach," Carly said brightly, her arm extended toward him.

As the opposing coach turned to face Ryan, he gave a quick prayer, wishing for a trick of the stadium's sound and lighting that would prove his new girlfriend had not in fact been chumming it up with his ex-wife.

***

CARLY'S HAND froze in the air, her cheerful wave to Ryan aborted as she caught sight of his expression. He was like a poster boy for shock and disbelief, almost looking like a caricature of himself. She watched as he fought for control, smoothing his features. But in his eyes fear was mixed with rage and indignation, and she involuntarily took a step back. Had he heard she was leaving immediately after the game?

She'd planned to tell him when it wouldn't disrupt his mental preparation, but had she inadvertently blindsided him instead? They hadn't had time to build on their newly proclaimed love, and she'd already ruined things with one of her patent bad decisions.

As Ryan marched forward, he seemed to recover, anger his predominant emotion. There was something triumphant and calculating in Coach Tyblone's gaze, and Carly realized that whatever was going on with Ryan wasn't about her Montana court date.

Coach Tyblone had straightened her shoulders and her voice was cool and even when she said, "Hello, Ryan."

"Your name is not on the roster," he replied, his tone sharp.

"Checking up on the other teams, are you? Afraid you might lose something?" Her emphasis on the word *lose* set Carly's heart pounding.

"There is nothing you can take from me that I can't replace."

"I love a bitter, simple man."

"I don't think you understand the definition of that four-letter *L*-word. Is it new to your vocabulary?"

Carly felt the sting of Ryan's intent, but the woman simply watched him, calculating her next move.

"You can't be on the field without your name being on the roster," Ryan announced. He craned his neck, on the lookout for an official.

Myles had edged closer, seeming larger than usual as he stood behind Ryan. It was as though he was acting as a bodyguard, and Carly stepped closer to him.

"Actually, I belong here," Coach Tyblone said sweetly. "They listed me as a backup on the team's paperwork. I've been working with these guys all season. But as you know, you can have only so many people on the coaching roster. As team newbie, I wasn't going to be on the field. But our head coach is having medical issues, so here I am."

"Did you cause the issue?"

The woman let out what could best be described as a mean girl laugh. Carly gaped at her about-face. Mere moments ago she had been friendly and effusive.

Carly said hoarsely to Ryan, "We should go."

"Aw. No more insider secrets from you?" the woman said sweetly.

Ryan's nostrils flared as he stared at Carly, and she opened and closed her mouth, unable to force out any words. She hadn't said a single thing to jeopardize her team or Ryan, and never would.

"It was such a pleasure getting to know Ryan's latest fling," Coach Tyblone said with an innocent bat of her lashes, before turning away.

Carly's anger rode to the top of a wave before it came crashing down, her mouth opening to speak. Myles gripped her arm, whispering, "Don't." He bodily pulled her and Ryan away, sending Tyblone into what appeared to be near ecstasy when she turned to observe the effect of her visit.

"She'll get you two ejected for foul language," Myles warned, as he practically strong-armed them to the other end of their zone. "She'll see to it, and the team needs you both."

Ryan was so pale he could have passed for anemic.

"What did you tell Priscilla?" he demanded, glaring at Carly.

She gasped and caught herself turning back for another glance. That was Priscilla? How had Ryan ever been charmed by that evil, two-faced beast?

The same way she just had. The woman had been confident and gregarious, making Carly laugh. But in hindsight, Carly realized she'd been picking her over through the entire conversation. She'd been familiar with both Ryan and "that cute tiny town of Sweetbutt Creek" as she'd called it. She'd made a point of flashing her ridiculously large ring a few times, and now that Carly knew who she was, she wanted to storm over there and rip it off her finger and pawn it on Ryan's behalf. Was it his money that had her all glitzed up? Or had she found a fresh mark and was taking him for all he was worth?

"What did you tell her?" Ryan repeated.

Carly's hands flew up. "Nothing!"

"I swear I'll strangle that woman," he muttered as Jackie jogged up to them.

"Oh, goody! Did I hear we're planning a murder? I'm delightfully brilliant at hiding bodies. I can totally make it look like an accident. Who are we putting the hit on?"

Myles, his Mediterranean-blue eyes stormy, gritted out, "Not now, Jackie."

"Well, obviously not *now*." She rolled her eyes, then caught Ryan's expression, her jovial mood vanishing. "Priscilla!" she hissed.

Ryan whirled as Jackie's gaze cut to Carly's, then back to him. "You knew she was going to be here?" he demanded.

Jackie inhaled so sharply her nostrils fluttered. "I'm right, aren't I? Is she on the field? Where is she?" She spun in a circle. "I'll kill her myself to keep y'all out of jail." She pushed up the sleeves of her sweatshirt and widened her stance. "Right here, right now. It'll be worth the jail time to put that woman in an early grave."

Myles took Jackie's elbow, murmuring, "No murder today, Little Satan. Ryan and I need you and Carly to feed us everything you see out there today."

"Oh. Little Satan." She brightened, giving him a radiant grin. "I like that. Can I get it stitched on the back of my shirt?" She dropped a shoulder and looked over it, checking the back.

Ryan was still shooting daggers, cannons and missiles in Priscilla's direction, and Carly tentatively approached him, mulling over the things she could say to reassure him she had done nothing wrong. No secrets spilled. No insights given. But everything she thought to say sounded like guilt, guilt, guilt.

Myles gave Ryan a worried glance, then said to the women, "I need you at your best, spotting things we don't. You hear? If you see something we need to know, tell us right away. Not in five minutes. Immediately."

Both of them nodded.

Ryan's attention had turned to Carly, and he was watching her with such an intense focus it made her want to sidestep, like a horse avoiding the saddle. Take-charge-angry Ryan was sexy, but angry-at-everything Ryan was scary. She swallowed hard, then reached to hook her fingers around his arm, to let him know she was there for whatever he needed.

He avoided her touch, storming off toward the team and leaving Carly with a sharp pain in her chest. He made it five paces before he turned, his eyes filled with determination.

He asked Myles, "Where are the extra headsets?"

"The headsets?"

"Get these ladies hooked up so they can talk to us."

"But you said you don't want extra voices in your ear." Myles's eyes cut to Jackie.

"What?" she asked innocently.

"There's no way we're going home defeated. Not today." Ryan's gaze met Carly's, and she felt the unspoken warning—he would win, even if he suspected she might no longer be on his side.

11

Ryan couldn't stop pacing the edge of the field. He hadn't heard from Carly or Jackie in minutes.

"What have you got for me?" he asked through his headset.

"Nothing new," Carly said, her voice calm and smooth.

He covered his microphone and muttered to Myles, "How can they not have anything? It's a disaster out there."

"We're ahead by a touchdown," Myles replied. They'd switched roles again, and Ryan much preferred being chilled out. Being jacked up like this wasn't fun.

"We need to win." He needed to show Priscilla she hadn't defeated him. He was better off without her and living his best life, her ultimate impact on him nil.

As much as he tried to avoid it, he peered down the sidelines, trying to catch sight of his ex. What was she doing? She hadn't been a coach six years ago, merely an avid fan who'd always claimed she could do better than the professional coaches on TV. He'd thought it was cute at the time, but now he wondered if she'd been right, seeing as she'd made it this far without him hearing about it. Then again, she wasn't the team's head coach, just an alternate. An assistant.

Still, he couldn't underestimate her.

She'd known he would be here.

But she wasn't getting in his head this time. He would not be vulnerable and lose.

Carly.

He'd told her he loved her, and practically the next minute she'd been laughing it up with Priscilla.

His heart rate ratcheted up a few beats, and he reminded himself to breathe. Carly was on his side. She'd feed him intel that would lead to victory. Her laughing with Priscilla had been nothing but a coincidence. He wouldn't allow his ex to unsettle him like she'd undoubtedly planned.

This time he would win.

"Carly, Jackie," he said into his microphone. "What do you have for me?"

"Nothing since two minutes ago," Jackie said, her tone dry. "Can we give you back the headsets? I don't like it as much as I thought I would."

He could hear Carly hush her, then say, "They're playing well, Ryan. Jackie, keep an eye on Wiggins."

"For what?" Ryan asked, his eyes tracking the player in question. Anything he missed out on the field today would come back to haunt him in the coming months as the citizens of Sweetheart Creek picked apart the game, analyzing his abilities and decisions as a coach. Some days he felt as though it was as much of a sport as the game itself.

"He's being blocked a lot."

"Tell me something I don't know. I need a win, girls."

"We're not *girls*," Jackie protested.

"Number 55 is favoring his right leg," Carly interjected, her voice full of triumph.

Ryan found him and confirmed what she'd seen. "Pull him," he told Myles.

His brother gave him a surprised look. "Pull him? Jackson's our best—"

"Get him checked. We can't handle a single mistake right now."

"I think *this* is a mistake." Myles folded his arms across his wide chest. The other day he'd mentioned he could bench 250. Ryan had a fleeting image of his brother bench-pressing him right out of the stadium for his uncharacteristic behavior, before he shook it off. This was Myles, his right hand. He'd be here through thick and thin, taking Ryan's mood in stride, as always.

"Are you the head coach or am I?" he asked, his voice low, but hard enough to show he meant business. "This isn't the time for questions. It's time to act, act, act."

Myles's cheeks puffed out. "Fine." He made the substitution.

Hernandez threw the ball and Jackson's replacement missed the pass by six feet.

"He's not warmed up!" Ryan exclaimed. Myles stared at him as though he'd turned into a monster. "Well? Do something!"

The players on the sidelines were supposed to always be moving, keeping their muscles warm. He turned and barked at the ones milling along the edges. "You want in this game? Jumping jacks, push-ups. I can't put you in cold." He gestured to Jackson. "What's with the leg?"

"It's fine, Coach. Just a small tweak. I walked it off." He took a few steps, showing he had no problems.

"Then what are you doing here? Get out there!" He turned to Myles. "Put him back in."

Myles made the trade and Ryan snapped, "What's Wiggins doing?" He was waving at the spectators, while waiting for the next play to begin. No wonder he was getting blocked; he was dazzled by the crowd and not focusing. "Pull him. Tell him to get his head in the game."

Ryan paced, shoulders hunched. How had this game gotten so

out of hand? How had he not known Priscilla was coaching? And what had Carly and Priscilla been laughing about?

Laughing. Reaching out and touching each other like they were friends.

And now Carly wasn't giving him anything helpful from the sidelines.

No. She wasn't in cahoots with his ex. He didn't need to worry about someone tainting the well. He and Carly were good, were solid.

He forced himself to be calm as he asked, "What do you see out there, Carly?"

"You're making a lot of subs."

He inhaled, ignoring the way Myles was looking at him, lips twisted in amusement.

"Who's hot out there?" he asked.

"Ask your quarterback," she replied tersely, her tone setting him off again.

"Fine. I will." He ground his teeth, muttering to Myles, "Why did I put headsets on them?" Nobody was feeding him anything useful, and he needed this win. He needed it more than any other in his life.

"Hey." Myles gave him a nudge. "Halftime."

Ryan ripped off his headset in frustration. As he walked toward the locker room, he realized that if he wanted to be victorious, he needed to do this the old-fashioned way. The independent Ryan way.

<hr>

CARLY REMAINED in her spot as the team headed to the locker rooms for the halftime break. She knew Ryan was gruff because he was on edge, with so much weighing on him and this game. She couldn't imagine what it would be like to go up against your ex in such an important playoff.

Ryan was more intense as she'd ever seen him, making rash decisions, relying on her too much for some magic she didn't possess. He was snapping at everyone, setting off chain reactions in his players.

She would have to wait until the end of the game to tell him she had to leave. Not ideal, but better than adding another weight on those strong shoulders of his.

"Don't take it personally," Jackie said, guessing Carly's silence was due to hurt feelings. "He got like this last year, too. Well, not really. But a bit."

Jackie's gaze cut to where the other team had gathered on the edge of the field, not heading to the locker rooms. It was a show of confidence, a way to throw Ryan off kilter even further with a nonverbal statement that they didn't need the break to rest, regroup or strategize.

Jackie tracked Carly's gaze to the other team. "He needs you to put his head back on straight."

"And how am I going to do that?"

"Kiss him."

"I don't think that'll help." She didn't know how he might react to her moving into his physical space when he was this stressed out. His body language had suggested he'd been thrown off by how chummy she'd been with Priscilla. She'd fallen for the woman's sly, smooth chitchat. As a result, she'd helped ruin Ryan's flow state. She sighed at herself. When would she learn who to trust?

"We have to do something," Jackie said, and Carly nodded in agreement. They'd been standing rather than sitting in their chairs along the sidelines, so they could see the plays better, and she pulled Carly toward the locker room.

"We can wait here," she said, when they'd reached the closed doors. Carly had been about to push them open, but paused, wondering if her friend was afraid of Ryan's mood. Normally at halftime they both marched into the locker room as if they owned it, knowing the players would be decent. Although, thanks to the headsets, there wasn't much more to say about the game other than to encourage Ryan to chill out.

Maybe Carly could do that. Find some strategy that would defeat Priscilla and prove to Ryan she was on his side and always would be. Otherwise it might take him a while to come around and be rational, and allow his trust in her to override his shock and anger over his ex blindsiding him.

As they stood near the locker room door, voices filtered out. A private time-out between Myles and Ryan just on the other side, by the sounds of it. Carly looked at Jackie. But instead of moving away, her friend put a finger to her lips and leaned closer to eavesdrop.

Myles was talking. "Her being here doesn't mean a thing. This is no different than any other game. You need to take it down a notch and be yourself. Be the coach we need."

"I'm being a team player, and I'm using my best resources. Just like you're always telling me to. And just like that course you took advises. I'm listening, but look what's happening out there."

"You're making poor calls."

There was silence.

"Then my team is feeding me worthless information. Why am I not getting useful info from my stats keepers?"

"Because our boys are playing well. Be proud of them."

"What if..." Ryan hesitated and the women leaned closer to the door. "What if there's a mole on our team? What if we've been infiltrated?"

"Infiltrated?" Jackie mouthed to Carly, who felt her jaw muscles slacken. He had really and truly become unhinged by Priscilla's presence on the field.

"Ryan..." There was an edge of warning in Myles's voice. "Ryan... don't."

Jackie clamped a hand over Carly's arm, yanking her away from the door just as the men opened it, spotting them.

"Oh, hey!" Jackie said brightly. "Looking for us?" She pushed past Ryan despite the way he was barring the door with his body. Carly stayed where she was, frozen to the spot. She knew what he was thinking. He thought she'd magically appeared in his life at the right time, wriggled her way onto his team, fed him some good information and now was giving him nothing after chatting with Priscilla at the biggest game of the year.

Even Carly could see how that didn't look good. It was too easy to leap to that assumption when the man was already tentative with his trust. But the team was truly playing well, and there wasn't much new she could offer.

"We need to come up with a strategy," she said, after clearing her throat. "A plan."

Ryan held out his hand. "Give me your headset."

Carly felt as though she'd been sucker punched.

"There are no more plans to make," he said, when she didn't react.

She pulled the device from where it was resting around her neck.

Jackie had returned to the doorway and was gaping at Ryan. "You're gonna lose."

Ryan's expression hardened, and behind him Myles's eyes fluttered shut as though he had an urge to leave and never come back. Carly understood how he felt. She'd been part of the team, and now that Ryan was facing his past demons, all the confidence they'd built up between them was suddenly worth nothing.

"It's fine, Jackie. We have nothing new to add," Carly said, her voice remaining neutral and calm despite the hurt she felt at Ryan's lack of faith. She understood he was trying to pull it all back in because it felt like everything was imploding around him. She also understood that he needed her to be patient and rational right now, even though it was difficult. "If we see something in the second half, we'll flag you down."

She turned on her heel and marched back to her position,

knowing it wasn't likely Ryan would listen to anything she had to say. As it was, her timeline was tight for getting to the airport, especially dealing with postgame traffic around the stadium. But if she left prematurely, she knew her actions would confirm Ryan's worst fears, and that was a risk she wasn't willing to take. She inhaled a steadying breath and picked up the tablet, prepared to do the best job she could despite the situation.

The teams hit the field again and Carly kept her fingers crossed that everything would go quickly and smoothly.

Just as the game was about to start, there was a swell in the spectator noise. Carly looked up from the tablet cradled in her hands to see a horde of teenage boys, at least fifty of them, streaking across the field. They were painted in the opposing team's colors, and wearing nothing but briefs.

She sagged into her chair as they ran, skittering this way and that as security guards flooded the field, trying to apprehend them.

Beside her, Jackie was killing herself laughing and the Torpedoes fell apart in a riot of hoots and hollers. Carly looked beyond her friend and caught the tension radiating off Ryan. A distraction like this was the last thing he needed when his sense of control was already razor thin.

The streakers continued running, delaying the game as they continuously outmaneuvered the guards.

"Can't they just round them up already?" Carly asked impatiently. She checked the time, tension coiling inside her. She was either going to miss the end of the game or miss her flight.

She stared at the tablet, which was ready and waiting. Ryan hadn't asked to see any stats at halftime, and she had a strong feeling he was curving inward, returning to his Mr. Independent persona for protection. He wasn't going to ask for help. She could leave now, catch her flight with absolutely no impact on the game.

But if he turned because he needed her, and she wasn't there…

Carly sighed, jiggled her leg and checked the time again. The game had been delayed by fifteen minutes already. Fifteen minutes she didn't have.

She turned in her seat, saying to Jackie, "I'm going to have to leave before the game is over."

"Why?"

They both inadvertently looked at Ryan.

"Don't take him personally. This is a super intense day and having that woman here doesn't help." Jackie jabbed a thumb in Priscilla's direction.

"I'm not taking him personally." Although his tone and lack of faith had stung a lot more than she'd care to admit.

"He'll still listen to us," Jackie said without conviction.

Carly gestured helplessly at the last of the streakers, who were still avoiding the tired security guards.

"I heard Ryan say he loves you. Did he freak you out?"

Carly's head snapped her way. "What?"

"I hear things."

Carly frowned. They'd been on the opposite side of the bus, with nobody else around. Then again, she had just eavesdropped on Ryan and Myles with Jackie, so it wasn't as if overhearing things wasn't one of her friend's habits.

"I know he's tough to love, but he's a good one." There was a note of sadness in Jackie's eyes. "He's opened up to you so much. Please don't leave because of his mood. He really cares about you."

WITH HER HEART RACING, Carly propped her fingertips together and lowered her forehead against them as the cab took her farther and farther from the stadium, from Ryan, from a game she wasn't sure the Torpedoes would win. When she'd left there had been twenty minutes left on the clock and the score had been tied.

Why did she have to face her past mistakes in a court of law right now? Why not next week or the week after? She'd gladly give up Christmas in order to stand beside Ryan and prove she wasn't like Priscilla, that she'd be there by his side through everything. Wins and losses. Whatever came their way.

She wanted to join Ryan on the ride home, rehash the game, talk about Priscilla, and add her energy to tonight's welcome-home potluck in Sweetheart Creek. She wanted to be a part of it all. Instead, she was flying fifteen hundred miles away.

She texted Myles, knowing his phone was off and would be for at least an hour, postgame. "Tell Ryan I'm sorry I had to leave so suddenly. Please know it was an emergency. I'll explain later. I hope you won."

Her thumb hovered over Ryan's contact information. She tapped it and formulated a message before giving up. There was so much to say, so much to reveal. He didn't know what she was facing. He'd never let her in far enough to ask, or to let her explain.

It wasn't just today that his trust had failed when it came to her; it had all along. They were like he'd said that day in the stable: two teams of one making a team of two. But always still independent. Apart. Alone.

And he thought that was just great, and never wanted it to change.

She had believed it was, too, but she'd fallen into her old trap. She'd let him dictate the terms of their relationship. She'd believed it was enough, but it wasn't.

She'd thought she'd changed and was stronger, but she was still making poor decisions, still not getting what she needed.

Carly pulled the gold wedding band from where she'd tucked

it in her purse, then slid it onto her finger where it belonged as a reminder to remain true to herself and not be swayed by others.

"The game so bad you had to leave early?" the cab driver asked her, his tired eyes meeting hers in the rearview mirror.

"I have to catch a flight."

"Bad timing," he said.

She nodded when he looked back for confirmation.

Carly blinked back tears and focused on the nicked gold ring on her left hand. Ryan was still independent and a team of one. He'd told her he loved her, but instead of pulling her even closer today to fight through this together, he'd shut her out. He'd taken the first excuse to discount her and his faith in her.

With her throat tight with emotion, Carly reopened the text message to Ryan and typed, "I'm sorry."

RYAN PACED, arms tightly crossed, his head pounding from the effort of focusing.

Seventeen minutes on the clock. The score was tied, and the Torpedoes had possession. Now the officials had paused the game for no apparent reason, and had been conferring with the head of security for what Ryan felt was too long. The players were shifting nervously, milling near the sidelines. Ryan had already spoken to them about keeping their head in the game, staying warm and being ready for the play to continue.

"Ryan? Ryan!"

He turned to find Myles and an official standing beside him. Ryan's gaze automatically cut to Priscilla, wondering what kind of underhanded trick she might be trying to pull. He hadn't broken a single rule, and neither had any members of his team.

But an official was speaking to Priscilla as well. Her face was red, her gestures aggressive. Her team looked alarmed and Ryan shifted to face the official speaking to him, not quite ready to look away from the scene unfolding on his opponent's sidelines.

"Coach Tyblone orchestrated a disturbance which led to an intentional delay of game," the official was stating, his tone level.

He had Ryan's attention now. "Say what?"

A resulting penalty this late in the game could cinch a win for the Torpedoes.

"You can play out the clock to determine a winner, or you may choose to accept her team's forfeit. Either way, she is being ejected from the game."

Ryan felt his jaw unhinge. He turned to see Priscilla being escorted out. She was uncharacteristically quiet, her gaze steadily kept on the ground in front of her as she was marched into one of the chutes that would send her into the parking lot.

"We choose their forfeit," Myles said immediately.

Ryan was shaking his head, still wrapping his mind around the turn of events. "So you're saying she was involved with the streakers?"

"The stadium's security team received word during an interrogation that she paid the streakers," he said. "We've confirmed payment."

"So we can accept the team's forfeit?" Myles said. "How does that work?"

"They take a time delay equivalent to the delay in game. That would end the game, declaring you a winner based on the current score."

"Sounds good," Myles said.

"What's the alternative?" Ryan asked, ignoring the look of incredulity Myles shot him.

"Play out the clock. She's removed from the game and you complete the championship with no head coach on the other team. Whomever wins takes the title."

Ryan dipped his head, mulling over the choices. The

momentum and energy was with his boys, not the other team. The Torpedoes had possession and were close to the end zone. Having their coach ejected would very likely negatively impact the other team. The Torpedoes could quite likely get a touchdown, then hold that score for seventeen minutes. They could win. Legitimately.

"It's not guaranteed," Myles said tightly, no doubt aware Ryan was seriously considering the option he'd already rejected. "Our boys deserve this."

"Our boys deserve to feel they earned the win, not that it was handed to them on a technicality. We fight for this. We play out the clock."

"I'll take your decision to the other team," the official stated, walking away.

Ryan nodded, confident in his decision. He still had Myles and Carly. They could fight for a true win. Sure, he was antsy and keyed up, and not the best listener but he could try. Try again to work as a team, something that would undoubtedly be easier without Priscilla smirking smugly from her sidelines and messing with his mind.

The game would no longer be about her. It would be about football.

And crushing her team and walking out of the stadium victorious.

"This is foolish." Myles threw his hands up in frustration. "We were sure state champs, and now because of your pride or vendetta or whatever's going on in your head it's all up in the air again."

"We're going to play our hearts out until the last second on the clock. We're going to *earn* those boys their scholarships. We're going to get them noticed."

Myles's chest expanded as though he was struggling with patience. "Did you think to consult the rest of your team?" He gave one shake of his head, caught sight of them being broadcasted on the seventy-two foot tall screen above the field, and fumed off.

Ryan looked over his shoulder to confirm his decision with Carly and found her seat vacant. He scanned the area around her chair, then did a quick visual sweep of the sidelines.

He didn't find her.

He caught Jackie's gaze and she quickly looked away, causing his heart to plummet.

Carly was gone.

"What do you mean she left? To where? The bathroom? Leaving in the middle of the game is bullcrap and you know it." Ryan could hear the edge in his own voice, saw its effect in how Jackie steeled herself. His words echoed down the concrete chute between the field and the locker room. The boys were inside, showering and getting changed. Elated for a win he felt they hadn't fully earned. The other team had fallen apart after having their stand-in coach ejected from the game. Sure, his boys had played hard, but it wasn't the same as winning off a purely clean game without penalties and disturbances, where both teams were playing at their highest level. It was like someone had kicked the legs out from under the other team—a team of kids. It had been so bad, his boys could have won without any coaching.

And they'd won without their chief stats-taker.

He felt Myles's presence as he came to stand beside him.

"She said she had to go," Jackie explained. "I told her to stay, that you still needed us and that you'd give us back the headsets."

Ryan fought for control over his thoughts. The timing of her leaving didn't sit well. Priscilla had been busted, dragged off the field and suddenly Carly was gone from their sidelines without warning?

Carly and Priscilla's laughter. The reaching out and touching of Priscilla's arm in the pregame chat.

Ryan closed his eyes and clenched his jaw. He turned to Myles, muttering, "Why didn't you say something about her?" He pinched the bridge of his nose. His brothers had acted like Carly was someone he could trust, and he'd been swept into that idea, but people who loved each other didn't leave without saying goodbye.

The hurt made the win feel hollow. It felt like Priscilla had won again. He hadn't seen her being here today, and hadn't seen the game disturbance for what it had truly been. He also hadn't seen Carly taking off on him.

He was lucky he wasn't still married to Priscilla. She'd paid teenaged boys to help her win today. And for what purpose? To defeat Ryan once more? She'd already won. Already stolen Ryan's money and his trust.

And this time, Carly.

At least he hadn't married her. He'd repeated falling in love with a woman who would leave him right when he thought things couldn't get any better. What was wrong with his ability to learn this lesson about women?

"What are you mumbling about?" Myles asked.

He straightened. "What could be more important than being here?"

"Maybe you should have asked her." Myles crossed his arms, the win not having softened his disagreement over the forfeit refusal. "Oh, right. You don't ask people about what they want or think is best."

"Okay, as fun as this sounds, I'm out of here. There are some folks in the parking lot who actually know how to celebrate," Jackie said, striding away.

Carly had left without a word. It hadn't even taken her

twenty-four hours to turn around and abandon him and their relationship. Just like Priscilla.

No, Carly was different. There was no way she'd come fishing around, waiting for him to be at his most vulnerable so she could pull his entire world out from under him.

Still, he felt the hole in his gut, the desperation and loss. None of this made sense. Priscilla. Carly.

Not even the win made sense to him right now.

Myles had bunched his coaching jacket in his hands, pushing open the locker room door where loud shouts filtered out.

"Where are you going?" Ryan asked.

"I'm going to celebrate. You could try it, too."

"What was that out there?" a man shouted. It was Davis Davies, Sweetheart Creek's DJ. Ryan's hand instinctively closed into a fist.

"Its called a win," Myles said, letting the locker room door close again. He gestured to a security guard, who, in several quick steps, redirected Davis away from the closed area. "Y'all are lousy coaches! You could have lost us the game. You should have taken the forfeit, you egomaniacs."

"We won," Ryan said mildly, his jaw tight, his temples aching.

Myles stared at him, his expression saying he agreed with Davis.

"That was the last game some of our boys will ever play. The lucky ones will get scholarships, and they'll be based on merit not a forfeiture," Ryan said, turning away. He needed to regroup before he went into the locker room to celebrate.

Davis, still not out of earshot, hollered, "Even your stats keeper saw how crazy that stunt was and wanted nothing to do with it! She left to save face!"

Davis disappeared and the two brothers were silent for a moment.

Myles crossed his arms. "Maybe Carly was right to leave.

Maybe she knew you were beyond listening to sense and that you'd never ask for help. If we'd lost—"

"We won, okay?"

Myles lifted his eyebrows. "If we hadn't..."

"I'm the head coach, Myles."

"I'm your assistant. I'm the man you keep in the loop."

"And if we'd lost, would you be there still?"

"Don't ask stupid questions."

Ryan huffed a sigh.

"I jumped in a river for you. Don't make me regret it." He pushed his red jacket into Ryan's hands. "I'm stepping down."

"Wait. What?"

"I'd rather be consulted, or make my own decisions. Riverbend asked me to coach their team next year."

"What? But you're not qualified."

"Actually, I am. Karen told me I passed the course."

His brother now had more credentials than he did? "But we're a team."

"You might want to look up the definition of team."

Ryan blinked at Myles. His brother was always there for him. Always. Through thick and thin.

Somehow, even winning against Priscilla she had stripped him of everything again. He'd believed he had nothing left to take, but this time she'd taken more than money. She'd caused him to be his own worst enemy and push away the people he loved in what was supposed to be a highlight moment of the year.

A cheerleader ran past, saying merrily, "Congratulations, Mr. Wylder!" She gave a squeal and shook her pompoms, giving a jump before disappearing back onto the field.

Ryan felt gutted. He'd spent so many of his free hours with Carly, spilling his secrets and plans. He'd even given her a headset on the sidelines of the most important annual event in his life. He'd given her a voice in what he did and what he decided.

He'd promised himself he'd never give a woman that much sway in his life again.

But he had.

And she'd left him.

CARLY SAT in the bistro across the street from the courthouse, exhausted after being raked over the coals. As she settled at a table with a hot chocolate and a sandwich, her phone vibrated with an incoming call. It was her mother.

"Hello?"

"Carly, it's your mom, Carlotta."

She relaxed, calmed by her mom's chill Jamaican accent and the familiar way she always introduced herself over the phone. "Hi."

"How did it go?" The concern in her voice brought an instant lump to Carly's throat.

"They won. But it was messy from what I've heard."

Ryan hadn't replied to the text she'd sent him on her way to the airport, but Jackie had filled her in on the team's win and the small scandal that had taken place. As to be expected, Ryan hadn't taken her leaving very well.

Carly knew if she didn't explain things to him, this was the end. Today, her hiccup of obligations and commitments could determine the rest of their future. She needed to go home, but the logistics of finding her way back to her Texas ranch tonight was almost enough to bring tears to her eyes.

She could crawl back to her family, but seeing her in this state they'd worry even more than they already were.

"I thought today was the preliminary hearing?" her mom said.

"Sorry. I thought you meant football. The Torpedoes won. But the preliminary hearing went..." She struggled to find the right word to describe having her character and story cut down at every turn. Doubt had been cast with every new reply, to the point where she had begun to doubt her own innocence.

Had she intentionally overlooked their company's financial situation? Had she purposefully avoided pursuing whispers from her gut for fear of what she might have to face? Had a part of her known what was going on with the contracts? Or had she truly been too blind, too busy, too grateful to see what was happening behind her back?

The same questions could be asked about her relationship with Ryan. Had she chosen blindness so she wouldn't have to face the unpleasant truth she knew in her heart? She'd known he would choose his long-touted independence and shut her out when push came to shove, and yet she'd convinced herself it would be okay.

On one level she understood why he'd done it, but she still felt hurt from his lack of trust and the sting of his words. She knew she'd made a grave error in character judgment by talking and laughing with Priscilla. The woman was smooth, sly and should have set off Carly's alarm bells. But she hadn't. Carly had been so excited about being at the game and over-joyed at how her life had taken such a positive turn that she hadn't allowed even a hint of doubt to penetrate her little bubble. She hadn't even suspected the woman was behind the game delay.

"Carly?" Carlotta said softly, returning her to the present. "Are you still in Montana?"

"Yes."

"Why don't you come home? You could rent a car or we could come get you."

Carly thrust her chin upward, fighting tears.

"Do you have to be back in court on Monday?"

Carly shook her head, fighting to keep her hurting heart from showing in her voice as she explained that the judge had dismissed her until next month's trial, where Eaton would be the one raked over the coals, and, as witness, Carly would provide the ammo. She was free to return home.

"Why don't you come here? You shouldn't be alone right now. I'll make some homemade cornbread and chilli for you."

The urge to go home for her favorite meal and a hug was so strong she could barely breathe. "I have a farm to take care of." Brant had taken care of her animals overnight, but asking for more right now felt like too much.

"We worry about you."

"I know. I'm sorry."

Her mother laughed, surprising her.

"What?" Carly asked.

"It's our job to worry." The humor had left and Carly heard the weight of truth in her mom's voice. She worried her daughter would struggle to follow her dreams, and be hurt or disappointed in the process. That she'd face unsafe situations as a woman, and that the color of her skin would mean she'd encounter prejudice and racism. That she'd have to work harder than some, or that she'd be treated unfairly. That she'd have her heart broken or get sick. Carly knew she'd have the same worries for her own children one day, but it didn't make it any easier, having her mother fret. It wouldn't be as hard on her mom if she'd stayed closer to home and found a simple, steady career.

"I know it's your job, but I don't make it easy on you."

"I love that about you."

Carly blinked in surprise. "You do?"

Carlotta's voice lilted with her faint, singsong accent as she said, "You don't listen to us or let our worries hold you back. You're independent and strong. And yes, you'll have the door smacked shut in your face sometimes, but look at you." Her tone warmed and deepened. "You're persistent. You get up every time someone knocks you down. Nobody's going to hold my girl back. Not for long!" Her voice lowered again, as though she was in awe. "And a landowner, Carly?" She was the first in the family, but only because her grandmother had left her a windfall that she'd been awarded in a lawsuit. "I couldn't be more proud."

"Or more worried."

Carlotta laughed, deep and rich. "It's worth seeing you out there in the world, not giving up. Your father and I aren't as brave as you are. We're old and tired."

"You are not!" Carly said indignantly, making her laugh again.

"We love you, Carly."

"I know. And I love you, too."

"Will you come home tonight?"

"I…" She heaved a sigh, thinking about Ryan. The longer she waited, the worse it would be. "I think I'd better go back to Texas."

"You need to be with Coach Wylder?" Carly felt her mouth drop open. "I saw him on TV today. It didn't even look like the win registered with him. He means a lot to you, doesn't he?"

"How do you know?"

Her mother gave a huff of satisfaction, making Carly realize she'd just confirmed her suspicion about her feelings for Ryan. Although the number of times she'd mentioned him during their weekly phone calls was likely a giveaway, too. "Keep being that trusting, bossy woman and he won't be able to resist." Her mom chuckled.

"Bossy?" Carly shrugged it off. She kind of could be.

"Go in with your heart open."

"Being trusting is what keeps getting me into trouble, Mom."

"I've heard the way you talk about him. Let me know when you've made it back to your farm. We'll see you there a few days after Christmas. I can't wait to see it."

Carly ended the call and took a deep breath, then tapped on Ryan's contact info before she lost courage.

She put the ringing phone to her ear and shifted in her seat to peer across the street through the Montana twilight. It was bitterly cold and felt bleak despite the cheery Christmas lights decorating the street, and she longed to be back on her ranch.

Ryan should be home by now, the long drive complete. The community's late-afternoon potluck over, although, for some, the celebrations might continue on into the night.

As the phone continued to ring, Carly wondered if she had it in her to fight one more time today. Did she have the energy and drive to tell her side of the story if Ryan picked up? She'd have to dig deep and find it.

When her call went to voice mail, Carly suspected Ryan was ignoring her. She was used to him picking up right away, and his voice becoming lighter when he discovered it was her. She lowered her silent phone, blinking back tears.

She'd fought the past today. Now she needed to fight for the future.

She booked the first flight to San Antonio she could find, left a tip despite not touching her meal, then called Jackie to see if she could pick her up at the airport. Jackie said she and April would meet her there in a few hours.

It was midnight when Carly, staggering from exhaustion, but bolstered by the support of her friends, knocked on the door at Ryan's place. The sunny yellow house, a small, two-bedroom single-story, nestled under two towering oaks in the heart of Sweetheart Creek. His dog Joe came to the front window and stood on the back of a couch, barking.

"What?" The terse reply came through the closed door. Ryan's gravelly voice didn't hold its normal warmth and Carly felt that familiar hurt of being shut out, of her issues not being worth bothering someone over.

"I heard about the game," she called through the door. "Congratulations."

Ryan cracked it open and slid a shoulder through the gap. Under the glow of the porch light he looked ragged and beaten. Not like someone who'd finally defeated his ex, or brought a major win to his hometown. When the dog tried to sneak past, Ryan shooed him back inside with a few curt commands, and Joe promptly reappeared in the window.

"I'm sorry I couldn't stay."

"I needed you."

"I'm sorry." She dropped her eyes, feeling guilty for not being up-front about her court date. She should have forced herself to blurt out the truth weeks ago.

"You left without warning," he said, his voice revealing hurt and disappointment that had her fighting tears. "Without even a goodbye."

"I didn't know until just before the game. I didn't want to add any uncertainty about me leaving to your plate. If it hadn't been for the streakers delaying the game, I could have stayed to the end." She rubbed her eyes. The game felt like it had happened weeks ago. "I had to leave. It was the only way I could catch my flight to Montana. I'm sorry."

"Is that where you went? Montana?"

"Yes." She waited for him to ask why.

"For a family emergency?"

She shook her head, waiting, hoping he'd care enough to keep digging.

"And you're back. Already."

"Yes."

"Because we won?" He was watching her like a spooked animal.

"No, because I love you. Because…" Words failed her. She was scared. She wanted to be that woman her mother saw, and she wanted to be strong enough to try again with Ryan. But a part of her wondered if she was just delaying the inevitable pain. He'd never allowed her into his life all the way, and she'd never trusted him with the full version of herself.

How could they do better if there was a next time?

"How do you know Priscilla?" Ryan asked suddenly.

"I don't. I met her for the first time today. Please, Ryan. I'm sorry."

"I trusted you. I needed you. You left me without any kind of explanation."

"I know." His look was hard and unforgiving, the hurt obvious. She felt herself become defensive even though she knew it wouldn't make anything better. She was tired of him being the one in control of where they went with their relationship and where their conversations went. "You made it clear we weren't allowed to share certain parts of our lives with each other."

A truck zipped past in the dark, music blaring, teens hanging out the windows.

"Put on your seatbelts," Ryan bellowed, hands cupped around his mouth.

A girl yelled back, "Hi, Mr. Wylder! Macey thinks you're cute!"

He was frowning after the truck. "Someone's going to get hurt tonight." He was reaching inside the doorway for his Jeep's keys. "Hernandez got the scholarship and now they all think they're invincible."

"What are you doing? Are you leaving?" He had closed his door and was standing there as though waiting for her to leave.

"Look, this isn't a good time."

"Ryan, it will never be a good time. If I walk away it's going to be over. I know you. I know me. Did you ever think to ask what might be going on in my life that I had to take a fifteen-hundred-mile flight at the drop of a hat? No, because you're afraid to know me, afraid to let me in. Afraid my painful past might trump yours."

He looked at her in surprise. Nervously, she brushed a curl away from her face, Ryan's gaze locking on her ring for one brief second.

His expression blanked, tone flat and emotionless when he said, "This relationship changed who we are."

The relationship had changed her, too, but for the better. She was stronger now. She could see where she needed to go, who to become. But she hated this part where she felt weak and without control.

"You said you loved me, but you're too afraid to know all of me, afraid you might really and truly become attached. We're not at our best when we're not sharing with each other. That's not a relationship, Ryan."

He was frowning down the street in the direction the truck had gone, the sound of music and laughter coming closer again. He gave a resigned shake of his head. "I've got to talk to these kids. Call Conroy." He took the steps two at a time, jogging toward the street.

"Who's Conroy?"

"The sheriff. Tell him the kids' celebrations are getting out of control and someone's gonna get hurt."

Someone already had, but not in the way he predicted.

RYAN, having flagged down the truck of partying kids to give them a verbal warning to play safe, leaned against the closed door of his house and exhaled.

Carly.

He'd always known it wouldn't work out.

Unable to sit, and knowing he'd be unable to sleep, he slipped into his running shoes and, despite the late hour, clipped Joe to his leash and started jogging down the sidewalks of Sweetheart Creek. He pushed his pace, trying to block the picture of Carly's bedraggled appearance from his mind. The deep shadows under her eyes and the sheer exhaustion that had left her swaying on his front step struck him with every step. She hadn't looked like that this morning.

He had won, so why did he feel as though he'd lost? Won

against Priscilla at long last, brought home the championship title, and yet it all felt so meaningless.

He wanted to say he'd given up his hard-earned and vitally important stay-alone mind-set the moment he'd met Carly. But her words about him not asking about what mattered in her life told him he'd failed. He'd tried to give himself to her while retaining his independence, but had ended up with a mess.

He wanted to say the game mattered most. It had been what he'd been working toward for five seasons. But without Carly there to hoist the trophy with him, without Carly there to talk to the press, to join the community potluck, or even just share a we-did-it smile...

What was the point?

Barely able to breathe any longer due to his punishing pace, he turned up the sidewalk to a small house a few blocks from his own. It was Luanne's Blackburn's old bungalow, the one Laura had been renting since early autumn, and had moved out after Thanksgiving.

The Wylders had moved April into the place that same day with a swiftness that still had Ryan's head reeling, and likely her husband's, too. Meanwhile, his brother was living out on the ranch. So what was Ryan doing here?

He bent over on the front walk, hands on his knees, breathing hard, heart pounding in his chest. He straightened and kept moving, pacing the short sidewalk.

The front door opened, and Ryan closed his eyes, tipping his head back. The last thing he needed was kind and caring April, with her no-nonsense attitude, asking him about State, or Carly, or pretty much anything. April had grown up among the Wylder boys and, unlike most others in his family, she didn't fear asking him tough questions.

As the door gently clicked shut and the sound of shuffling feet echoed on the porch steps, Ryan made himself look up to face April.

Brant was silhouetted under the light.

"What are you doing here so late at night?" Ryan demanded.

"What are you doing having a heart attack on my front walk? I'm not insured against that, you know."

"Family shouldn't sue each other."

"Doesn't mean they won't."

"Are you and April a thing, or are you doing that fake boyfriend thing to scare off Heath? I heard he's not letting her go without a fight."

Brant came down the steps, stopping a few feet away. "I was babysitting. April needed to pick someone up at the airport." He watched Ryan for a long minute before asking, "Since when do you go for a run in blue jeans?"

Ryan looked down. He was wearing a button-up flannel shirt, jeans and a pair of old running shoes he hadn't bothered to lace up. The clothes were stuck to him, the air chilly, but he hadn't noticed until now as the sweat dried. In fact, he'd barely even noticed Joe panting happily beside him, the leash loose in Ryan's grip.

"Are you trying to start rumors?" Ryan asked, pointing toward the house. "Her divorce papers are still unsigned."

Brant had been petting Joe, and straightened. "Since when do you care about anyone's opinion? And the papers were signed yesterday. It's almost final."

"I care about you," Ryan said. "What? Don't look so surprised. You know I care."

"Ditto." Brant was watching him out of the corner of his eyes, his head tipped down, as though afraid if he gazed at Ryan straight on it might spook him. His brother spent too much time around animals. It would take a lot more than talking about feelings to spook Ryan.

Brant was watching, waiting.

Why had he come here? Was he hoping his brother would absolve his feelings of guilt?

With Priscilla he hadn't felt this heart-wrenching sense of loss that made his entire body hurt, made him want to curl up in bed and sleep until he felt okay again.

"You broke up with Carly, didn't you?" his brother asked. Ryan let out a long sigh and Brant shook his head. "You're too independent for your own good."

"So's she."

"I thought it might work for your benefit, but I guess being a couple takes a lot more than that."

"But we were happy. We were both independent and yet together. It worked, Brant. It really did." He caught the look of doubt in his brother's gaze.

"It did?" Brant asked, the skepticism in his voice thick enough to spread over a piece of bread.

He'd thought it had. Obviously he'd been wrong.

Ryan aimed his gaze to the night sky above, the streetlight on the corner not quite masking his view of the stars. It was beautiful, and he wished he could share the heavens with Carly.

He swallowed hard, knowing he'd messed up. She'd come to him tonight to work things out and, instead of letting her in, he'd used the truckload of cruising students as an excuse to avoid talking about his fears and how he'd felt when he'd looked over to find her gone from the sidelines that afternoon.

"She let me down," he said, knowing he had actually let himself down. He just wasn't sure where he'd started and where it all ended—or if it even had.

13

arly sat hunched in a booth at the diner, with April and Laura across from her, Jackie at her side.

"Y'all want a warm-up?" Mrs. Fisher asked, waving her coffeepot. She had tiny green and red gems stuck in her teased hair to celebrate the quickly approaching Christmas Day.

Jackie held out her cup. "Yes, please."

Mrs. Fisher topped it up, then hovered the pot over Carly's mug. She shook her head, scooting it out of reach. She had the mix of cream and sugar just right and adding more coffee would ruin it.

"Very exciting to have the boys win State." Mrs. Fisher gave a low whistle, giving a slow shake of her head. "Ryan sure took a risk not accepting that forfeit. I don't know if he's a crazy fool, or the best darn coach this state has ever seen with iron-strength courage and conviction."

"Hey, Mrs. Fisher," Karen Hartley said, squeezing in beside Jackie and folding her coat in her lap. She half stood again, stretching to snag one of the clean cups sitting upside down on the table across the aisle. The waitress filled it without question while patting her teased hair.

200

"He knew all along that the Torpedoes could beat those cheaters," Karen said, adjusting her dark-framed glasses. "Myles sure wasn't happy though."

"None of us were. Talk about sending our hearts racing."

"It was worth it in the end," Laura said.

"Sorry you missed the windup party, hon," Mrs. Fisher said to Carly.

"Me too."

"A family thing take you away?"

"Something like that." She could feel everyone's eyes on her as she took a sip of her coffee.

Seeing she wasn't going to get an answer from Carly, Mrs. Fisher said, as the order-up bell rang, "I'll bring you girls more cream and sugar."

The diner was busy for a Thursday night, with Christmas decorations reminding Carly the holiday was mere days away.

"Your cheer team did well," Laura said to Karen. She was sitting up straight, her posture perfect as always. "Has anyone heard how Robyn's doing?"

As they started discussing local gossip Carly allowed her mind to drift. The past few nights had been sleepless, her thoughts on Ryan and what she could have done differently. She had about a thousand retorts she wished she'd said to Priscilla, a thousand ways to get that happily ever after with Ryan she still so dearly wanted.

As therapy, she'd spent hours with her hands in the dirt, planting her winter garden, and spreading the word that she would have fresh produce in a few months. It hadn't helped her thoughts, but it got her closer to her farming goals.

"How about you?" Laura asked, reaching across the table to gently tap Carly's hand.

"Sorry?"

"How are you holding up?" Karen asked.

"I'm fine."

"Ryan showed up around midnight the day you came home. He looked upset," April said, her voice lowering as Brant entered the diner. Her cheeks grew pink as they all waved at him, and he called out a hello from the other side of the diner as he met up with Levi, his eyes locking on April for an extra beat.

Clint, the local mechanic, joined the brothers and the three men headed out together.

"Ryan should be upset," Jackie said indignantly. "He broke Carly's heart. He told her he loved her, then when she had to leave the game he ended things with her."

"Why did you have to leave?" Laura asked.

"It's not our business," April stated. But she watched Carly, no doubt hoping to hear the answer to that little mystery.

"Oh, come on. Tell us," Jackie coaxed. Carly had steadfastly avoided the topic for days as well as on the way home from the airport last Friday for fear she'd break down and cry.

"I was called to a preliminary hearing as a witness," she said reluctantly. The words practically stuck in her throat, she'd kept them inside for so long.

The women gasped, and Carly braced herself for judgment.

The entire group leaned in, questions flowing. "Are you okay? What happened?"

"Are you in the witness protection plan?" Jackie asked. She straightened her spine and peered over the walls of the booth, looking this way, then that before hunching down again.

"No, no," Carly said with a laugh that dissolved her earlier urge to cry. There was something about Jackie that always made things feel lighthearted and easier. "I was running a business with a friend. We had a contract with the United States Army, but it turns out my business partner made some dubious decisions and some of his contracts got us in trouble."

They all gasped.

She hurried on. "I didn't know what was going down. I'm lucky I was so oblivious—as embarrassing as it is—because the courts decided not to charge me as an accessory." They'd come close, though, and she felt the familiar wash of shame for not knowing her own business. The guilt at what she'd helped Eaton do was a heavy weight on her shoulders, and she was no longer welcome in the Reserves as a result.

Carly allowed her eyes to flutter shut and inhaled through her nose, trying to find some serenity. The words of her ex-business partner washed over her. He'd called her gullible, naive, stupid, the real one to be blamed because she'd made it so easy for him to take advantage of her.

And he was right. She was all of those things. The worst of it was that she hadn't learned. She had worn that ring to remind herself not to be those things, and what had she done? Turned around and done it again. Her independence had been a false front, and she'd fallen in love with the first man to kiss her.

"That's so awful," Laura said, gripping Carly's hand and making her feel like crying again.

"Are you in trouble?" April asked. "Is everything okay?"

"But wouldn't you have known you had to go to court?" Jackie's forehead crinkled with confusion.

"The courts absolved me of guilt, but I was called in as a witness to testify against my business partner. I was subpoenaed for the preliminary hearing last Tuesday, but it got postponed until Friday. Only I didn't hear about the new date and time until I was already on the way to the stadium for the final game. I booked the last flight available right then and there, but didn't want to tell Ryan in case it would throw him off his stride. And then Priscilla was there, and the game was delayed by those streakers..." She swallowed hard, aware she sounded as though she was making excuses. "It turned into a giant mess."

"That must've been so difficult," Laura said, giving her hand another supportive squeeze.

"The bright side is that I'm not going to jail." She let out a bubble of pained laughter. It didn't change the concern she saw on her friends' faces. "I've definitely earned the labels of gullible, blind, and frankly, pretty stupid, though."

April was shaking her head, but it was Laura who spoke. "No. Don't do that to yourself. We have all made errors that make us think less of ourselves."

The group nodded in agreement.

For a moment there was only the clatter of dishes, and country and western Christmas songs playing in the background, as Carly waited for the judgment, the "How could you not have known?" questions.

"Where's Kurt?" Jackie asked suddenly, as if she'd just noticed the single mom was without her little guy.

"With Heath," April said impatiently. "So why did Ryan break up with you?"

"That's what independent men do. They tell you they love you, tell you they need you, and then when you start believing it they rip the rug out from under you and there you are, with a broken heart, crying all the way to Montana to get what's left of your soul stomped on by a lawyer and your ex-friend." Carly let out a shuddery breath, fighting the sudden flow of unstoppable tears.

She dipped her head as other customers turned to look her way, then buried her face in her hands, her shoulders shaking. Her friends immediately surrounded her with hugs and passed napkins to dab her eyes.

"Men are such bastards," Jackie declared, cracking her knuckles. "Is Ryan in school today? I'll go over there and give him a piece of my mind."

"They're on Christmas break," April said.

Carly looked up. "No. This is for the best. I knew it was coming, and I kidded myself that it wasn't."

The women were all watching her, their expressions forlorn.

"I just didn't think it was going to hurt this bad," she whispered.

"None of us ever do," April said wisely.

Looking up at her, Carly realized that her new friend probably had bigger things going on in her life than a little heartbreak after a short romance. She likely had an even better idea of just how awful things could hurt when true love turned around and bit you.

A FEW DAYS after breaking up with Carly, Ryan found his mom sitting in the ranch house kitchen. It seemed like every time he'd come by since her return from the beach town of Indigo Bay a few days ago, she'd been here rather than in her tiny home in the yard. And he'd been by the ranch plenty seeing as he was steadfastly ignoring his rodeo horses over at Carly's, taking Lucinda's word that everything was fine.

"Hey, Mom." He took a seat at the table. "What's up?"

She gave a halfhearted shrug, her hand wrapped around a steaming ceramic mug. His best guess was peppermint tea, based on the minty smell in the air. Peppermint meant she was feeling down, according to what Brant had once told him.

"How are you doing?" she asked, and he wasn't sure if she meant with all the ego-boosting kudos on the state win, the fact that Myles was still mad at him for his unilateral game-day decisions, or how he and Carly no longer spoke.

"Fine. The players are settling down finally."

"I remember when you boys used to play." Her eyes were kind and patient, and he sensed she was angling toward asking him something.

"That was fun," he said, waiting for her to get to the point.

"What's happening with you these days?"

"Nothing."

She gave him that unimpressed look that said she wasn't buying it and could wait forever. His mom was a good listener, a great problem solver, but spilling his guts about his love life wasn't something Ryan was comfortable with. He considered getting up and heading home to his dog, but knew she'd just find a different way to get the information from him.

"I was going to ask you the same thing," he said, leaning back in his chair.

"Just dealing with life changes."

"I don't want to hear about menopause."

She chuckled. "Well, that's flattering if you believe I haven't yet experienced that life change. Or else your health education is severely lacking and I've failed you as a mother." Her eyes took on a teasing glimmer. "Shall we talk about the birds and the bees?"

He gave a growl of disgust, then eyed her carefully. "Brant said you were hanging out with Clint during your trip to Indigo Bay." Levi speculated that the local mechanic had a crush on Maria. It was something her sons preferred not to think about, but Ryan couldn't help but wonder if the man was the reason for her sadness. If so, it could be time to find a new mechanic. "You two are friends?"

The sadness in his mother's eyes deepened and her mouth turned down in a frown. Ryan was tempted to change the subject, but remembered Brant's honest look of surprise when Ryan had told him he cared about him and the family. He cared, but maybe it was time to show it. He could start by making a point of letting them in and listening more. All that stuff Brant did so well.

"Or are the two of you more than that?" Ryan felt like he was talking to one of his students, prying out the truth with gentle, leading questions.

His mother flashed him a warning look to mind his own business. "Clint and I are friends."

"He's made it clear he'd like to be more than that?"

"Have you been talking to Levi?" She sat straighter, pulled her cup closer.

"You don't like Clint?"

"He is a very thoughtful man who…" Maria made a clucking sound. "You don't want to hear about your mother's love life."

"You have a love life?"

She snorted at him, her eyes flashing.

"Tell me." He was curious, feeling a need to hear how someone else in the family had foolishly put their heart on the line, and what had happened.

"Why don't you tell me about you and Carly instead?" his mom asked.

Ryan let out a large puff of air and sat straighter, just like his mother had. "Really? You want to hear about that menace?"

"Yes, I do."

"I forgot the golden rule. Women leave." He shrugged, feeling that painful sensation in his chest whenever he thought about Carly not being there on the sidelines when he'd looked over. Then how that pain had deepened when he'd discovered she'd left without even saying goodbye. That was always followed by the sensation that he was missing something, something important. Some reason or clue that would make it all fall together. Why had she gone to Montana, then spun around and returned home so quickly? None of it added up. His brothers were right; he needed to work on his listening skills.

"None of it makes sense, Mom."

Maria was silent for a long moment, and he waited for her pearl of wisdom that would help him make sense of it all.

"What?" he asked, when she remained deep in thought.

"Men leave. I guess women do, too."

"No. It's *women*." He hadn't left Carly or Priscilla. He shook his head before taking a moment to look at it from his mom's perspective. She'd come from a long line of leavers. Her dad first, then her husband, Ryan's dad.

He had a feeling that despite her history, she'd stepped up to the plate with Clint in hopes of a home run.

"Okay, fine. People leave," he said. "You gave it a shot with Clint, didn't you?"

His mom's cup was now clutched at chest level. "I tried, but he left."

The man had gone to Indigo Bay to help a friend put a scooter back on the road for the fundraiser his mom had been helping with. At the time Ryan had thought it was a bit of a coincidence, with both of them having friends in South Carolina, and both going to help with the same fundraiser at the same time. But then the more he thought about it, the more he realized it wasn't one at all. Clint had attempted to reach out to his mom, away from all the things that may have held her back. Like her boys.

She'd tried, failed, and was home again.

"He left," Ryan repeated.

Something about that proclamation didn't sit right. Clint wasn't the leaving type, for one. He'd been making eyes at Maria for years, according to Brant, who noticed stuff like that. Why would he go all the way to Indigo Bay just to mess it all up?

"He left for home. I told him I wasn't uprooting my life for him, and that I wanted to go slowly." His mother's tone was sharp, full of hurt and bafflingly unfamiliar.

"So he up and went home?" Ryan asked carefully, thinking about a promise Clint had made Levi that might have brought him here.

"Pretty much."

"Have you talked to him since?"

His mom was silent, revealing the truth.

"You know why he came home?" Ryan said.

"I told him to. I'm not going to put my heart out for someone who leaves me. I've been left by three men." She set her cup down with a thunk.

"Three?"

"I'm counting Cole in that number." She lifted her chin, covering her emotion just like she had when Ryan had been swept downriver in the flood. He now recognized it as false bravado.

"Why did Cole leave?"

His mom studied something out in the yard through the patio door for a long moment. "I can't help but wonder if Brant will have a chance with April now," she finally said.

"Cole left because of April?" That didn't seem right. They'd dated like wildfire as teens. In and out of a relationship so many times Ryan just assumed if they had a rodeo weekend they'd come home broken up or vice versa. Cole leaving and staying away for several years didn't add up, but looking at his mother now, he realized he wasn't going to get more from her than her whispered hope.

"Okay, so women leave," he said. "Men leave. People leave. Maybe we just need to get over it and move on with life—alone."

"I think it's worth the risk of heartbreak," his mom said, looking up. She stood, taking her cup with her, sweeping a hand over the spot where it had rested on the table.

"You do?"

"You're too young to give up."

"If it's worth the risk, then why haven't you spoken to Clint this week?" When she stayed silent, taking her cup to the dishwasher, he said, "You know he came home because Levi needed him to?"

She turned to him, unspoken questions changing her expression.

"He was supposed to go to Indigo Bay for three days, and he was gone almost a week. He'd promised Levi to fix the cultivator." Ryan had wanted to loan it to Carly.

Maria was still, her breath shallow as though in pain.

"Maybe he didn't leave you," he said gently. "Maybe he was respecting your wishes, and then came home to support your family." Ryan stood in turn. "I know you worry about how Clint would fit into our lives, but do you think Dad cared about that when he married Sophia? Maybe you need to take care of yourself for once. I don't think Clint left you, Mom. I think you're seeing what you want to see out of fear of getting hurt."

She turned to face him. "And then, if you're so smart, why did Carly really leave *you*?"

"Women have made a career of leaving me, Mom. It's really nothing new. Life's better when I run things on my own, and she reinforced that. I'm meant to be alone." And with that dreadful knowledge lodged in his heart, he pushed his chair in at the table, wishing his problems were as simple as his mother's.

"You were never lonely?" she asked, her interest genuine.

"Why would I be lonely?"

"You never wished for someone who understood you—the parts deep down inside?" There was a wistful longing in her question.

"No." He was lying. But it was also true. He hadn't wished for it, but now that he'd had a taste of it from Carly, he was certain he would wish for it in the future. It would be his own bitter reminder to keep himself in check.

"I think you need to go talk to her."

"What's the point?" he grumbled, wishing he could figure out how to start a conversation with Carly that might end up with her in his arms once again.

His mother paused thoughtfully. "You know who won't leave?"

"Uncle Henry?"

She rewarded him with a wry smirk. "Fiona."

"Mrs. Fisher?" The diner's aging waitress was in what appeared to be a lackluster marriage with a man who'd turned cranky after an accident had left him in a wheelchair. The conversations Ryan had overheard between the couple usually left him glad he'd made a vow to stay single.

"I suggested she leave William."

"But he needs her," Ryan said, surprised his mother would suggest Fiona leave her husband in such a condition.

"He's unkind to her. He's taking his frustrations out on her and she deserves better," she said simply. "She loves him, but she also has every right to leave him even if she feels she can't. But she loves him even though this has been very hard on her."

"Grandma Ruth didn't leave Carmichael, and he's an ornery old hound. Maybe it's a woman thing to be so stubborn about love." He immediately pictured Carly standing on his front step in the dark, looking positively drained, but still fighting for him, for them.

Man, he was a fool. How could his useless fears and pride be stronger than love?

"If that's true, then maybe there's hope for you, after all," his mom said with a teasing smile.

He let out a huff.

"You know, I heard something in the diner about Carly." When she paused, no doubt to bait him, he felt the predictable swell of curiosity. "It sounds like something serious took her to Montana on game day."

Ryan's throat went dry, a panic building inside him. "Is she okay? She said it wasn't a family emergency."

"Maybe you should ask her that yourself."

"Hey, thanks for helping us out," Brant said to Ryan at April's door. Ryan's brother had a distracted look, as though he'd bought stock at the top of the market and was just now realizing he was about to lose his shirt in a downturn.

Ryan entered the house, taking off his cowboy hat. To keep Levi happy, he'd been over at the ranch helping the hired hands, Hank and Owen, fix fences. He'd told Levi that afternoon that he wanted to remain a partner in the Sweet Meadows Ranch. He'd keep doing his share of the morning chores or hiring Blake to do them for him, but he didn't want the daily grind of every small decision, and wanted to keep his freedom to follow other pursuits. The brothers hadn't come to a final conclusion in regards to how the ranch would be run, but Levi had agreed not to buy out Ryan.

"Where's Kurt?" Ryan asked, looking around the living room. There was a Christmas tree in the corner, decorated simply, a few wrapped gifts underneath. Three days until Christmas.

"He's in the backyard kicking his soccer ball with April."

"Cool." Ryan began walking in that direction.

"We'll be a few hours."

"Okay." He had nothing on the go, unlike before State, and he was antsy, his mind finding way too much time to think about Carly.

"If Heath comes over, he's not allowed in."

Ryan's steps faltered, and he turned to look at his brother. "Say what?" The man wasn't allowed to see his own son?

"He has visitation rights."

"And…?"

"He's been…" Brant's mouth twisted, as he tried to keep from saying something unsavory about April's ex-husband.

"Is he violent?"

"He's been getting drunk. Saying abusive things when he's not trying to woo her back."

"So he's the same guy he was on the rodeo circuit?"

Brant gave him a look so much like their mother's that Ryan apologized, even though it was the truth. Heath had always been the life of the party, gregarious, fun, full of action and adventure. But when he'd emptied a few too many bottles he could be the back end of a donkey when he didn't get what he wanted. Having his wife leave him was likely bringing out that side with or without the emptied bottles.

"I can handle him," Ryan assured Brant. His job was to babysit

Kurt, so the kid wouldn't be subjected to the possibility of seeing his father at his worst should he show up at the lawyer's offices. "You go take care of April and get things settled."

The divorce was being finalized with surprising swiftness, and hopefully the custody agreement would soon be as well. Brant, April's self-appointed bodyguard, was riding along to the lawyer's office, where she'd sign yet more papers. While Ryan didn't love that he was getting tangled up in something that could go sideways on both of them, he appreciated his brother looking out for her.

Brant went to get April, and Ryan called Kurt inside. As April left the house, Ryan gently caught her by the arm. "If you need anything, we're all here for you. Okay? Anything. Day or night."

Her smile was sad, tired. "Thank you."

"We're family." He pulled her into a hug, releasing her to Brant, who took her elbow and guided her toward the door. "Brant will take good care of you."

She looked over her shoulder and smiled again, this time looking a little less sad, less tired. "I know."

"He's a good man."

"I know." She pivoted and placed a hand against Brant's cheek. In his memory, Ryan could practically feel Carly's hand doing the same to him. It was a touch that was gentle, reassuring and sweet. It meant you were cared for. "I'm lucky to have grown up with you crazy Wylders. You're good people."

"We try."

Her eyes darkened for a moment. "Well, except you could learn some lessons in listening."

He glanced at Brant to decipher the comment, but his brother was studiously digging his truck keys from his jeans pocket.

"I'll apologize to Myles for my unilateral coaching decisions at State."

"No, you need to..." April shook her head and exhaled. "Never mind. It's not my business. You know Carly would have been there for you unless something big got in the way. We're talking go-to-jail-sized reasons."

Without giving him time to ask what she meant, Brant whisked April onto the porch with a quick goodbye.

Go to jail? He dragged a hand across his mouth as worry set in. Why would she go to jail? And why hadn't he asked her to get a volunteer screening from the sheriff before letting her work with the team and minors? He'd really let his heart get in the way with her, hadn't he?

Wait, no. There was no way Carly was a criminal. She had to be the victim in all of it—whatever "it" was. Those trust issues of hers had to have come from somewhere. She'd said something about a shady business partner, hadn't she? Why hadn't he asked for details?

His own words about not needing to know, the pushing down of his own feelings of failure welled up as a reminder of why he'd never asked. If he was ever going to be the man Carly deserved he was going to have to face his fears, wasn't he?

Ryan turned to Kurt, who was standing behind him. "Now what?" he asked the little boy.

"I'm hungry. Can we have cookies?"

"Probably not." Ryan began moving toward the kitchen. "Where does your mom keep them?"

Hours later, with all the cookies eaten and just about every play in his football repertoire tested on the four-year-old, Ryan dozed on the couch, with Kurt snuggled against him, watching cartoons. The front door opened and he jerked upright, disturbing Kurt. His first thought was Heath and that he'd forgotten to lock the door, but Brant called out a quick hello, putting his mind at rest.

"We ate all the cookies," Kurt announced to his mom. She looked worn, but a weight seemed to have been lifted from her shoulders. Ryan took that as a good sign.

April fussed over Kurt while Brant saw Ryan to the door, just as Myles was coming up the steps. Their brother's expression darkened when he spotted Ryan.

"Hey," Ryan said, receiving a grunt in reply. Still mad over what had happened at State.

"Kurt left this at the Longhorn this morning," Myles wiggled the purple stuffed unicorn Carmichael had won at the library fundraiser fair and given to the boy.

"Thanks," Brant said, taking the soft toy. "He wouldn't have been able to sleep tonight without it."

Ryan shot Brant a look. His brother seemed pretty involved in Kurt's upbringing beyond his self-assigned protector duties. Brant returned his gaze without so much as a flinch.

"See you for coffee later?" Myles said to Brant as he headed down the steps toward his truck.

"Unless an animal emergency comes up, I'll be there."

Ryan raised his hands as if to say *What about me?* Neither brother looked at him.

"Hey, Myles? I'm sorry." Ryan's tone was all wrong, but the effect was a step in the right direction. His brother stopped moving down the sidewalk and turned. "I shouldn't have taken my frustrations out on you at State. You're an excellent coach."

"I know."

Ryan inhaled, then said, "If you want the team—"

"I don't want the team," Myles snapped, storming back up the walk. "I want to be a part of the team."

Ryan winced, his shoulders tightening as his brother's fists clenched in frustration. His brother felt as though he'd had no part in the final victory even though he'd been the magic behind the scenes that had brought their boys there.

"Cut him some slack," Brant murmured. "We don't know how we would have reacted in a situation like that."

"No." Ryan shook his head. "He's right. Neither of you would have ended up there in the first place. I lost my grip on reality and what was important." And at exactly the wrong time. "I should have listened to you, and had a conversation before making such an important team decision."

"You didn't need to shut everyone out when you saw Priscilla was there," Myles stated.

Ryan felt the weight of failure press down on his chest.

"You blamed Carly for leaving, but you weren't even listening to her anymore." The anger in Myles's expression surprised him. "She would have been in contempt of court if she'd stayed." Ryan's head jerked up. *Contempt of court?* "And you kicked her out of your life because you think you know what happened. You don't."

"I know. I need to listen more," he said hurriedly. He asked Brant, "Is being in contempt of court the jail comment April made earlier?" He turned to Myles, his sense of failure amplifying along with panic. "Is Carly in trouble?"

He'd thought April had made the comment in a flippant, female-solidarity way, not as an actual warning. But things were adding up way too quickly. Carly had needed him, and he'd been too wrapped up in his own life to notice. He'd noticed the way Brant was going out of his way to help April, a woman who was like family. Someone they all cared about.

And Brant was doing more for April than he normally did for a newly-single woman. He had a history of pretending to be a woman's new boyfriend in order to encourage her ex to take a hint and move on. But this was more. Brant was stepping in because he had a selflessness Ryan lacked. Had it occurred to Ryan to step up and help April without being asked? No.

And worse yet, he'd shut down the woman he loved any time she'd tried to go deep and tell him things he didn't think he wanted to hear. He'd said he loved her, but how could he claim that when he'd never fully allowed her in? He'd told her he had, but he hadn't. Not all the way. If so, he would know more than his family did about this apparent legal problem.

"Why don't you ask her?" Brant replied. "Carly, not April."

Ryan laced his hands behind his head and exhaled. "I'm sorry I freaked out when everyone seemed on board with Carly. I made a fool of myself."

"What do you mean?" Brant asked.

"I listened to you about where to cross the creek, and about marrying Priscilla."

"We didn't approve of Priscilla," Myles pointed out.

"I didn't know that, but I listened like I did with the creek. Then when Carly came along I think a small part of me thought you were all wrong again."

"The creek?" Myles frowned at Brant.

"The flood. If I'd crossed where I wanted to, it would have been fine. But I listened to my big brothers, and put your life at risk, Myles. We could have both drowned, and what would that have done to Mom and Dad?"

"You're holding the creek against us?" Myles asked, looking dumbfounded.

"You told me where to cross."

"You know what happened to Bonkers, right?" Brant leaned against the porch railing. His blue eyes were watching Ryan, dancing, picking up clues.

"He died of old age." The boys had come home from school and their father had explained that their family dog had passed away.

"No, the day you got swept into the floodwaters," Brant prompted.

"Yeah, he'd been running around with us. What about it?" Bonkers had been barking at the sticks Ryan had sent downstream, every once in a while taking a dip into the flood to retrieve one. Cole had snapped at Ryan repeatedly, worried Bonkers would be washed downstream and get hurt. Ryan was used to Levi snapping at him, but having Cole ride him had been new and slightly alarming.

"You know how he broke his leg?" Brant asked.

"None of us do." Bonkers had been like any ranch dog, sometimes disappearing for up to a day at a time. He'd appeared the morning after the flood with a broken leg. Their father had been prepared to put him down, as he'd been in bad shape, covered in mud and not looking like much. Brant had thrown himself over the dog, sobbing and saying it was a miracle he was alive.

Frankly, Ryan had found it all a bit dramatic, but together the boys had pooled their money and paid to have the dog's leg x-rayed, set and cast. That was when Brant had decided to become a veterinarian, but Ryan didn't know why else the story was relevant.

"He got run over or kicked by a cow or something," he said. It wasn't uncommon for dogs to get injured due to a momentary lapse of attention on a busy ranch.

"After you fell in, Bonkers tried to cross the river where you'd wanted to. He was trying to get to the other side, to save you. But the rocks suddenly gave way, sending him into the water."

It made sense that the pile of rocks they'd tossed in willy-nilly had weak points that had been expanded by the water rushing over and around the gaps. It wasn't a coincidence that after floods they'd often needed to rebuild their crossing points. But in his memory that path had still been solid. How had a light-footed dog been unable to cross?

"He was dashed against that outcropping just downstream from the path. He went under and I thought he'd drown. I don't know how he survived."

Ryan could still feel the icy flood, the unrelenting pull as it sucked him farther and farther from his brothers, the desperation to inhale whenever his head surfaced. He could still taste the muddy water in his mouth, hear the roar of an angry Mother Nature in his ears. His boots had filled with water, wet denim stuck to his legs making it nearly impossible to move. He'd been seven, older than Kurt was now, and still taking the first level swimming classes at the town's outdoor pool. Drowning had felt sure.

Sheer panic had helped him keep his head high enough for Myles to find him and pull him to safety. They had narrowly missed rocks, finally coming to a stop when Myles caught Cole's hand on a fallen tree as they passed underneath it, yards and yards downstream from where they'd gone in.

If Myles hadn't risked his life, Ryan knew he wouldn't have survived going down that river. He wouldn't have been tall enough to reach the tree or Cole like Myles had, and he would've been swept under it, gone forever. He gave a shudder at the near miss.

"If you'd gone where Bonkers did," Brant explained, "it would have been you dashed against that outcropping. And honestly, even with only three good legs, Bonkers was a better swimmer. You're lucky to have fallen in where you did."

That sobered up Ryan like a belly flop from the high dive. He nodded and adjusted his hat. Lucky.

His brothers had prevented a tragedy that day.

If only he'd built up enough trust that they could have told him the truth about Priscilla, they could have prevented that one, too. But they'd probably worried they'd lose him to the Wylder stubborn streak—the very one that had sent and kept Cole away. The very one that had prevented him from throwing himself at Carly's feet and begging her to take him back.

"I'm sorry I'm difficult." Ryan inhaled the crisp December air, settling his mind. His brothers were right. Right about the football game, about Priscilla, about the creek, about his attitude. Everything. "Thanks for getting Mom that day, and for telling me where to cross."

"I'm just glad you listened for once," Myles said dryly.

Ryan smirked in reply and Brant chuckled, any lingering tension between them dissolving.

"I love you two," Ryan said, giving them each a one-armed

hug. "You're a real pain in the butt sometimes, but apparently that's what I need."

His brothers nodded, understanding just how deep his gratitude ran.

As Ryan walked home, he realized that the day of the flood was just one of many where he'd needed his brothers, needed his family. They'd set him on the right path back then, just like they were trying to do with him and Carly.

It was time to let go of the past and start listening to them once again. And it was high time to set his stubbornness and pride aside and go talk to Carly heart to heart.

*E*arly had been working hard on the farm, and things were taking shape. Maybe not to an outsider, but she could see strings of future possibilities, extending out from each of her garden plots, giving her hope.

That was one place where loosening the reins on being completely independent had helped her. She'd allowed Ryan to give her advice and hone her focus.

She leaned on her hoe and looked out over the row of green sprouts poking from the ground, pride growing in her chest. It felt good to have something that was all hers. She owned this. She'd created it.

Her farm was a new beginning, but not in the way she'd expected. Instead of it being a way to hide out from the world, it had become a way to blend independence with allowing others to help. She couldn't have gotten as far as she had in such a brief time if she'd stuck to her original plan of doing it all on her own. Allowing Ryan to help hadn't turned her into a sucker, and his take-charge personality hadn't overwhelmed her. She'd messed up in a lot of ways, but in a different way this time. One that didn't destroy her life, just added another sizable dent to her heart.

Carly could see what had gone wrong with Ryan. She'd fooled herself into thinking that it was okay not to tell him about her problems. She'd been too afraid of what he might think, of how he might judge her for not being the brilliant, strong and independent woman he obviously saw.

Carly set down her hoe and began heading toward the stable. Catching herself, she changed direction and headed for her chicken coop instead, unsure what she'd do once she got there. She'd already fed the hens and collected their eggs at dawn.

Shivering in the gray, chilly day, she stopped to listen. Something seemed different. Had it been the growl of a new piece of machinery over at the Sweet Meadows Ranch? A bird she'd never heard before?

She turned in a circle, surveying her land. Just over the knoll, in the dull sunlight, she could see the glint off a windshield by the stable. A Jeep. Ryan's Jeep.

Without thinking, she began walking that direction again.

"Hello?" she called when she got there. The doors were open at both ends of the stable, allowing a breeze to cut through and causing her to wrap her coat more snugly around her torso. As she stepped inside, the aroma of horses, straw, dirt and leather met her with its welcoming embrace. The only thing to make it better would be to smell Ryan's aftershave.

She needed to move past him and the insufferable hope that wouldn't let her admit that they were over. Over, over, over. No more kisses by the stalls. No more early morning coffee together, watching the sunrise.

Ryan popped out of the tack room near the door, giving her a start.

"Sorry," he said, adjusting his cowboy hat as though nervous. "I didn't mean to scare you."

"What did you mean to do?"

"Figure things out."

"Problems with the horses?" She didn't dare assume he meant *them*, even though that was what her heart wanted.

"Somebody said you were going to jail?" His blue eyes pierced hers and she stumbled, surprise and shock hitting her at the unexpected question. He was giving her that look, the one that seemed to peer right into her soul. She wanted to cover herself, hide behind a wall, run.

She inhaled, bracing herself for the conversation and his possible judgment. "I'm not going to jail."

He took a step closer, still watching her from under the brim of his hat, as though using it as a shield. "Are you in trouble?"

"No."

"Good."

They were silent for a long moment.

"Are you still keeping your horses here?" she blurted, at the same instant he asked, "Why are people talking about you and jail?"

Carly drew in a deep breath, letting her long legs take her down the center aisle of the stable, her boots silent on the straw-covered dirt floor. Halfway along, she put her hands on her hips and swiveled to face him.

The whole town knew her business? So much for a fresh start. But what was the worst that could happen? Everyone had obviously had a chance to judge her, and she was still standing.

"The business I told you about? We were serving the US Army. It was pretty good, a secure food services contract, but my business partner found a way to make it more profitable."

Ryan remained still, watching her.

"He got involved in some financial dealings that weren't on the up and up. Charges are being pressed."

Ryan cursed under his breath, the severity of the situation not lost on him.

"I've been absolved of all guilt, thanks to my blatant naivety and blind trust in someone I shouldn't have." She'd been staring at him, shoulders back, but now felt her strength and resolve slide away as familiar self-judgment rode in, whipping her with its crop. "Story of my life."

Ryan moved closer. "He took advantage of your trust."

She closed her eyes. She'd been an easy mark, and content to remain so. "I should have asked questions. I should've been more involved in my own company. I shouldn't have been so happy to turn a blind eye to that aspect of things."

"Peter took advantage of your trust, too."

"Thanks for pointing that out."

"I didn't mean it as a judgment."

"I was subpoenaed as a witness. It was a preliminary hearing that had been postponed that took me to Montana at the last minute on Friday. I should have explained."

"Now I know why you..." Ryan's voice trailed off, and she involuntarily cringed. When he looked up at her again, his expression was one of confusion. "How could you trust me after those men treated you poorly?"

"I'm a slow learner," she said, swallowing the lump of pain in her throat as she turned and walked toward the open stable doors.

Ryan caught her arm, turning her to face him. "I want to be worthy of your trust." He licked his lips, his focus on her mouth. "I shut you out. I didn't trust you. I even convinced myself at one point that you and Priscilla were in cahoots."

"We weren't, I swear."

"I know. I blamed you for my own problems that were completely unrelated."

"I left when you needed me."

"You did."

Her chest ached and she longed for him to say he forgave her.

"But I'd left you long before that," he said quietly, taking her hand. "I shut you out and didn't let you talk about this court stuff. You tried, didn't you?"

"I loved you, Ryan."

"Past tense?" His voice was tight.

"You're a team of one and happy that way."

"What if I could have helped? I could have at least loaned you an ear if you needed to talk it out."

"We were our wonderful independent selves," she said bitterly, pulling back her hand. She saw her words hit their intended mark as his lashes lowered in shame.

"I know. We were." His eyes met hers again, sure and strong with a heat that started something warm in her belly despite her hurt and anger. "But I know now that we weren't great or perfect like we kept saying. We're our best when we're together and sharing our lives. All of it. It scares the crap out of me, if we're being honest." He lifted his hat with a giant exhale and shoved his hand through his hair. "I know I ruined things, and I don't expect instant forgiveness for how I treated you, or how I shut you out."

"I would have been in contempt of court if I didn't haul myself to Montana. They subpoenaed me. And every time I tried to explain, you shut me down by telling me we were better if we didn't unearth the past."

He opened his mouth, his face set like he planned to argue. He closed his eyes, re-centering. When he opened his eyes again they were a beautiful blue. "Push me next time. You're strong enough to, and I need that. Otherwise we're going to end up right back here again."

"Again?"

"Again."

Carly realized with surprise that at long last they were finally being truly, brutally honest with each other. And it felt good. Really good.

THE PAIN in Carly's expression was getting to him, along with the knowledge that he was the one responsible for it. This was nothing at all like how things had been with Priscilla. This was himself and Carly, their problems and their inability to truly communicate with each other. Breaking down that wall between them was difficult.

"I know you're probably done with me," Ryan said, "and I know I'm far from perfect, and that I'm probably going to keep screwing up, but would you consider giving me a second chance?"

Her head had lowered and he could see traces of dampness in the corners of her beautiful eyes. She had gone through so much with her failed business dealings and her court appearance, and he hadn't been there for her.

"I'm sorry I made you feel as though you couldn't share things with me."

Things were rough, but he could still see a future with Carly. They already had a history that forged them together. If they could move beyond this, they would be strong enough to face most anything.

He was starting to understand why Mrs. Fisher stayed with her husband. There were bumps in the road, but love wasn't something you could just turn your back on no matter how much you wanted to. Love was something that grew in your bloodstream, changed the way your cells and muscles worked. Removing it would compromise your entire being.

Carly remained silent, and he took a closer look, checking her reaction. Tears were streaming down her face, but her features weren't crumpled in anger or a good, old-fashioned, ugly cry. He couldn't determine if they were tears of happiness or joy, or if they were of pain, fear and sorrow.

She was wearing that damn ring again, twisting it around on her finger. Didn't she know she didn't need it? Didn't she know they could heal each other, and that their love was enough, if only they let down their walls?

"Well, say something. Are you having a seizure?" He waited impatiently for the corner of her lips to quirk into a smile. Instead, she turned and marched out into the gray December day, her arms wrapped tightly around her torso.

He followed her outside, stopping when she did. He stepped close, bracketing her feet with his own, cupping her chin and gently raising her face to his. "Carly, I love you. Not just my idea of you. I want you to be a part of my life. I want to try again and do better by you. Please, will you give me a chance to figure this out?"

Her bottom lip quivered and her eyes were wet with tears. "I don't want to be our best independent selves anymore. I want to be a team. A real team. And when we say we're being brutally honest with each other, I don't want it to just be us tossing around cutting comments about me shooting you or neither of us wanting love. I *want* love. I want us to open up our dark and scary pasts, our fears and horrors and worries, and every insecurity, and talk with each other. I don't want us to shut each other out."

"Can we share the joy, too?"

The fear and pain melted from her eyes.

"We can share the joy, too," she agreed, her shoulders relaxing.

"What else can we share?" He placed a gentle kiss on her lips, her response so familiar it filled him with longing and remorse that they'd missed almost a full week of this. When she kissed him back, joy and hope began to ease the chains that had been cinched around his chest ever since he'd discovered her missing from the sidelines at the championship game.

When the kiss ended, her hands were pressed against his chest, her focus on her fingers. "I should probably let you know I have some plans for next year's team." She looked up now, that playful sparkle in her eyes he so dearly loved. He grinned. He couldn't help it.

"We should run your ideas past Myles," Ryan said.

"Yeah?" she asked, eyebrows raised.

"If I can convince him to come back for another year. He got an offer elsewhere."

"Tell him I know a coach at the local college, and she might do a summer camp with the boys. I think our defense could use a bit of work."

"Is this what it'll be like on the off-season? Always talking football?"

"Is there something else you'd rather discuss?" she asked.

Ryan leaned back, watching the sky as he thought about that. The sun had finally broken through the steel-colored clouds, rays of sunshine and hope streaking across the ranch.

"You think you might ever want a roommate out here?" he asked.

"No," she said with disgust.

He chuckled and grasped her hand, giving it a squeeze.

"You should know by now that I'm the kind of gal who wants more than a roommate." She bumped his shoulder with her own.

He wiggled his hand in hers, then twisted his wrist to reveal the glint of gold on her finger. He gently lifted her hand and pulled on the ring, which came off without effort. He pushed it over the knuckle of his pinkie finger.

"What are you doing?"

"I think maybe I'm the one who needs to wear this. It can be a reminder for me to listen and to let others in."

Carly gave him the most serious look he'd ever seen. He chuckled, unable to help himself.

"Very funny. Give it back."

He yanked at the ring. "I think it's stuck."

"Everyone will think you're married—"

"It's the wrong finger."

"—to a jailbird." Her eyes grew damp again.

"Is that a problem? And anyway, you're not going to jail, right?"

"No, I'm not, but yes, it's a problem! Why do you think I took off the ring? Because it would hurt your reputation."

He pulled his hand away. "I thought you said removing the ring wasn't about me. And now that we've broken up, you're wearing it again?"

"It *wasn't* about you!" She growled in frustration and twisted in his arms, finally working the ring down over his pinkie finger with precise moves. He winced as it finally came free.

She held it up. "Now nobody's wearing it. I didn't want people to think you were running around with a married woman. But do you think you could have handled hearing me say that the other week? You would have freaked out."

That sobered him. "You're right." He would have lost what little nerve he'd had. "And as for the jail thing, honestly, I think everyone's just worried about you."

Her eyes grew shadowed with concern.

"Nobody thinks you're guilty, by the way. Although you did threaten to shoot me. Maybe if they knew you like I do, they'd be fixin' to put you an orange jumpsuit."

She glowered and reached out to pinch him. He dodged, laughing.

"You have bigger reputation problems than a ring," he said.

"Not funny!"

She was indignant, but he could see the humor sparkling in her eyes, as well. It was the best sight he'd seen all week, and he eased closer, letting her know playtime was over and it was time for kisses.

"I should have left that ring on you so you'd have to find someone to marry you." Carly lifted her chin with that defiant smugness he adored. He slipped his arms around her waist, pulling her close as he nuzzled her neck, breathing her in.

"It was the wrong finger."

"So? In Sweetheart Creek people don't care about those kinds of details."

"And who do you think might be interested in helping me out with something like a reputation-saving marriage?"

"I told you a long time ago that if you ever—"

He kissed her, then said, "We haven't known each other that long."

"—asked me to marry you I would punt you to the next county, and then some."

"I don't think that's a direct quote."

"Do I need to get my gun so you understand how serious I am about not marrying you?"

He laughed, rocking her in his arms. "Okay, okay. But so you know, I want to keep you on the right side of the law. The penitentiary visitation schedule doesn't mesh well with teaching high school."

"Seriously?" She tried to pull out of his arms at the teasing, but he held her tight and she melted into the embrace again.

"You could marry me. Two tainted reputations…" He let his voice trail off dramatically.

"Why don't we start with first things first."

"Okay. What's number one?"

"I agree to take you back for a second chance."

"That would be good. So today you become my girlfriend again."

"Yes."

"And tomorrow we get engaged, and the day after that we get married?"

"Let's just take it one day at a time."

"I thought I was."

She gave him a sly smile he couldn't quite interpret. But before he could puzzle out what she had in mind for their future, she gave him a kiss that obliterated all thought as her mouth angled over his. A perfect match.

Like Carly, the kiss was unrivaled and beyond compare. Simply the best he'd ever had, and he looked forward to a lifetime of many more of them, each one better than the last.

Christmas Day
Brant Wylder

Brant stood in the middle of the Wylders' ranch house living room. A fire was crackling in the fireplace behind him, Levi having stoked the flames. His brother sat shoulder to shoulder with Laura, whispering and laughing quietly.

Across the room Myles and Karen were slow dancing to an old record that Carmichael had put on. He'd been sipping eggnog but had his eyes closed now, no doubt remembering moving to the songs with his late wife, Ruth.

On the walkway above the sunken living room, Ryan and Carly were standing nose to nose, hands on their hips, chewing each other out. Brant knew that moments from now they'd have their hands tangled in each other's hair and be kissing as though the world was about to end and the only way to save it was to keep doing so.

His mom was bustling about in the kitchen and the Christmas tree was twinkling merrily beside him, the gifts beneath it having been opened earlier in the day. He'd popped by April's in the morning, delighting in Kurt's excitement over Santa having come. April and Heath were officially divorced, and right now she was sitting on the love seat near the tree, looking more relaxed than she had in months as she watched Kurt play with some horse figurines Carmichael had given him.

Brant had helped her feel this way and his heart swelled whenever he looked at her. She was beautiful, a woman with a strength he admired, no longer that scrawny kid with messy braids tagging along behind him and his brothers on the ranch.

He'd always been her confidant, not the one she'd flirted with, not her first kiss, like Cole had been. Brant was more than that. He was her rock, the one she came to in heartbreak and crisis. And over the past several months, she had shown him he was still that person, not just for her, but for her son, too. Brant had given them a safe home and provided April with a job in his veterinary clinic. Now he was ready to offer her more.

But was she ready? Did she see him as someone to lean on in a crisis and nothing more? Or did she feel what he did? That undeniable connection, the arc of electricity that happened whenever they touched?

April noticed him watching her, and her expression warmed as she patted the spot beside her on the love seat. He took the invitation, crossing the room to sit beside her. With both Cole and Heath out of the equation, maybe it was his chance to finally show her how he'd felt for years. He was a stable man she could rely on and trust. A man who would do right by her now that she seemed ready to let go of her wilder side and settle down.

Her figure had rounded out after having Kurt, giving her lush curves that were feminine and erotic, sexy and welcoming.

"Hey," he said, clearing a frog from his throat.

Her fingers clasped the simple locket he'd given her for Christmas. He'd asked the jeweler to place a photo of herself holding a newborn Kurt in it. She'd teared up when she'd opened it, then thrown her arms around him. Brant hoped it was the first of many pieces of jewelry he would give her on Christmases to come.

"Hey, stranger," she said, her lashes fluttering down as though she suddenly felt shy.

He was tempted to tug on a lock of her hair and use her childhood nickname to highlight the fact that their histories were intertwined, one and the same when it came to the most important threads. He was more than just the caring boy she'd grown up with, more than the shoulder she cried on.

It was time to act on the heat that had been simmering between them.

He gently took her chin between his index finger and thumb, and turned her toward him. Her lips parted in anticipation as he angled her face to line up with his. He lowered his lips to hers, a soft kiss. It was innocent and sweet, and not the kiss he intended to give her when they had more privacy.

He jolted, realizing he'd kissed her where anyone there could have seen, including Kurt. No doubt she didn't want to confuse her son, and Brant had just blotted out the entire world except for what he wanted. That kiss.

He wanted another.

April kept her lashes lowered and gently locked their hands together, sliding them between his thigh and hers, hiding the small embrace from view. Her palm was warm against his own. He gave it a squeeze, feeling as though he needed to look away before the moment vanished, a trick of the eye, a wishful dream, a fantasy.

Ryan and Carly were now cuddling, their arms around each other's waists. He'd noticed Ryan had given her a charm bracelet earlier in the day as a Christmas gift, and the two were smiling. Ryan caught Brant's eye and gave him a questioning look, his head tipped toward April. It was one of approval but also full of questions Brant couldn't yet answer.

April gave his hand another squeeze, and he glanced back at her. Her cheeks were pink, her eyes bright, her smile sure.

She looked calm and at ease, not at all the way he remembered her around Heath. She'd always seemed as though she was waiting for the other shoe to drop, always braced for the wild side to come out and take her for a ride.

"Supper'll be ready in less than five," Maria called from the kitchen doorway. Bingo, the rescue dog Brant had given his mother a few days prior, sat at attention beside her, surveying the room before looking up at Maria with an adoring look. The two had bonded quickly, the neglected dog lapping up Maria's love as her mothering instincts had kicked in upon seeing the skinny, dirty animal. The black-and-white pointer mix was already looking healthier.

"Can I help?" Laura asked, popping to her feet. She had become close with Maria, the two of them often working on ranch meals together, but half an hour ago Maria had shooed her into the living room as she put the final touches on the supper herself.

"Thanks, Laura. I've got it." She wiped her hands on the apron around her waist, her cheeks rosy from the warmth of the kitchen.

The front door burst open and Maria glanced up, her entire being alert as though expecting Santa Claus himself.

It was Uncle Henry and Jackie.

"Hey, guys, sorry it took us a while," Jackie said cheerfully as she slipped out of her coat.

"Jackie managed to hit the ditch trying to avoid Bill," Henry proclaimed, leaving the door open a crack so the ranch dogs, who had nosed their way in, could exit again.

"I wish armadillos hibernated," she muttered. "He's such a menace."

"Is your car okay?" Brant asked. Some of the Hill Country

ditches were steep enough to take out the oil pan or smash a bumper on a car as small as hers.

She waved away his concerns. "Nothing a little duct tape and twine won't fix."

"Spoken like a true cowgirl," Myles said with a laugh.

Henry harrumphed. "She darn near killed me with her reckless driving."

"Oh, I'm sorry. I didn't realize you wanted fresh armadillo for Christmas dinner," she said, leaving Henry scowling and the gathered Wylders laughing.

Jackie's gaze honed in on Brant and April, who were still on the love seat, holding hands.

"I saved you seats at the football games," she said simply, blinking at them as though stupefied. "Am I four-for-four?"

All eyes turned toward Brant and April, and he felt his body heat as well as the desire to hide their clasped hands. He knew if he wasn't careful about dating April it would look as though he had broken up her marriage. In a small town it didn't matter if a union was obviously ready for Breakupville pretty much the day the couple had agreed to marry. He'd still be the one blamed.

The door swung all the way open again, and Brant felt the energy of the room shift as everyone gasped, Maria the loudest and happiest of all.

"Who did you save those seats for?" Cole asked, standing in the doorway. His build was stronger and more filled out, his confidence and appeal larger than when he'd left Sweetheart Creek almost five years ago.

Brant felt April's hand slip from his and Carmichael's record stopped playing.

While Brant had often encouraged his brother to return home, right now Cole was the last person on earth he wanted to see darkening the doorway of the Sweet Meadows Ranch.

THE COWBOY'S OF SWEETHEART CREEK, TEXAS

Read them all!

The Cowboy's Stolen Heart (Levi)

The Cowboy's Secret Wish (Myles)

The Cowboy's Second Chance (Ryan)

The Cowboy's Sweet Elopement (Brant)

The Cowboy's Surprise Return (Cole)

There are more Sweetheart Creek stories set in Indigo Bay! Maria has her own special story, Sweet Joymaker. Their cousin Nick's story is Sweet Troublemaker. And you can't forget about the Wylders' cousin Alexa! Her story is Sweet Holiday Surprise.

Indigo Bay

Sweet romances set in a beach town—meet characters new and old in this spinoff series.

Sweet Matchmaker (Ginger and Logan)

Sweet Holiday Surprise (Cash & Alexa)

Sweet Forgiveness (Ashton & Zoe)

Sweet Troublemaker (Nick & Polly)

Sweet Joymaker (Maria & Clint)

ABOUT THE AUTHOR

Jean Oram is a *New York Times* and *USA Today* bestselling romance author. Inspiration for her small town series came from her own upbringing on the Canadian prairies. Although, so far, none of her characters have grown up in an old schoolhouse or worked on a bee farm. Jean still lives on the prairie with her husband, two kids, and big shaggy dog where she can be found out playing in the snow or hiking.

Become an Official Fan:
www.facebook.com/groups/jeanoramfans
Newsletter: www.jeanoram.com/FREEBOOK
Twitter: www.twitter.com/jeanoram
Instagram: www.instagram.com/author_jeanoram
Facebook: www.facebook.com/JeanOramAuthor
Website & blog: www.jeanoram.com

www.ingramcontent.com/pod-product-compliance
Lightning Source LLC
Chambersburg PA
CBHW050611190726
48283CB00007B/2377